BLACK
HOURS

∾

BLAIR MacKENZIE BLAKE

BLACK HOURS

ISBN: 978-0-6452094-8-8

Editor: Greg Taylor
Cover Design: Joseph Nagy & Blair MacKenzie Blake
Photography: Duncan Blake

TREASURIA PUBLISHING

CONTENTS

CHAPTER I

"Anything can happen," Pastor Hoburt asserted with a conviction that was boosted over crackling karaoke speakers. His gaunt face sparkled with perspiration as he moved from behind the pulpit on a burgundy-colored carpet to better engage with his inspired followers.

"Anything at all is possible," the words bellowed out with varied pitch before a carefully timed pause. "Because our sisters' uncut long hair sends signals to angels. It's like a magnet," he uttered softly while moving sideways in front of those caught up in the sermon, many of whom were already nearing a trance state, swaying with arms raised and waving their hands to mimic the pale orange glow of flicker flame lights in sconces along the walls. "As I stand before you, angels are winging their way through a bejeweled gateway to bestow divine gifts to those slain in the spirit," he shouted with a measured staccato. "Can you feel their shimmer?" he sibilated like one possessed. Some of the brethren reacted by closing their eyes, while others leaped onto their folding chairs, raising their fingers towards the sloped ceiling.

"Should I adapt to modern ways, saints?" he asked with a deprecating smile. "Engage in watered down spiritual warfare?" This was followed by salvos of deep groans from the faithful.

There was a satisfied gleam in the minister's rheumy eyes as he ran his fingers through thinning grayish hair that was combed back with Brilliantine sheen. Self-gratification was etched on his face, as he reveled in the murmurs of approval.

"My job is exegetical spadework." His emphatic tone had sunk to a conspiratorial whisper. "Yours is not to question my green-lighted authority. Touch not God's anointed one. I have to be hard between these neutral-painted walls. No surreptitious snips!" his voice swelled. "No treacherous trims! No beauticians! No stylists, sisters! Intricate coiffures aren't apostolic!" he uttered in rapid-fire succession. "And there's no preventing the efficacy of a woman's long uncut hair by genetic limitations here in Jaywick. Angels reward bland faces covered not with ostentatious displays, but naturally with glorious buns. Receive their gifts, sisters, in this theater of Gods glory! Gifts better than a Mary Kay Lexus. Amen."

With animating effective oratory skills and pausing at strategic moments, to the small congregation, Hoburt's charismatic delivery was the epitome of Pentecostal conviction. Given the opportunity to shine, his idiosyncratic techniques had them "catching the fire" without quoting a single passage from the scriptures.

Seated in the middle of the assembly, twenty-six-year-old native of the small town of Jaywick, Indiana, Dal Gordon, watched the theatrical antics with amused disdain.

To him, the dramatic gestures and rehearsed dynamics that whipped the crowd into a frenzy were nothing more than manufactured emotion. Bizarre behavior activated by the power of suggestion, if not staged like courtesy drops to please their high-octane leader. Others that squeezed out hallelujahs at the flip of a switch were just ordinary folk from rural suburbia looking for a spiritual fix – some supernatural pizzazz in their daily routine. That and an ink-stamped passport to Hoosier heaven. But he didn't give a shit about the bumpkins. The spirit-filled could bark like dogs for all he cared. It was his mother's participation in the church that concerned him.

Word had it that Hoburt demanded obedience from his flock and wasn't above humiliating a member for a minor transgression with some degrading punishment. From stories he'd heard, he was also prone to violence. Usually, he stuck to challenging the devil to a fistfight in the church's back alley, but if really pissed off about something, he justified paroxysms of rage by comparing his actions to Jesus' own meltdowns, like the time the Savior was hangry and cursed to death a barren fig tree.

"Holy magic hair contains cosmic powers," the pastor shouted with an emotion-charged resonance. "Right now, angels are fast approaching through a glorious passageway." Mopping the sweat off his hollow cheeks, he shut his eyes tightly before continuing with a commanding, almost incantatious tone. "Descend, ye angels, into this simple refuge so that we can feel your magnificent touch?" After a suspenseful pause, he uttered some unintelligible speech-like sounds.

Though Dal rarely attended the services, there was always the same insanity about apostolic hair, an obsession of Hoburt's that went far beyond the passages in Corinthians, he thought.

Hearing his mom parroting the hinky fuck at home, he did his best to convince her that the minister had gone off the rails. She responded by calling his criticisms unwarranted potshots. He also attempted some humor by using a toothpick to pierce the skin of a banana and trace satanic graffiti that would 'magically' become legible an hour or so later. Even after he revealed the simple trick that was his way of showing how gullible she was, she still maintained that the "devil's black pictures" were made by spirits of deception that had control over him. After months of listening to her faulty reasoning and unsound arguments, he wasn't sure if anything he did would convince her that Hoburt's unchallenged interpretations of the Bible weren't worth a rubber nickel. Because she was a recent convert, he maintained hope that there was still a chance to deprogram her. He just wanted his spunky mom back.

He was only there that night because of a promise that he made. It was the only thing his mother wanted for her birthday. For days he had remained uncommitted, finally agreeing after she reminded him (with a wink) that by showing up, he would also be invited to the church picnic on Saturday, and a "certain pretty sister with a lovely singing voice would be there."

He knew that she was referring to Derethia with this obvious sweetener. He had once remarked that she was good looking even without a trace of makeup. Yes, she was quite attractive, but with hair hanging down to her long skirt, was she salvageable? At times she shook and wailed and uttered made-up words like the other Rapunzels. When he glanced back at her during Hoburt's babbling to see if she was dancing in spirit or seizure-like shaking off whatever it was, she made a funny face before recoiling into her chair as if she had lost the protection of God by merely making eye contact with a guy who rode a motorcycle. She was damaged goods. Subjected to too much toxic theology in her young life. Let the angels fondle those brown tresses. For a flimsy paper plate of burnt weenies, watermelon and potato salad the kid who kept his promise would have to endure another hour of the whack job with plastic buttons on a gray flannel suit.

****

The blue-uniformed mother and daughter crew from 'Indy's Nightly Janitorial Team' were standing at the rear of a white company van that was parked in the small lot behind the church. In the haziness of approaching nightfall, the smell of fresh mowed hay wafted in the warm breeze as muffled energetic music could be heard outside the brick edifice.

"Mama, why's the cloud look like that?" the daughter asked with a puzzled tone while looking up at the puffy mass of vapor with a perfect ovoid shape that was hanging motionless directly above the steeple, so close that its wispy edge almost touched it.

"Don't pay no nevermind to that, child," the stout woman drawled as she smacked her Wrigley's. Leaning inside the cargo bay, she was rummaging through storage bins that contained buckets and cleaning supplies.

"Just look at those pretty colors," the girl said with her eyes riveted on the luminous discharges that danced in a rhythmical pattern within the strange natural formation. No sooner had she spoke when the vaporous oddity started to take on a faint metalized sheen. Devoid of its fleecy cloaking, when fully transformed into a structured object, its shape appeared as a white oblate ellipsoid that gleamed with subdued silver tones. Adding to its puzzling nature, at times, its actual color was hard to distinguish due to a wavy effect on the finish that created cryptic transitions. As the girl remained transfixed by the machine's unworldly presence, from the rippling gradient of its underbody, matching appendages unfolded with delicate biomorphic fluidity.

"I don't know, momma," the girl's voice was barely audible as she cocked her head to see if the mercurial structure would undergo a further transformation. As she did so, in the partial darkness, the dully lucent ovoid with its obscure silver tinges and bewildering organic mimicry morphed into what looked like a midsized white shuttle bus that appeared to be stuck on the towering church spire. The solidity of its reflective surface was so convincing that her stomach tightened at the thought of it falling onto the building. As it remained perfectly still, she recognized it to be the same vehicle she had often seen in the church parking lot.

She even knew that its model type was called a Ford Starcraft. Adding to the absurdity of it hovering there, its warning lights flashed on with an amber glare.

"Momma, look."

"Don't puzzle yourself over it," her mother said with a trace of annoyance while turning around. "Just get the sweeper, polish and scrubbins… but leave the wax remover."

Before the incongruent specter winked out and the funny egg-shaped cloud reappeared, she had glimpsed the indistinct outline of what looked for all the world like a white compact bus floating in midair.

"That don't make no sense at all," she mumbled to herself.

The church service was in full swing. Worshippers were clapping their hands furiously to drumbeats and the swelling organ when a large stained-glass window depicting the 'Holy Spirit Fire Dove' of the Pentecost flared with startling intensity. The silent explosion of dazzling whiteness that instantly filled the nave was brighter than a clear summer day and, though its source was not discernable, the light had an ineffable quality that some giving joyful praise reached out to touch as they would a tangible presence.

Spontaneous displays of emotion escalated to a startling degree in the divine effulgence; with bobbing heads vibrating so fast that they looked like pneumatic paint shakers in a home improvement center.

Though also dazed by the flood of light, Derethia was the first to spot what looked like several oddly white toy balloons floating in the enveloping brilliance. At first she didn't give much thought about the strings that glided along with them, despite that they appeared to be considerably thicker than usual party favor tethers. When one of the buoyant objects brushed against her cheek, instead of feeling its smooth latex surface, a sudden burst of electrified needles pricked her skin. There was a jarring flash of movement of something that looked like darkly luminous teardrops. At the same instant she heard a tinking sound that was quickly followed by vivid imagery appearing in her head like sharply focused scenes from a home movie:

> *Her and two other sisters were crawling on their hands and knees in a cow pasture. All three were completely naked and each had a cowbell around their neck. As pastor Hoburt walked slowly behind them, their heads were bent down as they sobbed unstoppably while struggling to bite and chew the coarse blades of grass. "If any of you gotta poop the stuff," Hoburt could be heard saying, "let it drop in the field like cows do."*

While fighting off the disturbing imagery, *that contained more details of the traumatic incident than she previously recalled*, she was startled by a flash of motion in the corner of her eye.

When the grayish bulge that bobbed about came to an abrupt stop, she realized with stunned disbelief that what she had mistook to be a balloon was actually some kind of freakishly oversized head. The repulsive face had a mottled, pearlescent-grayish cast with a pointy chin and scant vestigial orifices. The most prominent feature was its slanted, glossy black eyes. These huge, endless voids held her spellbound for a moment. With their penetrating glare, she knew that the liquid dark globes were capable of extracting her deepest secrets. Those she had tried to erase from memory. As the epileptic-like spasms of those 'seized with spirit' continued, she got a glimpse of two more of the grotesque configurations; both having identical un-

settlingly thin bodies that somehow supported their disproportionately large heads.

Whatever the ungodly things were, they were unnervingly
quick. Between the colorful blur of those who violently convulsed,
she had a hard time following their wispy appendages as they engaged in some devilish ballet. Why, she wondered, weren't others
in the fold alarmed by the satanic attack, and why didn't Hoburt
confront these infernals with divinely inspired tongues? What
happened to his repertory of tricks to banish malignant spirits now
that they were *real*, and pursuing some unknown agenda within
the very sanctity of the Lord's House? With the hellish gleam in
those lidless black stares, there could be no ambiguity about their
true nature. Even so, what her nostrils breathed in wasn't the expected demonic reek. Not burning flesh or the stinking vapors of
hell expelled from their pores. Instead of the sulfurous breath of
burning matchsticks, there was a more unique odor. A complex,
synthetic smell that was equally overpowering.

Bathed in the glaring radiance near the podium, the pasty-
faced pastor was gyrating like a tightly wound clockwork toy;
seemingly oblivious to the intrusion into his world by spindly
entities with soulless glares that appeared to be anything but
the seraphic visitants he invited to descend into the Holy space.
Again, Derethia wondered: What happened to the natural covering? The power on the head referred to as "precious amulets."

When she somehow managed to let out a scream, it was so
resoundingly shrill that all three of the diminutive beings fell to
the floor like knocked over bowling pins. As someone cupped
her mouth with their hand, the misshapen things quickly bolted upright. With bouncing strides that were in perfect lockstep,
they vanished among the hyper-jittery profiles seconds before
the overwhelming brightness that had engulfed the congrega-

tion suddenly flicked off. In its absence, a narrower luminous burst of light appeared from above.

Derethia watched as a powerful beam that looked like a sparkling green cone swept rapidly towards her. Murky delineations could be seen within its shimmering greenish hues. The spidery shapes might have been the dangling silhouettes of the malformed things. She tried to scream again, but this time not so much as a whimper escaped from her lips.

Unlike the chaotic behavior of the others, Dal was rooted to the spot by a soothing subvocal command. Prickles coursed through his body, along with a pulling sensation. When a mysterious optical force lifted his limp body, the tingling flurries of bio-fluorescent energy felt exhilarating. As the beam angled upward, he twirled about, swimming in vibrant jewel tones that flecked a mixture of subtle greenish tints.

Outside in the parking lot, the matronly cleaning woman snapped her chewing gum while shaking her head with a bemused grin as her daughter vigorously swung her wet mop over vivid purple, red and yellow reflections that had appeared on the gritty asphalt.

"Child, now what you mopping the street for? That don't make no sense at all."

She hadn't realized that she, herself, was leaning on a commercial vacuum clearer, whose cord had been plugged in. Nor did she give a thought as to how it was possible that both of them were standing in the middle of the elaborate tracery and detailed motifs in illuminated panes of colored-glass – the church's only vibrant accent – that by some enigmatic process had been duplicated in the oil-stained blacktop as a fixed image.

"Momma, who took our clown ball?" the younger girl asked while glancing up at the antenna on the cargo van.

When the evening service ended, as members in the gathering shook the pastor's hand and began filing out of the church, Derethia tapped Dal's mother on the shoulder.

"Corina," the girl said with a warm smile. "Did your son get bored with a service done God's way? I noticed he left halfway through."

"He told me that he had to get on the bus," Corina replied with only a hint of exasperation.

"Oh, I see. Where's he going?" Derethia asked with raised eyebrows.

"To the church picnic... tomorrow," Corina stressed the last word to emphasize her son's obviously poor excuse. "Ha-ha, he's always joking. I'm sure he's planning on zipping there on his Janus."

"I thought maybe it was because there wasn't enough enthusiasm for him to participate," the girl said. This was followed by a taunting laugh. "Well, I'll see you both there. Oh, did some of the balloons for tomorrow get loose in here?"

* * * * * * *

In a spotlessly white, clinical setting, Dal's surgically cut apart head protruded from an aperture in a cylindrical tank, whose surface blended seamlessly with the hazy, featureless surroundings.

The lower portion of his face had not been dissected, and discolored lips were moving without making a sound. In stark contrast, with muscles, blood vessels and tissue exposed to view in a bizarre manner, the upper part resembled a teaching anatomical model.

With bodily fluids firmly fixed in place, some of the perfectly excised smaller cubes of flesh that had been separated by a high precision cutting device were attached to delicate support rods that extended from deeper biological layers. These had also been pulled apart, and were spread out in blocks arranged in front of the opened head. The larger oblong slice, that included the orbital region, contained a pair of twitching hazel-gray eyes. After one of the blinks, like pulled down roller shades, both eyes were completely encased by a thin layer of glossy dark tissue.

Dal felt a pleasant numbness as a young girl with blond pigtails appeared in his field of vision. She was licking a blueberry ice cream cone while seated on a swing in the dappled shade of trees. As he observed her in this idyllic setting, he felt off-balance in the moments when his perspective changed, as if she was being viewed from various angles and distances. When she seemed to be so close that he could reach up and touch her, he noticed a green fly crawling on the sugar cone by her fingers. The next thing he saw were the reddish goggles of some intricately detailed monster that was overlaid with puzzling calibration grids and technical marks. There was also an achromic cascade of computer-like code, whose minuscule rows were only perceptible because of their rapid movement.

When he realized that the compound eyes were part of the housefly as viewed under extreme magnification similar to the zoom mechanism of a digital microscope he'd used in a high school glass, he couldn't understand how such powerful amplification was possible with his naked eye alone. After viewing the enlarged insect, his enhanced vision was suddenly blocked by the approach of a rapidly expanding, spinning black circle.

At the same instant, in the sterile environs of the operating theater, multiple robotic arms gracefully unfolded from a glinting tubular contrivance that slowly lowered itself above Dal's opened head. As agile, slender fingers repositioned the square chunk that contained his detached orbital region, the hazel-gray globes within darted about.

When his sight returned, he found himself seated on a park bench in the receding light of dusk. As he glanced about, ordinary-looking people shuffled about in a dazed state around a single lamppost. None of them were talking or looking at each other. After a moment, a wiry fellow with a dirty silvery ponytail sat down next to him. There was a yellow smiley face on his unwashed gray sweatshirt. In his dazed state, Dal didn't notice any resemblance to himself in the man's features, including his hazel-gray eyes.

"You look a bit confused, sport," the guy said while scratching his chin stubble. "But, that's good. Or else that Frisbee gets tossed your way. See it being flung?"

When Dal turned to have a look, in the distance, he could see two figures playing catch with a solid black Frisbee as those between them drifted about aimlessly.

"It gets thrown at your eyes," the man continued, "but also into your mind, and then, WHOOSH, everything goes blank. They just want to make us think everything is okay. Yeah, sometimes it's better to not be aware."

When the fellow got up and wandered off, a slim, middle-aged fellow with a sun-creased face and droopy mustache approached. He was wearing a straw cowboy hat and the rest of his western getup included a dark teal shirt, denim jeans and fancy snakeskin boots.

"Howdy, name's Toppy," he said. "You hear about the old-timers reunion in Magdalena? You ought to come, friend. There'll be a chuck wagon taste-off, roping, fiddling and even the ugliest truck contest. You like fry bread?"

Dal's gaze was fixed on the shadow flicker on the ground. When he looked up to determine the source, he was bewildered to see that the lamppost was now a sepia-toned old windmill, whose wooden sail wheel turned against a bruised magenta sky. The surroundings seemed slightly warped, which caused him to wonder if he was dreaming.

That would explain the disconnected sequence of events. Thinking he had fallen asleep during the church service, he fought to wake himself up. "In Smoky Jack's Tavern," the man continued, "I once heard some old-timers talking about things from space and flying pie plates and such. Legends told by grimy-faced miners, I reckon, but maybe it was the trail's end for those folk, too... the visitors that came. We've a saying about Magdalena. Everything is unfussy on the outside, but take a step inside, and you'll be darned surprised."

* * * * * * *

With the shrill pulse of crickets in his ears, Dal opened his eyes and slowly rose to his feet in a forest clearing. In front of him, several shabby lawn chairs were placed around a freestanding blackboard. There were colored chalk sticks in its wooden tray that had been used for the list of names and dates written on the slate. Some were neatly printed while others were barely legible scrawls. He'd been to this place a couple of times when he was younger. Situated near a flat ledge at the edge of a ridge, it was once a popular hangout for locals to view the glittering night sky. Over the years people reported strange happenings and weird lights in the area, with some who witnessed unusual activity adding their names to the "guest register." Why hadn't rain smeared the list, he wondered?

Brushing the forest loam off his clothing, he tried to recall slipping and hitting his head on something hard. His next thought was that he had wrecked his bike again and wandered up to the clearing with a head injury. Though he didn't feel any bumps or contusions, he couldn't stop thinking about blacking out due to some accident. Suddenly it dawned on him that he had been watching a vague white shape moving between the dark outlines of conifers. He guessed this blurry object was some kind of new military drone that was able to conceal its presence, but as the result of a glitch he caught a glimpse of it.

Even with this hiccup, none of its features stood out in stark detail except for a plastic Jack-In-The-Box ball that some joker had affixed to one of its electronic sensors.

As thoughts of being zapped by some energy beam and losing consciousness because of something he wasn't supposed to see played over in his mind, he paced the length of the opening, looking for any telltale signs on the shadowy ground. Unbeknownst to him, glowing yellow eyes in the rotatable head of an owl perched high in a nearby tree followed his every movement. With mottled brown markings and other realistic details, it would be hard for anyone other than a wildlife expert to realize that the raptor in its nest was one of a dozen or more similarly camouflaged trail cameras placed about in these woods.

When he heard the sound of branches snapping, he thought it would be best to high tail it out of there. As he hurried down a narrow path, there was a crunch of footsteps behind him. Glancing over his shoulder, he could see several figures following him. All seemed to be dressed in metallic outfits that glinted in the faint moonlight. Their faces also looked strange, as if they were wearing dark masks. When he picked up his pace, jumping over dead tree limbs, the steps of his pursuers also quickened. No matter how fast he moved, they were quickly gaining on him.

At a bend in the track, two masked figures jumped out from behind a tree, blocking his way. The purple eye masks were of the cheap simple kind, which looked ridiculous, especially on the tubby shorter guy with puffy cheeks. Both of them had on the same purple jackets with shiny geometric prints and matching baggy jogging pants that had tinselly silver designs.

When the other three guys surrounded him, he saw that they were wearing the same flashy outfits as those standing in front of him. Since they were all dressed alike, his first thought was that they might be part of some bizarre cult. Two of the figures were holding old-fashioned glass bottles. He could smell beer on their breath, so assumed that's what was in the amethyst-tinted containers.

"What are you doing snooping around here?" the squat guy asked in a deliberately aggressive manner. "Spying on the klatch?"

"The what?" Dal replied with a faint smile. "Did you guys see a funny object a while ago?"

"Oh, you're one those, huh. Like the pokey things," another guy chuckled.

"Nice try, fuck!" the would-be toughie sputtered with a generous dribble of spittle. "He's looking for our stash, Boyd. Wants to take what's ours alone... the klatch's. Wadaya wana do with him?"

"We didn't see you come into Sullivan's field," a calmer voice said. "I think I've seen you around. You ride, don't you?"

"Yeah, a Gryffin. That's how I got here."

As he said this, he realized in a moment of clarity that he didn't know how he had got there, but he definitely didn't want these guys to know that. Though the possibility of the roly-poly twerp who couldn't hold his suds getting in his face was laughable, there were five of these clowns.

"I just like nature," Dal said while looking down at the ground. "I'm not spying on anyone. Whatever you're doing is your thing."

"There is no nature here," chubby blurted out with a lingering trace of his courage booster. "So, find a new place to scope out creepy owls. But first, we wanna know what you saw, bro? Tell the truth."

As the guy was about to shove his hands into Dal's chest, his eyes nearly popped out of the silly mask and all the color drained from his bloated cheeks. Whatever he saw caused him to flinch back so quickly that he stumbled, having to grab hold of a tall pine sapling to keep from landing in a thickly overgrown patch of vegetation.

"What the fuck's wrong with you?" the guy uttered as he moved behind the pine's splitting trunk. "That's some YouTube shit!"

When the others leaned forward to see what it was about Dal's face that had caused such a shocked reaction from their friend, one of them dropped his antique bottle. It didn't shatter, but gurgled foamy brew onto the leaf litter. Without exchanging glances or uttering a single sound, all of them backpedaled, comically bumping into one another before scrambling up the footpath. At the same instant, the visibly shaken figure cowering behind the sapling ripped his mask off and bolted into the dense woods.

* * * * * * *

Dal picked at the food on his plate. Not only was he tired from spending most of the night walking back to the church to get his motorcycle (luckily, he hadn't parked it in the section that had been taped off as an emergency crew jackhammered the asphalt to repair a broken gas main), his eyes burned and watered as the midday sun beat down on his face. Though he'd never had a migraine before, he thought he might be experiencing one as neon white blobs appeared across his field of vision.

20

Most of the church members were seated at picnic tables in the park. Those enjoying "the wondrous glory of potluck" sitting around him, including his mother, were joking about the similarities of a bag of Grippo's barbecue chips to "the fire of eternal damnation."

"I don't know how he can eat 'em," Corina said. "Those things were surely dusted in the Ordeal. Same with those other flamin' things Lucas likes."

"With long squirts at the bubbler, praise Jesus, that's how," another lady replied.

As they harped on about the chips, Dal couldn't stop watching a little tyke playing with a classic Mr. Potato Head plastic toy that was placed next to a Tupperware container of potato salad. With his cheetle-stained little fingers, the kid pulled out the detachable eyeballs and then reinserted them back into the holes, repeating this without touching the other facial pieces. Seeing him doing this for the umpteenth time, something in him snapped.

"Stop doing that!" he shouted. "Leave the thing alone!"

"What else can you do with this?" the kid asked while shrugging his shoulders.

"You don't have the right to do that, you little shit stain."

"Dal, what's gotten into you?" his mother blurted, surprised by his rude outburst. "That was uncalled for."

"I just don't like what he's doing to me," he snapped back, still irritated by the kid's messing with Mr. Potato Head's eyeballs.

"To *you*? You mean to the toy, don't you?" his mom said with an uneasy look.

"I think I'm getting a migraine," he said while rubbing his temples. "Sorry, Lucas, I didn't mean to be so testy. It's there for people that have trouble identifying side dishes."

"Snarky is better than huffy," his mom said while repressing a smile. "Lucas, honey, why don't you go play with something else."

The kid shrugged his shoulders again and slid over to the open spot that was right next to where he had just been seated. There, he quickly began pulling out and pushing back in the eyeballs attached to the plastic cucumber "friend" of Mr. Potato Head that was placed in front of a mixing bowl of cucumber salad.

"Here comes Hoburt to slap the demons out of me," Dal mumbled after spotting the pastor walking briskly towards the table. As he approached, the pastor was nervously stealing glances at something in the parking lot. "If that perve lays his hand anywhere near my head, he'll be the one dropping to the clover, and I guarantee it won't be a courtesy drop."

"Why don't you go and get some sleep," his mother suggested, hoping to avoid a confrontation. "No wonder you're tired – mowing the lawn in the middle of the night. I'll bring home a plate in case you're hungry later. Derethia's peach cobbler isn't canned and is crackling as always."

"Does she make fry bread?" he asked absent-mindedly. For whatever reason, he had a sudden urge to leave Jaywick and maybe head out west. "The grass has been cut?"

✳ ✳ ✳ ✳ ✳ ✳ ✳

Night had fallen on the cornfields surrounding a narrow back road in northern Indiana's Amish countryside. Seeing the amber headlights of his pedestal lamps on a triangular red reflector, Benuel reined his horse and slowly applied the brake of his market wagon to stop behind the dark boxy carriage parked on the gravel shoulder. He was returning from his roadside stand and wanted to make sure there wasn't anything wrong with the driver or his speckled draft horse. After climbing down from the padded seat, he walked up to the charcoal-black buggy and leaned against one its matching spoke wheels.

"*Gut daag*," he uttered with the distinct accent of a distant German dialect while shaking his head at the lack of hazard lights. Didn't the new brother know that young kids raced their cars on these rural lanes and that if there was a crash the buggy never wins? Even though there were no interior lights, after pulling on his suspenders and adjusting his straw hat, he tapped on the carriage's fiberglass siding. When the lowered blinds were raised halfway, a heavily bearded face with wire-rimmed glasses appeared in the opening. The man also wore a black trimmed straw boater.

After being assured that everything was fine, Benuel headed back to his sizable buggy. Instead of leaving, he gathered up some baked goods and pickled treats and returned to the carriage. Rather than knocking, he climbed up the entry step and pulled back the leather screen behind the flip up window.

"*Ach.*"

Along with a simple dash setup, the enclosed canopy was crammed with high-tech electronic equipment. There were tactical radios, portable modules, charging cells and computer monitors with color displays. The man in colonial attire even had a bendable display affixed to his wrist. On its gray scale display, a black dot rotated clockwise around the circumference of a larger white circle before stopping at the edge of a particular radius.

In the process of decoding a cryptic message on the mobile unit's flexible screen, the man had scribbled on a note pad the words:

BLUE GATE

With a surprised look on his face, Benuel held up the plate with the red beet eggs and chocolate whoopie pies.

"*Appeditlich.*"

* * * * * * *

Kingston 'King' Mockenhaupt knew he was about to get his head chopped off, and he'd just driven through what locals call a gully-washer to meet with the man who wielded the sword. At least he no longer had to wear that beard. Spirit gum had irritated his skin, and a different adhesive that had been recommended caused an allergic reaction. In the glistening wet parking lot of the "Blue Gate" – a popular restaurant for tourists visiting the Amish settlement in Shipshewana, Indiana – he awaited further instructions. With his gaze fixed on the wearable computer, while seated behind the tinted windows of his black Jeep Wagoneer, he was keeping track in his head rather than writing down the 'invisible letters' that were represented by a series of black dots that were distributed along the equally invisible line segments near the perimeter of a white circle.

"Is there another T?" he uttered under his breath.

As he continued to observe the monochrome display, the colors suddenly reversed and a configuration of several orbiting white dots veered outside the bounds of the black sphere and came to rest along the periphery.

"Pat, I'd like to solve the puzzle. Is it PIT STOP?"

Despite having a youthful appearance, the retired lieutenant colonel with a shaven head and twinkle in his brown eyes was a former Air Force intelligence official and combat controller with a Tier-1 Unit. With his involvement in covert operations, he was one of only a few highly trained assets recruited to participate in an unauthorized Special Access Program (uSAP). The program was ultra-black from its inception, unshackled from congressional oversight and concealed within an impenetrable labyrinth of spurious programs designed to confuse and mislead anyone on the outside. To protect the most closely guarded secret in the classified realm – the recovery of advanced technology of non-human origin – nothing was deemed out of bounds, and through the decades the outcome for many that ventured too deep into the maze was the stuff of lurid fascination.

His current duty involved going undercover in order to get chummy with an Amish boy named Abram. When he wasn't rotating soybean crops or churning butter, the kid was posting advanced theoretical concepts on subreddit threads about higher dimensional realities from the privacy of a barn's hayloft. Some of the speculative ideas involving space-time metrics were so novel that, while one astro-physicist in the working group expressed zero confidence that the assumptions were within the realms of possibility, those more desperate to make something happen were willing to toss the 'hypothetical' dice, especially in knowing that they, themselves, had "impossible things" under wrap. After much debate it was agreed that the equations of this potential Einstein with a stem of hay in his mouth required further investigation. The first step involved a carefully arranged farm accident. In ensuing MRI scans, a specific part of the boy's brain lit up like a Christmas tree. Even with contrast dye, it was an extremely bright signal. Others who shared heightened activity in the same region were believed to be more receptive to unknown influences. They were more attuned to anomalous phenomena, and often referred to themselves as experiencers.

After being made aware that Abram's subcortical nuclei were on fire, he became a prospective candidate to have a crack at a stubborn piece of hardware that was part the inventory spirited away in a uSAP cubbyhole that was off limits to all but a select few.

It took some doing, but once King gained the boy's trust, when asked about how someone brought up in a community that was frozen in time gained the knowledge to conceive and develop putative formulas involving arcane field resonance theorems in a cowshed, Abram claimed that "a rock had told him."

At first this was a head scratcher, but the crazy explanation became a tad bit more plausible when he added that it wasn't just any rock, but a lithophonic boulder. As a child living in Upper Black Eddy, Pennsylvania, while visiting the nearby ringing rock fields in Bucks County, after repeatedly striking the diorite stones with a hammer, certain harmonics of the hauntingly beautiful bell-like tones created also whispered into his ears the secrets of slipping between realities.

For the 'minor indiscretion' of committing two words to paper, he would most likely be removed from the task of probing further into the dimension-hopping Amish boy's sonorous rock claims. That and vetting him prior to recommending he be given the necessary clearance to access the location where one of the prized finds was kept. He could blame the momentary lapse on buying into his cover of living a simpler life, though most likely he was drowsy after popping too many Benadryl tablets. With the skeleton in the cupboard he'd been entrusted with, he wasn't concerned about being dissolved from the program.

He assumed he would either be transferred to a security-oriented detail, or become part of the disinformation campaign. The latter was work that involved creativity, but kept him out of the thick of things, he lamented as he started the ignition. There was no point in psyching out over it – he would learn of his new assignment after a half hour drive.

* * * * * * * *

"Benuel asked me if I had a Glock inside my mutza," King said while grabbing a handful of popcorn that he washed down with a gulp of one of the sports bar's on-tap pilsners. "If you're infiltrating a fentanyl ring preying on teens experimenting during a rite of passage, than you need to be packing. Yeah, he swallowed it. Benuel is the real deal. I've had his butterscotch fudge and it's better than Betsy's. *Appeditlich*, as the Amish say."

"Well, it would be wouldn't it?" the man seated across from him in the booth said with a telling look. Though along in years, Spiller Andrews maintained a hard visage that was furrowed and darkened from his time in the program. As one of the senior figures in an elite cadre of gatekeepers, he had lived with an explosive secret for so long that he found the cheery faces in the room to be unsettling. With a hotel-barbershop cut of silvering hair, he wore a rumpled tan overcoat despite it being a humid summer's day.

"I'll give you points for your reflexes, but this isn't about being compromised," he said while stirring a glass of scotch with a long, thin finger.

"I thought that might be the reason for the switcheroo," King said.

"I'm sure you've had enough hog offal. By the way, what's worse? Scrapple or Spam?"

"I would assume scrapple is nastier, though I couldn't tell you because my cover wasn't that deep," he joked. "It wasn't all that bad. The clatter of horse hooves in the buggy lanes lulled me to sleep. The clip-clopping. Hell, some of the carriages cost more than my Jeep. Those with add-ons like fog lights. Shag carpet. Cup holders."

"Don't forget a speedometer?" Spiller added with a derisive chuckle.

"I almost forgot something I learned incognito," King said after being distracted for a moment by some rowdy customers. "The true secret is Southwestern Dust."

Spiller's jaw dropped.

"What does that mean?"

King reached into his pocket and pulled out a small shaker bottle filled with brown powder.

"It means this spicy seasoning the Amish sell might just put some life into this stale popcorn."

"Oh, that dust," Spiller said while regaining his composure. He didn't like being caught off balance, and accordingly drained his scotch.

"But, to circle back, you'll be provided with additional footage from the trail cams," he lowered his tone despite the cacophony of multiple games played on endless flat screens along the walls. "In the brief clip you were shown, I trust you saw this Gordon person's eyes… the dark casing that appeared over the sclera and had those other kids crapping their silly pants."

"Yes, it was clear when analyzing the screen-grabs – a smaller version of the black wraparounds. I wasn't expecting that – the biosynthetic film on a verifiable Hoosier kid. They're really pushing it, aren't they? With those things exposed to view, even if only in certain instances. We'll go with a congenital condition. Persistent pupillary membranes something or other."

"So, now he's a camera, sending hyper-spectral imagery with his eyes. I remember the days when they used cows for peepers," Spiller said while eyeing his half-eaten cheeseburger. "They'd take 'em apart and put their own optics in and then put them back together again. Then we'd take them apart to try and find the stuff, though we didn't have the means to put them back together. Thus, all those mutes that had ranchers befuddled. Anyway, the recent incident with a trickster in Jaywick involved aspects of the same exotic predation. Your standard bionic module vectored in with a made-to-spec 3-pack of bug-eyed foldouts that, like a transport beam to the welcome mat, is now a fucking trope just like our social engineers intended. There might have been a few extra features in the package... besides the talons... to carry out *his* add-ons. I wonder what they're looking for?" he mumbled with a straight-on glance.

"So, what's up with those purple guys?" King asked.

"Oh, you mean the Wixley klatch? They're entrepreneurs," he said as he eased back into the seat's red leatherette fabric. "They found a large stash of pre-prohibition beer buried near the shortcut. After drinking the stuff, they make a killing on the vintage bottles sold as collectibles. Breweriana, it's called, that's sold at flea markets and antique malls and such. Since the glass hasn't been artificially nuked, it's highly sought after on the eBay. I guess the purple colorization is from traces of manganese that was added way back when as opposed to recently color-altered glass."

"But, you said they first drink the beer. How could it still be good after all that time?"

"Indeed," Spiller said with a mischievous grin. Once again, he eyed the remains of his lunch before looking down at the paunch under his coat. "The long and short of it is," he said while leaning forward and discreetly glancing about, "that the recent Jaywick encounter takes precedent. We've a rare opportunity here. As interesting as the Amish kid's story about the rock sounds are... well, to exploit what we think this Dal Gordon guy was fitted with... you can see why we need to get you – a specialist – involved. So, we're putting Abram on the back burner while you get acquainted with this new fellow."

As King dusted his popcorn with a generous amount of the spicy powder, a man with a shaved head and round acetate glasses wearing a Colts jersey paused by the booth and gestured to a photo hanging there. It showed a 1940s Indianapolis 500-style racecar painted blue and emblazoned with the number 3.

"The winner in 1947," the man said without a distinctive accent. "But, only because of a mistake with the pit strategy that allowed him to catch up. Instead of a battle to the finish line, there was a friendly wave."

After saying this, the fellow calmly walked away.

Even though the bar was packed with racing enthusiasts, and the man spoke with a typical midwestern dialect, there was something about his choice of words with regards to a faded piece of memorabilia that caused alarm bells to go off in Spiller's head.

"This Benuel's fudge might be better than your prudence with comms."

* * * * * * *

Dal returned to the clearing on the forested ridge at night a few days later. While checking out the immediate surroundings, he pressed his palm against the bark of a tree, running his fingers over it, feeling every coarse furrow to convince himself that the rough layer wasn't an artificial veneer that disguised some liminal threshold like those invisible portals and energy vortexes in other places he'd recently heard about in a number of documentaries on YouTube. Glancing about, he lifted his ears. There was even something about nature's melodious share that seemed a bit odd.

Having seen an enigmatic object with egg-shaped symmetry gliding between the pines, he had cause to wonder if the luminous displays and unexplained activity really were just misinterpreted events repeated by beer guzzling teens. Even stranger were the stories from older folk that claimed to have glimpsed what looked like a drive-in movie screen showing a clear day-light sky framed by the night's twinkling stars. Maybe they weren't just joshing a new generation about the wooded hangout. While standing in front of the blackboard, for some reason, he picked up a piece of blue chalk and wrote his name under the others that had signed the guest register.

After a few minutes, he decided to head back to his bike. While taking a less used path to avoid any possibility of running into the purple-garbed gang, he suddenly found himself standing in an ethereal greenish glow. For a second, he thought the eerie shimmer had emanated from above. However, he quick-ly realized the ghostly chartreuse aura that enveloped decaying wood radiated from luminescent fungi. Yet, as his gaze remained transfixed on the foxfire, the pleasing tonality of a voice sang from deep within him.

Faint impressions unfolded and shifted before his eyes, though he was unable to hold on to this confusing imagery. It was fleeting like the details of a dream upon awakening. While he didn't know what it meant, he knew that it was something not to be ignored.

* * * * * * *

CHAPTER II

The town historian didn't have many details about the incident and a search on an online database failed to provide any results to back up the elderly woman's strange account. Finally, after days spent viewing yellowed newsprint on an old microfilm reader in the library, King was rewarded for his effort. The entire article had been printed on the front page of the *Indiana State Sentinel* in the summer of 1885. Although the preserved text was of poor quality, with some eyestrain, even smudged, run-together words were readable:

MY GOD, WHAT IS THAT?

Heaven! We are given an account that is said to be perfectly true, the particulars of which savors strongly of the marvelous and will certainly puzzle naysayers. While coon hunting in deep thickets sometime before nightfall, Elbert Gordon, a gentleman of highest respectability and unquestionable veracity, claims to have seen a most remarkable character noiselessly gliding about near a small structure with mortared stone walls and timbered buttressing that functioned to protect a natural spring or to store perishables, perhaps even used for mortuary refrigeration as a crude, purpose-built charnel house.

According to a description furnished by the witness, the personage he observed with mute amazement was of diminutive proportions, having a delicately molded form with lustrous golden eyes and pleasing features like "polished ivory with an oddly yellowish cast." The mysterious visitor was clad in spotless, brilliant white tight-fitting coveralls, with a matching nightcap-like head covering and "funny shoes that didn't touch the ground" completing the bizarre costume. With absolute sincerity, the truthful citizen also reported that the being carried what looked like a cheese plate on which were situated several bottles of beer that he recognized to be the exemplary product of Indiana's own Wixley Brewing Co.

Upon realizing that Mister Gordon's eyes were glued on it, to avoid dire calamity, the timid figure made a bee-line into a nearby "curiously constructed metal hut without any windows." Suddenly, with a rapidity that seemed to be a work of magic, there was a faint swishing noise as the weather changed, whereupon the inhabitant's white tin shack became enveloped with a light cloud or vapor of un-wavering shape. A strange feeling came over the one taking his peeks, and the entire scene of wonderment disappeared in a twinkling, with scarcely a vestige remaining. In a state-ment to the skeptical, he said this wandering apparition was no troubled dream. So far, there have been no invitations for Elbert to visit a clinic as small gatherings wait on the small hilltop for the mischievous specimen to reappear, hopefully with the tray of local hop-juice.

Though this coverage of the "wandering apparition" smacked of the newspaper games of the time period, written as a circulation booster (with tongue planted firmly in cheek), after reading the piece a couple of things stood out. The location of the encounter was near the "shortcut" and the witness to the event might have been an ancestor of this Dal fellow. This was something that could be useful when it came time to jolt his memory.

But why was someone's stockpile of beer hidden within a submerged storage bin many decades before prohibition? Were they also aware of certain anomalies in the vicinity and used one of them to ensure the brew's longevity? Or did the visitors themselves stash the beer there, using the place that once served as a hillside root cellar, lime kiln or dead house as their personal cooler? Perhaps, from time to time, they also enjoyed kicking back and having a cold one, as the 1885 incident seemed to suggest.

* * * * * * * *

The remnants of stone masonry were swallowed in shadows cast by moonlight sifting through spreading tree branches. Twigs crackled as King paced about the exposed old foundation, the sharp beam of his flashlight sweeping back and forth from slatted retaining walls with a silvery tracery of lime-mortar wash to an unlatched wooden plank covered with artificial shrubs that made for a cleverly disguised trapdoor.

Soon, a figure emerged from the narrow opening, holding an antique purple bottle that was still sealed with a ceramic plug.

"You've got to unfasten the gravitating stopper to take a drink, sir", the gangly redhead with freckled cheeks and protruding Adam's apple said while climbing out of the below-ground pit. Not wearing the colors of the Wixley Klatch, the fellow named Boyd handed King the fancy beer bottle.

After running a finger over the bold embossing, King pulled the metal clasp and 'uncorked' the porcelain stopper. He took a couple of long sniffs before taking a sip of the chilled, sudsy contents.

"A little skunky, but not bad for being pre-prohibition belch. Not bad at all," he said while wiping the creamy head from the blob-top.

"There's still over two hundred bottles left, along with an old flask filled with some kind of powder, sir. Probably something used for what's called glassmaker's soap, a mixture of stuff like pyrolusite or other alkalines that were added to the formula as decolorizing agents. I went online, sir, to learn this for our eBay listings so buyers didn't think we were selling fakes."

"Right, the recipe for the unusual coloration. So, you think the brewery went out of business but the owner planned to start up again at a later date? Okay, that makes sense."

King wasn't at all surprised how dutifully the kid accommodated him. Upon learning that he was considering enlisting in the military, Boyd had been chosen, not only to reveal the entrance to the subsurface storage hold, but for the specific purpose of keeping rumors about alien-human hybrids, shape-shifting reptoids or a taxonomy of otherworldly beings that blend in with the population that were circulating among the town folk from spreading on social media forums.

With members of the vintage beer bottle club having glimpsed Dal's dark sclera casing – features that King had reason to believe were surgically implanted as multifaceted optical instruments – it would be best, he felt, to keep any back-fence talk contained to an isolated podunk.

"You said you wanted to talk about what we saw," Boyd said while shutting the hinged wooden hatch.

"Have you ever heard of congenital conditions involving pupillary tissue?" King asked. "Things like mydrasis dilation. I can understand your and the others initial reaction. Seeing something spooky like that. And what about novelty black contact lenses they sell?"

"But, I saw it as it happened. No, he didn't put anything in his eyes... So, we're not supposed to talk about it... the scuttlebutt," Boyd said with a sly grin, as if he wasn't buying the explanation.

"No, say whatever you want. This place isn't far from Wright-Patt. Hell, maybe something escaped from Building 18," he said while recalling what a former CIA director once said: *If you want to keep a secret, then pretend to share it.* "Made a getaway from cryogenic suspension in the Blue Room... or is it pink like the pinkish-gray skin-tone of the recovered little guys in the glass coffins looks under deep-freeze lights? You know, something kept on ice... in a maze of cold storage... just like your beer here."

"You're kidding, right?"

"If you want people driven by curiosity flocking here in droves to your private reserve, be my guest. It's not my valuable glass. I'll tell you what – as a change – I'll forget what *I* saw," King said while gesturing to the trapdoor.

"Yeah, you're right, sir. I don't think there are any bogeymen in these woods."

"Did you feel a sense of dread?" King asked.

"Well, yeah, sort of. It was that and this voice in my head... my own voice... telling me to turn and run."

* * * * * * *

On weekends when the weather was nice, Dal liked working at the outdoors liquor dispenser station in the rustic setting of the Muddy Boots Tavern. Popular with local bikers and their "hell babes," the out-of-the-way joint had live music and a smoke shack kitchen in which buried beef sandwiches were served from a scaled-down version of the more famous "crock-pot" in Parke County. Like the brick-lined pit there, foil-wrapped packets of beef were simmered over layers of coals and chunks of scrap wood covered with sand.

Keeping watch of the glowing embers when the pit's steel lid was opened was an off-duty fireman (who joked about being on the grounds to put out any "Prairie Fires", referring, of course, to the half-price tequila and Tabasco shooters).

"What's the matter, barkeep, you got something in your eye?" a heavily tatted dude wearing a patched leather vest over a "City Moto" tee uttered to Dal. "What – am I supposed to get a refill from the fucking dirty creek? Also, the sauerkraut on my rye was a little gray. Did you hear me – a little gray," he chuckled while stroking the goatee on his ruddy face.

"Hold your horses," Dal uttered back while pouring a foamy draft from the brass faucet of the triple-tap Kegerator. "This guy was here before you, so you're riding pillion, bro."

"I'll have a tall blonde," King said as he tilted his polarized silver mirror shades to glare at the obnoxious fellow standing a little too close to him.

"So will I," the biker said rather gruffly. "Or any color. I don't care. You're all sisters from the waist down, right honey," he said while turning to face a tanned strawberry blond that was dressed similarly to the other young knockouts on the patio. The bloodshot eyes of the grungy dude with a soiled red bandana moved leeringly from her lace-up skinny shorts to a ribbed white tank that accentuated her cleavage.

"You've got some loud pipes," the woman said, seemingly not offended by his crude remark. "I haven't seen you at any runs. Does your scooter also bark that loud?"

"Try, Ducati, hon."

"Might be a little too much mustard on that kraut," she said before pursing her lips in a comical manner. "Next time ask a Yelper."

"Yeah, sugar lips, I outta to have ordered the beef from that dutch oven thing. It's supposed to be out of this world, right barkeep?"

Though he emphasized the last sentence, as with previous attempts to poke fun at Dal for the idle chat about of him being a disguised alien of some type, Dal hadn't heard the rumors, and, as such, didn't have a clue as to what the guy was referring to.

"Make it a Deal with the Devil, scrambler, but not fucking glassy like the last one," the dude with the bullying attitude croaked while pounding the counter with a fist of wadded-up cash.

"Do you want a pretty swizzle stick?" Dal asked dryly.

"No, but I could use some pretty fingernails like this bitch's claws to scratch the chigger bites on my veiny balls," he said while turning around and winking at the woman.

"I'd tell him to go catch some wind," King said in a voice that was devoid of emotion, "but road rash might improve his looks."

"I'm not afraid of you," the dude mumbled with his unsteady gaze directed at Dal, "no matter what the fuck you are."

Unfazed by what he perceived as an idle threat from this weekend warrior with his boutique rags, Dal sighed with mock-exasperation. Instead of the DIAP the ass-clown ordered, he poured him a hazy amber, citrus sweet "nonny." As his mom would say, *beware making a bargain with the Devil.*

When the bar back arrived with a bucket of ice, Dal handed him a plastic cup.

"Take over for a second, I've got to make a call."

"Yeah, he needs some space," the buzzed shithead stressed the last word while spilling most of his zero proof. "Up yours... again."

To get better reception, Dal headed towards a shady stand of trees at the side of the tavern where customers parked their rides near the edge of a small creek. It was on one of the banks that an actual vintage motorcycle was suspended on a pole as part of a quirky promotion. Adding to the elaborate gimmick, not only was the bike's headlamp on, the wire-spoked front wheel rotated.

As he was about to make a call, his gaze was drawn to the flicker of shadows on the ground. Though he'd stood by the tavern's famous sign many times, the shadow cast by the spinning wheel had never been so pronounced.

When he raised his gaze, what he saw didn't register at first. With profound shock and utter confusion he stepped back from the jarring sight of an old windmill silhouetted against a dramatic twilight streaked sky. Even more startling, the summer foliage that had surrounded him was now a boundless expanse of desert scrub and distant jagged ridgelines tinged with fading hues of orange, magenta and crimson. As sand spouts rolled over thorny bushes, a rider approached on horseback from the direction of a barren creek bed. When several yards away, the man dressed in southwestern attire softly commanded the horse to a halt and climbed from the saddle into the pulsing shadows of serrated wooden blades. Tipping his cowboy hat, he walked up to Dal with a friendly smile.

"Howdy there friend. If'n you don't recollect the first time I made your acquaintance, the name's Toppy. I'm the caretaker of these grazing lands – not the owner of the spread."

"Okay... seriously, what you people are beaming into peoples' heads isn't funny," Dal said while rubbing his disbelieving eyes. "Seriously, it isn't fucking funny, people – "

"Seeing how I'm pretty good at spotting an unbranded calf," Toppy said, "I wanted to tell you that feller back there with a mighty bray has more tricks than I've seen in a domino parlor. Like a seal in a circus, he is. But, he isn't the only one dark as Angus hide."

"Okay, that's enough," Dal said while diverting his gaze from Toppy to the intense shadow flicker of the slatted sail wheel. "What is this shit even supposed to mean?"

"It's an invitation… and a warning, partner. If'n you think that beef cooked to a frazzle is dandy, by golly, you should visit Smoky Jack's for a right proper green chili cheeseburger. We're more than hoisting beans aplenty from a tripod with a spoon here."

"I'm not talking to this. I'm not talking to this, okay – "

"Back in the day, while most were panning with broken teacups for a nugget to gladden their eyes, some had bulging pockets from other ore bodies. Like the manganese deposits in these parts. About these shabby prospectors with their tale telling, I reckon some were able to talk the hind legs off a mule. But some might not have been swappin' lies with their yakkity about fallen pie plates and canary-colored kinfolk with dwindled faces. I'd be much obliged if you looked into this. As they say, Magdalena might seem penny-plain from the outside, but take a step inside and you'll be darned surprised. Now for the warning. Riders on coal-black horses will be coming. Coming from way off yonder."

At that moment, a thick plume of dust blotted out Dal's sight. When the swirling brown haze passed and his vision returned, the surroundings returned to normal.

Pausing under the motorcycle on the pole, he made a call on his smartphone. As he did so, a couple of cute twins in sequined jeans and leather bustiers passed by.

"Hey there, two-fifty," one of them said, "how are you supposed to start our prairie fires from here? Look, Dal, we've both got the exact same mud stains on our heels," the other giggled as both girls raised matching ankle boots.

"I'll be with you in a sec, ladies," Dal replied while leaving a voice mail. "Hello, mother. From my bar on casters I get whiffs of burnt flesh that's been tormented for an eternity in some infernal region. You want me to bring some home for dinner, or is it the ineffable glory of the Lord's providing at the Waffle House?"

* * * * * * * *

Jix Black wasn't sure about which footprints to feature in the next episode of her show, "BLACK HOURS", so she flipped a coin. The loser, tails, would have taken her to Cloudcroft, New Mexico, where "convincing" over-sized tracks in the mud had been filmed under the cracked branch of an aspen tree on which a cluster of assorted Tootsie Pops had dangled as bait for a relic hominoid suspected of dumpster raiding at a local eatery.

Heads brought her three hours northwest to Magdalena, where a newly discovered cave contained ancient rock art that included prominent six-toed footprints composed with an ocher pigment.

Had there not been a battery drain with the game camera, and it captured something shaggy and large with human-like features, she would have opted for the shady forest and possible clean stick award presented by the owl mascot of the sugary bouquet, though she harbored doubts that any self-respecting Sasquatch would enjoy hundreds of delicious licks to get to the chocolate core without reciprocating with so much as a dead mouse, twig bracelet or trinket from whatever extra dimension that it popped in from.

As viewers that got their "Fix of Jix" were made aware, the show's engaging host felt it was important to maintain a sense of humor when dealing with high strangeness, especially when it came to those elusive creatures that hundreds of brawny out-doorsy types wearing camouflage fatigues and bedaubed with tricolor military face paint hoped to attract with Ritz crackers and sparkly marbles. She was even prepared to help by gifting gourmet peanut-butter treats that had a rating of "four-and-a-half grunts." But, as to the latest video upload, a coin toss had other ideas for the lovely "DarkZone Drifter."

With a degree in journalism from Syracuse University, Jix worked for a popular Las Vegas news station. A couple of years ago she started doing podcasts dealing with unexplainable events to earn more income. Increased upload frequency resulted in more viewers and subscribers. After tracking the metrics that mattered most – views, subs, likes, shares and the all-important ad revenue – she launched her own channel on a streaming platform that was a competitive alternative to YouTube. The analytics looked good, receiving high ratings for informed content and production values, as well as (unfiltered) positive feedback from those that tuned in for her witty comments when it came to handling fringe topics. The show also boasted insider knowledge, which made some of the more cynical types suspicious of disinformation tactics, though most credited this to her being a dogged investigator. It also didn't hurt that she was easy on the eyes. As a striking natural blonde, she had turned down numerous offers to be a fashion model (and more unsavory propositions). Though not overly concerned with the graphs that obsessed others, she kept an eye on them. If the current trajectory of the various indicators stayed the course, factoring in potential brand deals and merch sales, there would soon be enough income to go full time. She had found her niche and was having fun. She was also genuinely interested in UFO/UAP activity and its associated phenomena, though she remained careful that her enthusiasm for dissecting inexplicable happenings was balanced by a healthy dose of skepticism.

Some of the details were scarce, but the story of the cave paintings involved a group of local teenagers that frequented an abandoned mine to engage in juvenile mischief like kids have been doing for generations (which the graffiti-marred rock strata attested to). While further exploring the rusted machinery and wooden hoppers in a tunnel for a Facebook post, a couple of the teens discovered an inclined passage with a false wall that was made to look like a collapsed working.

Removing some of the spoil heaps and rotted timber revealed a canvas-draped opening that led to a circular chamber that was used by indigenous people for ceremonial purposes in the remote past.

Having seen the vibrant images on the Internet, an expert in ancient Native American pictographs from Albuquerque managed to convince one of the finders to allow him to examine the cave (there might or might not have been a couple of variety packs of "the claw" involved). Part of the agreement was that the location (which was on private land) would remain undisclosed to the public. The kids wanted their secret gathering place, and the specialist realized this might prevent the site from being vandalized again. Likewise, to get footage for her show, Jix had also promised not to reveal the teens' hangout.

Since they still hadn't found the original access point, the host had been warned that she and her cameraman would have to deal with the usual surface hazards in defunct mines. Things like sketchy flooring over a stope, sagging roof supports and the possibility of rattlesnakes. On the plus side, the ventilation was good and there were no undetonated explosives.

"Just up ahead," the young preservation anthropologist said. Though Chayton was part of the Navajo Nation, there was no trace of the distinct accent that many of the older members had.

In the dark recess behind him, the glare of flashlight beams swept across swathes of exposed breccia deposits in the uneven bedrock walls of the hidden chamber.

"What's that smell?" Jix asked while wriggling her nose. "Maybe rat piss?"

"It's definitely messing with your notes of vanilla," her cameraman, Aiden, said while pivoting his caving light to the rock-strewn floor.

"So, Chayton, how long do I have to provide a blood sample to see if I'm infected? What's it called – Weil's disease?" she asked with a light-hearted smirk before flashing an expression of mock horror at the serious-faced researcher.

"Oh, you're fine," he replied with a dismissive gesture. "That's teenager urine. This is their favorite spot to drink that boozy seltzer. No Weil's disease here."

"My cavenaut outfit will protect me," Jix mumbled while raising a sturdy boot. For safety's sake, she wore a reflective short sleeve shirt and jeans with kneepads. Mindful of style (and the possibility of wheeling bats), her blonde plaits hung from a lariat-brown, wide-brim fedora.

"Here's the panel."

In the wavering glow, the buff-colored rock mural was filled with strange imagery that had been composed with vivid mineral pigments. Along with abstract geometric patterns were the silhouettes of enigmatic figures with hourglass-shaped torsos. Painted with red hematite clays and yellow ochers, the fantastical assemblage of elongated trapezoids also included six-toed footprints that were arranged on a 'staircase' of clouds.

"Not being patinaed, it's very difficult to date, but this was done by the ancestral Puebloans. Perhaps Mogollon. We don't like the word Anasazi because of the negative connotations. I'm also one of those that don't like the word, rock-art... even hyphenated. You can make the aesthetic argument, but it goes well beyond that. What the designs represent, even if it seems obvious to the casual observer, we simply don't know what's being conveyed."

"It's like Pictionary. They're stories?" Jix asked. "Or, hunting magic. Is it multifaceted?"

"Perhaps. You've got the squatter man anthropomorphs and typical hexadactylic footprints on stepped clouds. Polydactyl digits might have been associated with a type of divinity here in the Southwest. Again, it's speculative, but this could be a graphic expression of the specific boundaries of the spirit realm and material world."

"No antennae on these forms," Jix was quick to comment.

"Correct, no elk antlers," he responded curtly to the ancient astronaut allusion.

In the middle of the panel where the stylized outlines of the composite figures danced (or floated), a small section of the rock surface, itself, was missing. The remaining hollow space was egg-shaped (an ellipsoid, to be more precise). Measuring several inches across and about an eighth of an inch thick, the depression was perfectly smooth with uniform edges, suggesting that an advanced cutting tool had been used.

"Why a piece was removed, and by whom, I don't have a clue, but it's sad. Looks to have been done fairly recently with a specialty blade."

"What about this thing with nothing on it?" Jix asked while pointing to the lower right corner, where a whitish-silver elongated oval with a totally blank surface appeared to be the exact same size as the machine-cut cavity.

"The proportions are the same as the scoop-like cut, but what's more puzzling is the coloring agent used. It's more lustrous than calcite or powdered gypsum. Almost having metallic tints. And there is no trace of splatter along the edges that I could detect…

even under magnification. Whatever was in the artist's palette, it definitely wasn't blown through a tube. Applied with a thin bone, indeed. As to why they left it blank, your guess is as good as mine. One other thing, it doesn't reflect light."

Interspersed among the spirals, squiggly lines and zigzags were unusual glyphs that resembled modern math symbols or graphic devices that had been applied in a vivid bluish hue. Seeing that Jix noticed how the markings sparkled at times, a smile spread across Chayton's face.

"Wow, these are something," Jix remarked. "Ancient Puebloans did this?"

"The stylistic differences of these intrigue me. Not only the design aspects, everything about them, including the tertiary colors. Looks like they got a chunk of azurite to mix with some binder, and the fine-grained crystal flecks that are attached or embedded might be local blue smithsonite. I've a hunch they're territorial markers, with topographical features represented by some ambiguous tribal symbol code."

* * * * * * * *

Smoky Jack's had long been the favorite watering hole in Magdalena, New Mexico. Inside, wood-paneled walls were covered with faded photographs of atomic history, bullet-riddled license plates and shelving with dusty antique liquor bottles. In the days before Budweiser glass lamps hung from rafter beams festooned with red chili pepper string lights, scientists from Los Alamos working on "The Gadget" frequented the place, claiming to be part of the mining community if anyone asked questions.

Though country heavy most of the time, a polka was playing on the jukebox as regulars drank alongside out-of-staters that had stopped by because of its storied past and to try a green chili cheeseburger, cactus fries and pecan pie. For more adventurous tourists, there was a grilled elk steak sandwich with frijoles and traditional flat bread.

"My last boyfriend hired a private detective would you believe it to see if I was cheating," Jix told the Hispanic bartender, who was listening with an amused expression. She had changed from her "cavenaut" suit into a watercolor print V-Neck blouse, tight jeans with a silver conch belt and turquoise leather booties. "Okay, full disclosure, Jose. He had a good buddy that was a snoop. Anyway, one day he points a finger at me and says the guy has explicit photos. When I asked how revealing they were, he says they're pretty damning. One actually showed the thing in my mouth, and another actually had me swallowing. But, he was okay with it, because he cheated, too. Thus ended our pact to go vegan. So, have the cook put a brand on the bun and bring it on," she said after noticing the dark imprint on a bun of the Zia sun symbol that was made by using a custom branding iron. "Also, brand one for Aiden here, even though he wolfed down a Lotaburger for breakfast… and whatever my friend, Don, wants."

"Just a diet Pepsi," the clean-shaven middle-aged man sitting next to her said. "I'm on duty tonight," he added while tugging at his forest service uniform. Being part Mescalero Apache and part Spanish, Don had spent many summers working on his grandfather's ranch near the Magdalena Mountains.

In the past year or so, as the old *caballero's* health continued to decline, he had heard bits and pieces in breathy whispers about the crash/retrieval of an unknown object that occurred right after the "big war." According to other old-timers, this might have been connected with the famous Roswell incident.

"And a Corona without a lime to slake my thirst," Jix said while bobbing her head to the lively meter. As the bartender turned to get a beer from the case, the entertained look on his face remained.

"Sorry, Don, please go on with the story."

As he began to speak, Aiden framed a shot with his action camera.

"My grandfather, Josiah, was a young boy at the time. After finishing his evening chores, he and his friend were playing checkers with matchsticks on the porch when suddenly they saw this thing – "

"Better idea," Jix said as the drinks arrived. "Let's go to a quiet booth."

After sliding into the booth, the man continued with the story.

"He said the figure looked like one of the sacred clowns of the Mescalero Apache. It had a yellowish-white color that glowed faintly at night as it glided past them. He couldn't see its face… just a black circle. Over a period of a week, it appeared at various times. Whenever it did, it spooked the livestock. Goat bells went silent after hearing its terrifying laugh. It had a horrid laugh to keep things away. Some times it pretended to be invisible, remaining motionless for hours behind a scrub oak clump. At other times it acted crazy, sliding along the arroyo like a sand spout. The two frightened boys were given dumb explanations, like it was just a migrating sandhill crane that was covered with flour that came from burlap sacks dropped by B-17 bombers on practice runs over the area. Josiah still talks about it when he finds his tongue after licking teaspoons of brandy. What you need to understand, he doesn't think it was one of the clown impersonators that he saw in Apache ceremonies – but a real one that came from a sacred dimension. If you ask me, though, it was a star elder that survived the crash."

* * * * * * *

48

Dal was seated on the couch in the family room, eating a messy burger from the Tasty Freeze drive thru while watching the flat screen. He had recently found Jix's show and like many others was drawn in by her dynamic personality and intriguing subject matter.

In the soft, even light of her studio setup, she was reading comments from viewers.

"The thing Don's grandfather described made me think of the tale of the Sandown Clown. The incident that took place in the 1970s, when a couple of children playing in a marsh were greeted by a 7-foot tall specter in motley tatters that approached the kids with a peculiar hopping motion. It held a sign that read: 'Hello, and I am all colours, Sam.' The entity invited the boy and girl into its metallic shack that didn't have windows, and performed some tricks with a berry. Its face was paper-white with triangle and square markings like a robot's mask that spoke with unmoving yellow lips... Geez, that's creepy," Jix responded, "Let's hope the encounter with this ludicrous thing really occurred in a paranormal bubble or was some kind of imaginary playmate instead of just being a sicko wearing a clown costume preying on curious children."

The motion graphic backdrop of a southwest desert landscape at sunset switched to Aiden's footage of a well-lit section of the rock art mural. The camera zoomed in on one of the clearly delineated six-toed footprints.

"We were discussing earlier about how individuals born with duplicated fingers and toes in ancient pictographs found throughout the southwest might have been members of the tribe that were exalted or even worshipped like gods. You know, VIPs.

A new subscriber – welcome and thanks, my friend – writes: Yeah, we all know the grainy Alien Autopsy film from the 90s was an outright hoax. A latex-based life form with pigs brains, that when dissected, oozed blackberry jam bought at a local market. Tabloid shit, right? Well, not so fast. Has anyone seen the new frame-by-frame analysis?

Forget about the goofs in the fuzzy staged recreation of the genuine original that had mostly deteriorated and pay close attention to the few usable frames that were inserted into it. A careful examination of these few precious seconds reveal distinct differences. In one, the being's six toes are a different length than those on the dummy. In another, the piece of metal debris doesn't have embossed symbols. And there are other telling discrepancies. By the way, according to the cameraman, this crash didn't happen in Roswell. It occurred just west of Socorro near Magdalena. Keep an open mind, and don't get fooled again, people."

Jix made some adjustments to her equipment before continuing.

"Sounds like this might be a game changer unless a couple of rubber dummies were used with bad editing. Again, we're being tight-lipped about the location, but that's the general area of the mine. Before it was decommissioned, sizable ore bodies were extracted. Manganese used in alloys and to bleach glass that turned a pretty amethyst color used in specialty bottles back in the day. Also, it's on private land, so shoo all you pothunters."

The camera footage focused on a close up of the ovoid-shaped cavity where a small section of the panel had been removed with a precision cutting tool.

"Okay, so check this out. Part of the rock wall panel has been detached with a modern tool like a core cutter or mason's saw. You have to wonder what was so alarming that it couldn't be seen?"

The camera panned to the whitish-silver colored ovoid feature in the lower corner.

As Dal bit into an onion ring, he thought it was a little strange that the egg-shaped feature on the shadowy cave wall contained a red symbol that looked like an inverted V with 3 horizontal lines running through it. In contrast to the other crudely drawn geometric shapes, it looked like a modern insignia. Both the sharp lines and even color stood out.

"Here's the same elongated oval shape," Jix said, "that looks like something was covered up with super paint. Again, what was someone trying to hide?"

With a confused look on his face, Dal drained his soft drink. While shaking the ice, the annoying kid from the church picnic named Lucas walked into the room. He glanced up to see what was on the flat screen before turning towards Dal. As he did so, his eyes locked on Dal's. For a few seconds he stood motionless, as if paralyzed with fear. He then stared blankly at the floor for a moment before running out of the room.

"Lucas, they're just Indians with crayons," Dal said as he dropped the wadded junk food wrapper back into the paper bag. When his attention returned to the flat screen, a series of stills taken from the footage showed the unusual bluish glyphs that were scattered about on the mural.

"The specialist doing fieldwork thinks they might be territorial markings. I'm by no means an expert, but to me they look pretty modern for pre-contact time. Sort of like those unicode math symbols. Yeah, they could be weird topographical objects like you'd see on a map, but if they are I can't identify any of the identifiers. Except for this one with eight stokes that I call a spider trapped in a cup," she joked. "Here's another take from someone that wants to remain anonymous: Hello, Miss Black. In watching your video showing ancestral rock art, it might interest you and your viewers to know certain findings linked with a classified study for military applications of exotic atmospheric phenomena, in particular the close-range exposure of plasma-related manifestations that engage in complex behaviors and even interact with the human brain, often causing disturbing effects, hence the military interest. Though I cannot discus this aspect of the project, I am willing to divulge something in the data pipeline that involves your cave markings as well as those of other cultures. Such archaic snap shots of observed anomalous presences in the skies, witnessed worldwide and recorded for posterity, when juxtaposed with overlays of plasma bursts in various phases generated in laboratory settings bear striking similarities that extend beyond the overall shapes. That is to say, using advanced imaging techniques, stylistic comparisons with petroglyphs and pictographs and highly charged plasma entities closely match. Intelligence assessments using digitally stratified sets make this abundantly clear. The morphology of buoyant plasma formations, including warped toroids, spheroids and jetting rays were depicted by the ancients not only as ladders, columns and scorpion heads, but as other abstractions, like strangely elongated figures with prominent eye features and arm-like appendages. Weird creatures as visual representations of cosmic forces.

Those enigmatic trapezoidal bodies one sees on rocks. Again, the research is classified, but if one were to lay their cards on the table, Miss Black, these elusive, coherent structures display a range of awareness as if they are either guided by an intelligence or are, themselves, sentient life forms."

"He's saying what's shown in the mural are conscious blobs of electrical activity?" Jix said as her eyes widened to convey a scary thought. "The swirls and radiating patterns. That's an interesting theory I haven't heard before."

Dal's mother rushed into the room with a face stained with anger.

"That wasn't funny – your little prank. Lucas is really upset."

"What are you talking about?"

"Tell that little boy and his mom that it was just a stupid trick. And show him the dark coverings. The black contacts or whatever it was."

"I don't know what his problem is – "

"Well, maybe someone should put the fear of God into you."

* * * * * * * *

"What the fuck are violet crumbs?" Dal asked while standing behind the dimly lit bar inside the Muddy Boots Tavern. Last call had been given earlier and all the patrons were cleared out except for one, who was seated on a stool. As Dal put away some clean glasses, King Mockenhaupt sprinkled a generous amount of his "Southwestern Dust" seasoning onto a complimentary bowl of popcorn.

"Violet Crumbs is a person. It's on the nametag of her uniform. She's the one that claimed to see a man lifted by a burst of greenish light into a hovering object in the parking lot of a church. Of course, this hallucination was most likely caused by her inhaling the fumes of a toxic germicide used by sanitation experts like those with Sacred Spaces Church Cleaning Services."

"Yeah, I think the pastor also got too many whiffs of the stuff."

"That preacher's quite the theological anomaly, and you can bet he's on the radar of local law enforcement."

"We've got some Grippo's chips back here that you don't have to shake all that powder on if you want."

"So, you didn't see anything unusual in the woods? Haven't had any puzzling experiences as of late?"

"Not really," Dal said with his best poker face.

"Because these fellows that dress funny saw something."

"So?"

"Well, let's just say there are owls with really big eyes in those woods, and they use them to keep watch on what's going on. I read this microfilm record about one of your relatives named Elbert from long ago that saw something out of the ordinary at the very same spot where you signed your name on the guest register. And I've seen the MRI results from that motorcycle accident you had –"

"I was going in hot, that's all –"

"The scans didn't show any damage, but what it did show was rather interesting. It showed enriched gray matter in one of the subcortical structures, meaning you might have a gift, Dal. Might... With this more developed region – the brain within the brain – some are able to see things that others don't with cool rationality and without being predisposed to fantasy. These antennas, if you will, are referred to as intuitive empaths."

"Shit, I've heard about this. They're people who can find things by only using their minds. Where submarines are and underground pyramids – it pops into their head."

"You're talking about remote viewing to explore targets. That's different. There were no remote viewers really. The program actually involved synthetic telepathy. It was a test by the military using experimental technology that beamed images – coordinate axes and such – from behind the walls in a separate room. There was nothing special about the subjects. They had no psychic abilities. It was just a trick played on them to determine if the gadget worked. There's a lot of bullshit out there. Nowadays, you scroll on YouTube and see stories about black ops with unmarked shadow units engaged in human trafficking of people with heightened mental abilities that are needed to interact with alien technology. Most of the things revealed by whistle-blowers coming out of the woodwork – sinister forces and tech harvesting – that's disinformation clutter. But, the program I'm involved with is the real deal. Thus far, we've reached no startling conclusions with the small sample of experiencers. There's no starseed nonsense. People from some higher dimension who think they're guiding humanity. You should think about participating in a series of tests and experiments. Nothing invasive. If nothing else, it will get you out of these cornfields. How do you even know if you're having a bad day in a place like Jaywick?"

"I don't see how I can help, and I'm not sure what you want. It all sounds kind of crazy honestly, except the part about the cornfields. I can't believe I'm asking, but where is this program?"

"Las Vegas."

* * * * * * *

Dal's mother, Corina, had some unexpected company when three men turned up on her doorstep that evening. One of them introduced the group as chief officials that had traveled from the UPCI headquarters in Missouri to ask some questions about church affairs involving Pastor Hoburt. Surprised to be visited by members of the general board, she invited them inside. After showing them to the dining room table, she served coffee and slices of peach cobbler.

"It's my lazy peach cobbler," she said with an apologetic smile. "Nothing fancy. It's canned. I hope it's okay, being made with peaches in cans."

"Thank you, Miss Gordon," one of them said with an expressionless visage. Like the others, he had a smooth olive complexion with ambiguous features and thinning ashen hair that might have been a toupee. All were wearing sharply creased dark suits, whose spotless linen had a chemical smell of new fabric. Oddly enough, each also wore tight-fitting gray polyester gloves even though the area was in the midst of a heat wave. "We won't take much of your time." The words were noticeably spaced in a tone that seemed too deep. "The council is interested to know if your ordained minister has been negligent of his assigned duties? Has he done anything that is contrary to biblical teachings?"

"No, not that I'm aware of."

"Does he adhere to the rules such as modest dress and hair guidelines?" another asked.

"Yes," she replied.

"How do you explain those female members of the congregation that were recently wearing facial treatment masks?"

"I beg your pardon," she asked with an awkward glance.

"Those snap-on, shell-like masks that promise overnight miracles. You know, therapy for dark spots and oily skin that have green LEDs with a light setting on maximum intensity. They have genuine silicone eye protectors. Masks with protective eye cups... that's what you and the others saw. They're supposed to be collagen producers and prevent sun damage, but there are lots of complaints and the company responds with a bot generator. Did anyone report this to the Better Business Bureau? Report these snap-on masks."

"I've never seen anyone wearing facial masks inside the church," Corina said.

"Are you a licensed esthetician? What beauty school did you attend? Was it in Las Vegas, where people play a game of chance for stakes?"

"What? Heavens, no."

"It's hard to believe you. We are from the Show-me state, and I don't see any cans in this dessert," one of the men said while poking his fork into the cobbler and making a mess of the biscuit dough crust. "You said it was made with cans, but where are they? There's cornstarch, nutmeg and buttermilk in this, but no cans. If you were untruthful about the cans, I fear you're also not being honest about not seeing the masks with the eye cups."

"I'm not lying to you."

So much for straight-talking people from Missouri, she thought.

"I don't see a hearth in this house. If you are cooking peach cobbler over an open fire, you run the chance of burning the house down. Maybe you should serve Entenmann's instead. It's at the end of the store aisle if you need us to show you."

"What are you talking about?" she asked with a confused look. *Was this some kind of trick played by Dal?*

"We are the highest authority, Miss Gordon, looking into this matter to make sure no one crossed any boundaries. And we don't want you to make peach cobbler with or without cans with an open fire inside the house because that might result in an uncertain outcome on the basis of chance."

"I'm not feeling very good," Corina said while pressing her hands tightly against her temple. "Sorry, but would you gentlemen mind leaving. You can find your way to the door."

"So long for now and take care of yourself. Remember what we said about the facial treatment masks with the protective eye cups," he said with a penetrating stare. "We are the highest authority looking into this… to make sure no one crossed any boundaries."

Corina watched with an incredulous stare as all three stood up in unison and headed towards the front door. Instead of turning the knob and exiting, one of them paused and began knocking on the door, waiting for a response. When no one answered, he rapped on the wood again, louder than the first time. This time, the door swung open, with Dal casually walking in, startled and confused to see the men backing up. Without acknowledging his presence, they stepped outside in single file, each having a slow awkward gait. After closing the door, Dal turned towards his mother with a questioning gaze, unable to get a reaction as she sat there transfixed by the glint of the brass handle.

* * * * * * *

CHAPTER III

Dal was ready for a change of scenery. Having grown up in the corn-belt, he glanced at the endless farmland, looking for something different even though he knew he had another full day before he'd start seeing the desert.

As part of the deal with King to participate in some tests, he had been given a black Jeep Wagoneer (with tinted glass, no less) along with an ample amount of cash to cover expenses on the trip to Las Vegas. He was also handed the keys to a rental house in a neighborhood called Summerlin that had a view of a picturesque red rock canyon.

Knowing that it would be a couple of weeks before he would be cleared to take part in any "behind the door stuff", he planned to spend a few days in New Mexico – the home of real cowboys and Indians. While doing research online for places to visit, a festival called the Old-Timer's Reunion in a small town called Magdalena had caught his eye. It seemed like the perfect way to become acquainted with the flavor of the southwest.

Though he was upbeat about the changes in his life, he still had bouts of anxiety when thinking about what he might be getting himself into. He still wasn't exactly sure what he had signed up for, having only been told that certain elements of the program were classified and involved what King called transmedium communication. As always, King remained vague about specific details and said that he (Dal) didn't need to know the big picture, asserting that it wasn't anything that would cause conspiracy junkies to trumpet to the masses, especially, he added with a cryptic smile, if they didn't get wind of it. While he hadn't been plucked out of the blue, and was a potential candidate because of his unique brain morphology, there was always a chance that he would flunk out. If he did, so be it, Dal thought. What the hell, he kicked the sod off of Jaywick and would try to get a bartending job in one of those ultra-lounges on the Las Vegas Strip.

When he mentioned concerns about lacking any special abilities during the initial meetings, King had told him not to stress and that he was highly confident of getting positive results. Though Dal maintained that he didn't have any vivid interactions (to use King's words) with whatever he glimpsed in the woods above Sullivan's field, King reminded him that the object had affected his vision in that he was able to perceive with uncanny clarity the goofy antenna ball on one of its protrusions – something that he normally shouldn't have been able to discern from such a distance. This peculiar optical trick associated with the craft (that Dal assumed was a secret test of a new drone) would be a disadvantage to any military asset, except, that is, for the observer.

Though he had been completely up front in describing the physical characteristics of the unusual object, he refrained from mentioning the series of confusing images that flitted through his mind shortly after the sighting. Whatever it was that passed swiftly before his eyes (that he couldn't lock on to), he felt he should keep silent about it, at least for the time being. Ditto with the strange visitors that showed up at his house.

Sure, there was something a bit off about them, but the same could be said about the person they were asking questions about. If they weren't really church officials, maybe they were law enforcement agents working undercover to snare Hoburt.

To his mother they were imposters all right, but the masquerade was the work of the devil. Satan was infinitely devious, and men pretending to be the head of the church were more of his clever tricks. She had all but said that he (Dal) had unwittingly invited these dark forces into her living room by refusing to except church doctrine and outright mocking the divinity of Jesus (here, she was referring to a T-shirt he had worn that read: YOUR SAVIOR IS 70% WATER).

Like the witchy marks on a banana skin, he had no regrets of engaging in such antics (what his mother called "blasphemous escapades"). By using these tactics, he hoped to get her back to being her old self. After having surgery, she, like many others that suffered pain, had become dependent on prescription drugs. When she was the most vulnerable, the church had all the solutions to her problems. It was like a beacon of light that she and others gravitated towards after becoming sober. But, with her faith-based recovery, she had merely traded one addiction for another. She insisted that the church gave her back a sense of normality, but how she could feel that way after listening to the pastor's insanity seemed contradictory. Talk about things beyond conventional understanding! Before the painkillers became an issue, he had fond memories of better times, when the two hung out together like friends. There were fishing video games, campouts and cave systems to explore. She even taught him how to ride a motorcycle.

When he told her that he was moving to Las Vegas, the first thing she asked was why on God's green earth go there of all places? He said that he had an offer of a high-paying job in a posh nightclub. Had he told her that he was getting paid to be a guinea pig due to a correlation between an over-connection in a part of the brain with those that have experienced unexplained phenomena, she would have been deeply concerned. With her current mindset, any involvement with these profound events would be lumped together as further evidence of demonic possession if the personal experience didn't involve a baptism with the Holy Spirit. After giving her the news, she threw up her hands and said that maybe he'd run into his dead-beat dad there. That was his last known whereabouts. Neither of them had seen nor heard from him in twenty years. Growing up, he'd been told that his father started having problems when he returned from the war in the Middle East. He became detached from reality and rambled in subdued tones about participating in covert operations that sounded to his mother like the stuff in science fiction movies. Whether he suffered from PTSD or some other mental illness she didn't know, but at times he stared blankly for hours as if in a catatonic state. And then one day he was gone.

As the red orb of the sun was setting over cornfields, Dal was getting drowsy and decided to start looking for a motel. He was also hungry, and one of those fried onion burgers that Oklahoma is known for sounded pretty damn good.

After continuing for another half an hour, the radio started crackling with static. Instead of trying another station, he cocked his head when the man doing the broadcast started saying things with a clipped monotone voice that didn't make any sense:

"Be here now...
Be there right then...
Be here on time..."

When the oddly unmodulated voice repeating this over the speakers seemed to also be emanating from inside his head, he had this sudden feeling that there was something very interesting up ahead. Having an urge to check whatever it was out, he slowed down and took the next exit, not knowing where it would take him.

"… Be here right now," the voice repeated.

After driving for several miles on a desolate two-lane black-top that ran parallel with the freeway, he made a right turn onto a wide graded road that was bordered by hayfields. A short distance away, he saw numerous bright orange dots winking on and off against the starry horizon. Because of the manner in which they were skimming above the ground, as well as the synchronized blinking, he didn't think they were fireflies.

While cutting across the flat ground in their direction, the reflection from the beams of his headlights glared on an oblong metallic shape in the middle of the field. As he got closer, he could see that this was a trailer of some kind, whose riveted aluminum frame resembled the backside of a vintage Airstream camper. After parking, he climbed out of the Jeep and walked towards it. While doing so, he heard peals of laughter, cheers and whistling.

When he rounded the corner, the front of the silver bullet-shaped trailer was trimmed with garish pink neon lighting. The iconic camper had been converted into a mobile kitchen with a brightly lit service window. Placed in front of it were a couple of small plastic tables and chairs. In the semi-darkness, just beyond the trailer's glare, a group of exuberant teenagers tossed Frisbees that were studded with blinking orange LEDs. He recognized the lawn game that they were playing to be "Beer Bash."

Inside the vending trailer named, TRAILIN' SMOKE, he could see the kitchen gallery with its stainless steel sink and grill hood. The menu was painted on a sign, and as Dal looked it over, the items listed surprised him:

SHREW
JACK RABBIT
WOOD CHUCK
SQUIRREL
PRAIRIE DOG
GOPHER
MUSKRAT
AMERICAN BADGER
SKUNK

"They're really givin' 'em a whirl, aren't they?"

When he turned his head, he saw a middle-aged man standing next to him. The scruffy fellow with long, dirty silvering hair was wearing a stained gray sweatshirt with a un-smiley face emoticon. He looked vaguely familiar, though Dal couldn't quite place him.

"You look confused, sport," the man said with his voice pitched in a low tone. "They want to know what you can see on the menu. It's a test, that's all. Don't tell him they've got prairie dogs or American badgers or fucking woodchucks. Instead, it's chilidogs and American burgers made with ground chuck or whatever's on a normal food truck. Sometimes, it's better to be aware –"

"Have we talked before?" Dal asked. "Who are you, mister?"

"The rescue squad," the man replied, keeping his voice low in case someone else was listening. "Listen to me, son – you don't see wascally wabbit or other road kill on the menu, but there's also no fried onion burger, so do yourself a favor and go elsewhere to find one."

He gestured with a glance that Dal should take notice of the colorful life-sized cardboard cutout of the cook that was standing at the service opening. Behind him, the backside of a foam

64

board standup of another life-sized substitute was holding a spatula as convincing drifts of smoke rose from the sizzling grill.

After seeing these comical stand-ins, when Dal turned back to get an explanation for the absurdity of their presence in an otherwise normal mobile kitchen, the man was no longer there. While glancing about to see where he might have gone, a figure seated at one of the plastic tables with his back to him turned around to face him with a dark expression. He had exotic features that were similar, if not identical, to the men that had visited his mother. Instead of wearing a dark suit, the man was garbed in a brand spanking new black hunting outfit, complete with a matching 'Elmer Fudd'-type cap with a stiff brim and earflaps.

"You look hungry," the stranger said in a flat tone with notable spacing. "What looks good on the menu because you are hungry?"

"Yeah, I like chilidogs and burgers like those at the Tasty Freeze –"

"There is no Tastee Freez in your state," the man stated matter-of-factly.

"There's a place called the Tasty Freeze, but I'm not that hungry."

"Is it because it does not have a funny advertising ball like the one you saw?"

"I just thought they might have an icee."

"We are the highest authority looking into this to make sure no one crossed any boundaries, so let's try again, shall we," he said. "What would you like to select from the menu because you look hungry?"

"I'm just gonna find a gas station or something and get one of those fried onion burgers."

"We know much about onions caramelized when griddled, but this is not the state of Oklahoma. Everything looks good on the menu of Trailin' Smoke. If you do not make a selection, our fear is that your head will melt like Tee and Eff's – the Tastee Freez attraction that is not in your state. Who repainted your eyes like Tee and Eff's when the twins were restored? The people playing with flying saucers out there are not listening."

"Oh, you mean the Frisbees. Like I said, I just want an icee –"

"Icee, icee, icee. So long and take care of yourself. Icee, icee, icee."

Though his lips were no longer moving, the man repeated the last word like a stuck recording. As Dal slowly backed away from the monotonic glitch that was steadily increasing in volume, everything in his field of vision abruptly came to a complete stand still. Not only the movements of the indistinct forms playing the beer-drinking game, but even the gliding motions of the Frisbees, themselves, remained suspended in mid-flight with only their blinking orange LEDs still visible. With the teenagers now resembling cardboard cutouts, as faintly perceived by the glare of the trailer, Dal scanned the frozen tableau with a perplexed gaze. After the mobile kitchen and hanging Frisbees went dark, there was a loud thud that caused him to flinch.

As his eyes twitched and his vision cleared, he saw a black Frisbee pressed flat against the windshield of his Jeep where it had just been tossed. Seated behind the wheel, he squinted as the first light of dawn appeared over a wide barren field. In the dusty orange haze, two figures approached, both dressed in what he considered to be farm clothes. When the older man in bib-overalls gestured for him to roll down the window, he did so without hesitation.

"Whatcha' doing – havin' some troubles?"

"Sorry," Dal said while rubbing his eyes. "I'm traveling and got sleepy. I just meant to rest my eyes for a minute but must have dozed off. Hope I didn't trample any crops."

"We just cut our grass hay so ain't much left even for the grubs," the older man said while kicking the hard soil with his work boots. "My wife seen you while coming back from the Circle-K and we just wanted to check if you was needing something. Couldn't see who was inside through that dark tint and found this thing sitting in the field," he said while picking up the Frisbee. "Maybe, you ought to have got some coffee or Red Bull with yums boughten from the Circle-K. Not much else around here near the Tripoint. Where you headin' if you don't mind my asking?"

"West."

"From Indiana, I see. Well, at least you're not from Inferior. That's what we call Missouri. I like your ride. Not too used up. The I-44 is just a yonder. Go about 200 yards and you won't be in Kansas anymore."

When the farmers turned and walked away, Dal wheeled the Jeep around and angled off towards the graded track. After turning onto the two-laner that would take him back to the freeway, he spotted a road sign up ahead that said, "ICY." As he passed it, something flashed in his mind.

"I see," he mumbled, "what? What do I see?"

* * * * * * *

"The last freeway was also a freakin' Safeway," Dal told King on his phone's Bluetooth connection while driving on an interstate south of Albuquerque, New Mexico. "I guess everyone's picking up road kill to save on their grocery bill. They've a pretty good selection of fresh carcasses from what I could see. And these people weren't hobos or whatever – they were driving nice cars, not pickups – those scraping up the stuff with shovels."

67

"A lot of deer get hit. You Hoosiers didn't have a recipe for carrion casserole or fender fricassee? Pull the Lexus over honey," Dal said with a thick Texas drawl. "If that one's not too flat, we're having roast pheasant with parsnips for supper. Can't you see them in Amarillo draining the blood into an oil pan and soaking the damn thing in milk with a dash of thyme."

"From asphalt to the skillet without the long grocery lines," Dal joked.

"So, where are you stopping?"

"Magdalena, New Mexico."

"Why? What's there?"

"The Old-Timer's Reunion. Navajo tacos on fry bread instead of raccoon hoagies."

"Isn't that near Socorro?"

"Yeah. Pretty close. Why?"

"I hope you have a PRD."

"What's that?"

"Personal Radiation Detector to measure the fallout from the last nuclear fission weapon detonated."

"C'mon, you don't need a Geiger counter to have a Navajo taco. The doses aren't high."

"I didn't say it was Chernobyl or Fukushima. But, the background radiation levels are elevated... comparatively speaking. Higher than in Jaywick."

"You can check when I start having tests. Speaking of which, you know the weird thing about all the road waffle I saw was that the night before I had a dream about it. They don't have food trucks out here that only serve road kill do they?"

"Sounds like you might be hungry," King laughed. "Enjoy that Navajo taco in the plutonium-laden dust," he said before hanging up.

After tucking his phone back into a pocket, King knelt down at the edge of a large ovoid-shaped impression in the same Kansas hayfield that Dal had been compelled to enter. Using an eyedropper, he squeezed a few drops of water over a portion of the scorch mark to see if it would be repelled. As he suspected, the whitish crust was hydrophobic. Though it was the middle of the day, he also knew that the impression emitted a faint luminescence. Seeing the plume of dust from a fast approaching pickup, he straightened up and leaned against his black Jeep Wagoneer.

"Looks like you haymakers have some kind of fungus in your field," he said to himself in preparation for any questions.

* * * * * * * *

Dal pulled into the dusty parking area of what looked like an old 1930s gas station that had been re-painted in earthly tones. Written in sandstone red lettering, the sign on the dingy yellow facade read:

NATIVE AMERICAN TRADING POST
BERT'S AUTHENTIC CURIOS & CEREMONIAL SUPPLIES

When he climbed out of the Jeep and headed towards the dilapidated structure, traces of the Texaco logo could be seen bleeding through the peeling 'new' layer. Passing the remnant of a rusty pump with a missing globe onto which a flybown tin sign advertising Nehi grape soda had been placed, he entered the store through a tattered screen door.

Steaks of sunlight filtered through slatted window shutters, casting prisms on the pioneer artifacts on the adjacent wall. Permeating the cluttered interior was a redolent, slightly acrid smell of burning pinion and sage from a smudge bundle placed on a smooth, oval-shaped buff-colored plate that masked a mildew odor from textile fabrics.

"What you're looking for, it's here," a voice rang out as a man emerged from the shadows. He was a Native American with a pudgy face and tawny complexion framed by longish black hair that looked like a messy Elvis Presley-style pompadour. Wearing a plaid shirt and faded denim jeans, there was a faint glint from the presence around his neck, being a traditional squash blossom necklace of 'pearl' beads and a crescent-shaped pendant studded with turquoise cobochons in silver bezels.

"Hello," Dal said. "Do you have cold sodas?"

"How about a bottle of Nehi grape like the sign out front says? My name is Bert Sandoval, and I'm the proprietor of this Indian Trading."

"Really? I mean, I meant the grape soda. That sounds great in this oven. Looks like you've got some really cool stuff here," he said while glancing at the bedizening selection of native herbs, jewelry and colorful pottery, trying to take in the unfamiliar motifs on crafts and fetishes displayed against a backdrop of woven blankets and pictorial baskets.

"If you're visiting, you've got to watch out for fakes, and that includes trinkets in gift shops," he said while fishing out a bottle of grape soda from an old metal ice-chest. "The white man gets duped by scam fests like eBay, whose non-native sellers list lopsided vases with sloppy designs. Plated silver without sterling marks. Do you have a magnet in your pocket?"

"No," Dal replied, feeling kind of stupid after touching his pants pockets.

"I guarantee my silver and pottery is handcrafted by Native Americans that don't eat snakes, owls or burnt toast. My people – they've got the knack for this. Everything is authentic, not lookalikes like a cartoon of Charlie Brown trying to pass himself off as a real human. How about some Sleeping Beauty turquoise studs for your lady?"

"I currently don't have a lady."

"What about your sweet mother? The turquoise comes from Globe. Rare as rocking horse shit. It's almost mythical."

"Her preacher won't allow her to wear jewelry."

"Then maybe some ghost beads for you to ward off evil. Genuine juniper berries gathered on tribal land, peeled and hollowed with the assistance of genuine squirrels and chipmunks that don't ask for a percentage from the five-fingered creatures also involved in the process. Ain't nature the shizz. Thirty bucks and I'll throw in some magic chants and corn pollen. If you've got some cloud nine for my peace pipe, we can make a trade."

"If that's what I think it is, I don't."

After taking a long drink, he noticed a browned paper chart hanging between the shelves of curios that contained a series of tribal symbols. The one in particular that caught his attention was an inverted V with the caption:

THUNDERBIRD TRACKS

"What does this symbol with the upside-down V mean?"

"Thunderbird tracks. Not from the gas-guzzler. The supernatural creature that swoops down from the sky with eyes that hurl lightning bolts. But, that mark is for the eyes of the profane… the non-initiated. It's not the true, complete symbol. Want to see it?"

"Sure."

Bert stepped into a storage closet and quickly returned holding what appeared to be a piece of antique pottery. The cream-colored vase had an elongated oval shape that contained a red glyph made with an ocher pigment that was still vibrant beneath the chipped beveled edge of its rim. Dal was surprised to see that the inverted V intersected by 3 horizontal lines looked identical to the marking on the cave panel as featured in the Black Hours show.

"This is a museum piece that came from a member of a tribal secret society. It's been passed down for generations. Notice the distinctive sheen? It's been sealed with pine pitch. I shouldn't sell it, but others have expressed interest, and times have been tough for many moons. Seeing how you were drawn to it, for three K you can put it on your shelf.

"I don't even know if I have a shelf. Anyway, its out of my league."

"I've horsehair pottery that makes for a less bruising financial experience, but this is a real treasure."

"I'll take some of those ghost beads in case I need 'em in Vegas."

"Give me forty and that will cover the grape Nehi, Uncle Sam, and I'll include a mud toy in case you have a shelf. I'll even chuck some nuts at the critters that assisted the five-fingered beings without asking for a cut. You should check out the dark veining on my spiderweb turquoise from Bisbee. Keep in mind, what you're looking for, it's here."

* * * * * * * *

The Old-Timers Reunion was even more colorful than Dal had anticipated. The crowned Queen was in her nineties, the best super-looper in the kid's rodeo was an adorable little girl, and the banjo plucking, quick pickin' fellers were awed by the frenzied yodeling of a bluegrass punk band. Craziest of all, the "cookie" that received the trophy for the chuck wagon cook-off had it quickly taken away for cheating.

His period garb might have been authentic enough, but part of the sauce consisted of a bottle of Kraft Original that sold for two dollars at a local mini-mart. A fellow contestant that noticed the plastic container while snooping around in the top cookie's pantry box to try and improve his own sauce provided video of the prohibited ingredients to the judges from Ruidoso. After being disqualified, the running joke was that Heinz made the three-time champ's whistle beans. This silly fart joke really had the rope-slingers slapping their knees.

Dramatic flashes of sheet lightning bounced at the horizon while darker patches of sky glittered over the expansive landscape. After most of the replica kitchen on wheels had been towed from the grounds, Dal and a group of locals remained seated in lawn chairs brought to the "big picnic", where whiffs of cow manure in warm breezes mingled with the smell of burnt cinnamon. While drinking bottles of beer and toasting churro-flavored marshmallows over a wagon's glowing firebox, tales from the old cattle trail turned to the space trail after a reporter from Albuquerque started asking questions about the rumored crash/retrieval of an alien vehicle and bodies that echoed the events surrounding the famous Roswell incident of 1947. Further complicating the story he was working on were the various impact sites of the downed craft. Some said the wreckage was found near the Magdalena Mountains, while others claimed it was on the Plains of San Agustin. A ranch near the White Sands Missile Range was mentioned, as were the rugged canyons in the Cibola National Forest. Quemada, Datil and Carrizozo were also thrown into the mix, as was a grazing area near the Lurea Mountains in Catron County. He was hoping that one of the old-timers could help identify of the actual location.

"My grandfather here doesn't know the exact location of the recovery operation," the smooth-faced forest service worker that Dal recognized from Jix's video said while peeling a tangerine, "but some think the conflicting reports of the chain of events could be explained if the main object and its escape pod were found in separate locations and got lumped together because both finds were in Catron County. Yes, while it is true that details of the incident have become fragmented over time, the odd child that was one of the occupants of the craft is firmly etched in his mind. And other town folk, besides ranch hands, also recall seeing the quiet little one that they called Shysie."

"Why did they call this thing a child?" the reporter asked. "Was it because of the being's small stature?"

"She looked like a child to them," he replied. "She was similar to us, but not an earth person. Some that saw Shysie without her disguise said she looked like a strangely beautiful doll. She had chalky yellowish skin. The features were somewhat oriental or Mongolian, especially the eyes, but they weren't bulbous like an insect's. She looked fragile and curious, but not like some space freak made by a Hollywood creature shop," he emphasized.

While listening intently to what Don was saying, Dal kept glancing at the ranger's grandfather, Josiah, who was seated across from him in a wheelchair. The old *caballero's* bronzed skin was deeply furrowed under a battered Stetson, and the tapping of the pointed toes of his fancy shit kickers kept time with the live fiddle tunes that could be heard coming from the square dance taking place in a nearby pavilion. At times his ears would seem to perk up by what his grandson was saying, and occasionally he would nod in agreement while scratching gray stubble or adjusting his silk kerchief.

Too young to understand the conversation, the old-timer's great-grandchildren spun rainbow pinwheels and licked the charred gooey mess on their fingers. While watching them, an image suddenly flashed in Dal's mind of a slender being with an unsettling fragility and pear-shaped head with subtle facial distinctions that he perceived with startling clarity. Slanted golden-hazel eyes, the glistening fixity of which caused him to flinch, dominated the mysterious visage. Though he tried to shake off their magnetic pull, it was too late. In that brief instant, feelings welled up from deep within him. He was overwhelmed with sorrow for the isolation and desperation this delicately complex lifeform had felt while stranded in the harsh desert environment. He didn't understand his reaction to something that mere seconds ago he had no awareness of. Yet, he couldn't help but wonder if this affinity to some otherworldly presence was connected to what King had said about him being able to absorb the feelings of others. If this truly was the case, did his unique brain profile momentarily create a psychic connection that put him on the same wavelength with this "quiet little one?" The idea seemed crazy, so he dismissed the vision as his imagination getting the better of him. He was sleep deprived and the sauce on those Navajo tacos was questionable at best. It definitely wasn't store bought.

"Not a dummy stuffed with animal butchery?" the reporter chuckled. "With all the eye-popping claims, none of the locals ever found any of the strange alloys?"

"Like what happened in Roswell, I'm sure the debris splatter was crawled all over after being discovered by the rancher tending to his cattle or looking for a new grazing area."

"Don, you mentioned a disguise. Do you know what this was?"

"A wig, aviator sunglasses, tattered velveteen shirt and jeans," he replied before taking a bite from the tangerine. "The lady that worked at the thrift shop back then – now the Samaritan Center and Food Panty on Main Street – told the story of how some of the donations were stolen one night. Guess what these were?"

"The stuff used to disguise the alien's looks."

"In return, Shysie left several small green crackers."

"Are you pulling my leg, Don? I know some of the cowhands in these parts were in a story telling group – "

"Yeah, sure, there was a Liar's Club in those days, but the witnesses weren't members. Shysie avoided people other than some kids from the Alamo band. Only they got close to her... and some got sick with nasal infections and such. But, mainly she hid in secluded places near the rez... sometimes seen on an eastern side of a small canyon or in an arroyo. Some of these kids' parents believed she had witchy ways that frightened the locals and the livestock. Sheep were found huddled together in the corner of a pen. The tribal elders tried to calm their fears. She wasn't a skinwalker, but a mischievous sky kachina."

Those gathered around the wagon were silent as Don's grandfather's jaw quivered.

"I am going to tell you one thing," the old man said with a weak raspy voice while inching his wheelchair forward.

"Joshia is feeling chipper," Don said with a wide smile. "He's been sipping coffee so thick that you could float a horseshoe on it."

"It didn't go on all fours like a wolf or skinwalker does," the old man said with labored breathing. "And it wasn't one of the delight-makers from a tribe ceremony either. When I locked eyes on it... it was like I was in a dream, but it had a real-life solidness. It wasn't an apparition like some would have you believe. And it wasn't a midget clown. I was on a single-track trail when I saw the air-roller for the second time... not playing piturrilla with Pino or Alvario as before. It was zigzagging back and forth... but it was not a devil dancer. This was one of its clever tricks – "

"Wait a minute, I'm confused," the reporter said. "Is he talking about the same being?"

"It didn't have a face in the normal sense," Joshia continued with his breathing becoming more strained and his already gruff voice getting more hoarse, "but it was good at feeding things into my head. It didn't want you to touch it because it could make you sick... so I covered my face with my mascada. This thing was her second skin... the second body that she peeled off. It was putting things into my head."

"Tell him about the other thing – what you felt after it slid away," Don said.

"The places where it once stood, the air was cooler than where it hadn't been, which was normal. There was no breeze –"

"He's talking about a difference in temperature. Pockets or bubbles of air that were cooler."

"This was directly," the old man said before having a wheezing fit. "I didn't hang around to find out if it petered out," he croaked, "but when I returned days later, the cooler spots had dwindled away."

* * * * * * *

Even though he hadn't got much sleep in the past couple of days, Dal was restless in his tiny motel room. Try as he might to rationalize it, as he sat on the faded bedspread, he was still haunted by the disturbing image and inexplicable surge of emotions he had experienced hours ago. For all the female humanoid figure's mysterious features, it was the magnetic quality of those striking eyes that affected him most. He wasn't sure if he had glimpsed a ghost or an angel or the entity they called Shysie, but when he perceived whatever it was, it felt like he was dreaming. This despite the overpowering smell that engulfed his nostrils. His mother sometimes talked about supernatural aromas. The foul stench of demons was far worse than the uncleaned frog cage he had when he was younger (or his sweaty socks!), she told him, while the fragrance exuded by angels was a feast for the palate of the nose. The sweetness of pure sanctity, she once described it (ironically, while eating at the Waffle House). The peculiar aroma with the mental image was delicate and ambery(?), but for some reason he associated the odd sweetness with the future. Instead of putting on pajamas, he grabbed the last energy drink from the mini fridge and went outside to gaze at the sparkling infinity of stars over the desert expanse.

While walking in the courtyard of the motel's fake adobe facade, he spotted something glimmering atop a nearby ridge. From where he stood, it looked like a ring of flickering lights, but it might have been someone's campfire off in the distance. Above whatever this wavering glow was, broad discharges of sheet lightning flared silently from cloud to cloud. After watching this for a while, he decided to go see what they were.

Having driven for a few miles up a bumpy dirt road, he stopped on a sandy track and got out of the Jeep. Near the ruins of an old timber-roofed, domed stone dwelling, dozens of Navajo and Apache people stood in a wide circle, holding lit candles and chanting in their native language. The men were dressed in bright velveteen shirts, corduroys and sneakers, while the women wore long skirts, shawls with sharp geometric patterns and knee-high moccasins.

As Dal observed the ceremony while keeping his distance, a white Chevy Blazer pulled up with a quick flash from its light-bar. A man wearing the uniform of the Navajo Nation Police got out and approached him.

"Hello there. I'm Lieutenant Emilio Grayeagle. I was on my way back to the substation when I saw your lights. Can I help you?"

"No, sir. Everything's all right. I was just watching it?"

"The settlement – they're holding a candlelight vigil," he said while gesturing to the solemn facial expressions in the glow of quivering candle flames. "You should probably leave them at it, because with your dark vehicle they might get suspicious."

"Oh, okay. Sorry. Who's it for?"

"The falling stars. Kindred spirits."

* * * * * * * *

When Dal walked into Smoky Jack's at around ten in the morning, a dozen or so locals were seated at the bar. Country music playing on the jukebox was drowned out by spirited conversations.

"How'd you enjoy the festivities?" the lady behind the bar asked.

"This town sure knows how to throw a party," Dal replied.

"Some of them fellers got pretty roostered," a regular said. "Be needin' some extra words from a gospel sharp," he chuckled.

"There's a fresh pot if you're in need of some coffee, and there's still some magdalenas left from the batch if you like muffins."

"Add a little bee sweetenin' and you're in business, though I'd go straight for the pecan pie myself," another local said. "Either one's better than those cook-off sinkers. That sure was something, wasn't it? That belly-cheater caught with more than a dib in his gravy by that feller shiggin' for his secrets. Sheesh, I'd copper a bet that others with a middlin' sauce – even ace-high cookies – do the same kind of sneakin' or at least have a wave at it for a shiny trophy."

"They tell some good stories about the UFO crash here," Dal said while climbing onto a stool. "I'll try one of those muffins with orange juice, please."

"Well, something played out, I reckon, that stumped them. What, who knows," another regular said. "There's all shades of opinions."

A middle-aged woman sipping coffee looked over at Dal.

"When I worked for the paper, before all the juicy tidbits about flying saucers there used to be stories about Spanish galleons and Viking ships stranded in the middle of the desert near ancient river channels. Oh the vivid yarns that the editors took to an art. Same with the tall tales of Liar's Clubs. It was a pastime back in day. Connoisseurs of lies worked hard to come up with their magnum opus. Li'l bitty lies didn't win them anything."

"Like the malarkey from flannel-mouthed miners I read in the High County Round-up," another local chimed in.

"You're saying the UFO crash was made up?"

"A lot of those miners worked in the Manganese district," the lady said. "Manganese Madness was an occupational hazard. Some absorbed far more than trace amounts of toxicity. It affected their brain. Accumulated in the basal ganglia, if I remember correctly, and caused symptoms similar to Parkinson's disease. Hallucinations. Even psychosis. It's called Manganism."

"They had lots of difficulty. Just look what it did to old Toby here," a local chuckled while pointing to a mannequin dressed in rancher attire that was seated at the end of the bar. His plastic fingers were clutching a bottle of whiskey, whose antique glass had an amethyst tint.

"I didn't know his name was Toby," Dal said. For some reason, the name resonated in his mind, though "Toby" didn't seem quite right. *Who was he thinking of?*

"The miners worst affected were sometimes seen bathing in a cattle tank with far-off stares," the lady said. "This was in a part of a canyon called Dreamy Dust Gulch. What they suffered from was known as Haunted People Syndrome, and might explain all the alien mischief they spoke of."

When the door opened, all eyes turned as a short, stocky figure wearing a desert bush hat and khaki fatigues entered the bar & café. The man looked to be in his late twenties and like many in these parts was heavily tanned from years of exposure to the desert sun.

Following him was a group of nine ordinary-looking people of various ages, genders and races.

"Speaking of alien mischief," the woman behind the bar muttered. "Oh, brother, another tour group."

"Do I detect lemon?" the tour guide asked while sniffing the air. "That means muffins, but we're here for the famous green-chili cheeseburgers those scientists that put together the A-bomb ate when they came to unwind along with honest to God cowpokes... as did those who later whispered about other things. Okay, folks, grab some booths and menus, though you already know what I recommend."

"Still looking for old tin cans?" one of the locals asked.

"And other telltale signs, Vern, like burn marks on the top of trees. Earlier, we were out on the plains. Been retracing Barney Barnett's steps. We just came from the area by the old homestead near the Kelly mine where another silver avocado fell from the sky."

"That place is popular with rock collectors. Is that what them aliens was looking for – rocks?" a rancher joked.

"You mean like this?" the tour guide replied while reaching into one of his cargo pockets and pulling out a small chunk of rock, whose bluish luster looked like melted wax. "Local smithsonite. I wish the aliens had left some that had gem quality. A cabinet specimen with electric-blue facetable crystals would fetch about ten grand. Terribly rare stuff, those with well-formed crystal are. But, considering they came a long way to get the druzy ones, exiting off the cosmic freeway, I can't blame them. I'm still trying to figure out how they extracted it from the matrix. Maybe they used some light-beam technology? You can see bluish-green mineral concentration melted and splattered around the crater with the host rock."

"Like I told you last time, I need one of them there crystal energy cells to get my poor pickup running," the rancher named Vern joked.

"So, who's driving the black Jeep Wagoneer I see parked here?" the tour guide asked.

"I am," Dal replied. "Why, is there a problem?"

"Just checking. Funny, it's the second one I've seen this morning. Both identical with darkened windows. At least they're not black Escalades."

"Where you fixin' to go after this?" Vern asked the guide.

"Oh, more greasewood desert. The Socorro landing of 1964. I've got room for one more in my van," he raised his voice so that everyone in the bar could hear him. "Someone with no mobility issues, who's not wearing flip-flops. There's no alien kitsch on my tour. Alienabilia, or whatever they call it. No circus like in Roswell – just my personal expertise shared at the place where history happened. Anyone here interested in the Socorro landing?" he half-shouted.

Though Dal had pegged the guy to be the enterprising type when he first opened his mouth, after being told that the sighting at

Socorro of an egg-shaped metallic craft and short humanoids witnessed by a police officer was one of the strongest UFO cases, he signed up for the tour. After paying half admission, he was handed a typed form letter stating that FOUR CORNERS UFO/ UAP CRASH/RETRIEVALS TOURS was not responsible for "any challenges to one's belief system, negative hitchhiker effects, equipment drains, visits by unpleasant sorts and medical issues resulting from scorpion or rattlesnake bites." Anxious to see what cognitive dissonance (to use the guide's words) awaited him, he boarded the 10-passenger van along with the others in the group.

While gazing out the window at the passing desert vegetation, Dal happened to glance down at what he thought was a foil wrapper glinting in the sunlight near his sneaker. When it began to move, he bent over to have a better look. While doing so, he was startled by something shiny that scurried across his pant's leg down onto the black vinyl seat. It was some kind of insect about three inches in length that had a big ugly head and almond-shaped black eyes. The thing looked like a cross between a giant ant and a grasshopper, but even weirder, parts of its body were covered with a sheeny material.

"What the fuck's that?" he uttered. "Look at that damn thing!"

"Shit, someone left the lid off the jar," the tour guide said with a trace of anger in his voice when he saw the bug crawling across the seat. "Be careful, it can bite with those jaws. It's not venomous, but it's painful. Believe me, I know. Let me get it back into the jar," he said while quickly switching seats with Dal.

"There are two of them," Dal said while pointing to the one that remained motionless by his foot. "This one looks dead."

"It's just playing dead. That's what they do."

As he watched the guy attempt to scoop the one on the seat into a mason jar, Dal was trying to figure out how he (or someone) had managed to glue aluminum foil onto its abdomen and thorax. As a further attempt to mimic the popular depiction of an alien insectoid, two of the creature's legs and antennae had been detached before it was painstakingly wrapped in its tight-fitting 'flight suit.'

Not a circus! Dal laughed inside.

When both bugs were back in the jar and its lid was screwed on tight, the tour guide explained that they were used for demonstration purposes because many of the witnesses in the 1940s, when asked to describe the alien crew (or cadavers) they saw, compared them to an insect with a conspicuously large head that was a common sight in region. He even showed Dal one of the bugs that was floating in an orange solution inside another clear container.

"They're Jerusalem crickets. Nino de la terra. The child of the desert."

Dalton was a rock hound from Los Lunas, who also hunted and sold meteorites before starting his UFO C/R tours. After rattling off details about alleged crashes from those claiming to have the inside scoop, Dal asked why some witnesses described bug-like creatures while others spoke of beings of slight build that resembled humans with only slight differences. As a reply, Dalton speculated that there might be several different species of non-human visitors, or that some are laboratory products – a living technology designed by the others to do their dirty work. Some of the cosmic automata, or bio-machines might even be detachable components of the alien spacecraft, itself, he added.

Only a few clouds drifted across a bright blue sky as the tour group stood at the exact location of the landing site of the famous Socorro UFO encounter. Against a backdrop of dark rocky slopes, the ground in the ravine was uneven and rugged, not the ideal terrain for a landing by any aerodyne, even an experimental prototype of a NASA lunar lander as Dalton had mentioned when offering some insights as to the list of possible candidates for the strange object sighted.

"A teenager speeding in a black Chevy gets a lucky break after the cop following him hears what he thinks might be a dynamite shack explode," Dalton said as he began to recap the information he had provided earlier. "So, he ends the pursuit and turns towards the shack. On the way, he glimpses a cone of bluish light over the arroyo. When he arrives, he sees a white object that at first blush he thinks is an over-turned car. He then notices a couple of figures inspecting it – little guys dressed in tight-fitting white clothing that resemble coveralls. One seems startled after noticing the officer, who, himself, does a double take. It's not an upside-down car he's looking at. The object is a whitish-colored ellipsoid… today we'd say it looked like a large Tic-Tac. What on earth is this funny-looking butane tank, the officer wonders? A classified military probe from nearby White Sands, maybe? Before he can respond, there is a loud roar that causes him to hit the dirt. His glasses fall off as the object lifts off with a bluish energy beam. He watches as it rises above a mesa and gets smaller in the distance very quickly until, in total silence, it disappears over a mountain. That's one hell of a Pogo stick, isn't it?"

After some laughter, he continued.

"What about the physical traces left behind – the landing site geometry? Indentations made by the versatile landing gear that suggest a machine more technologically sophisticated than NASA's future lunar lander… in that the system could compensate for uneven terrain. That should rule out an experimental prototype of a can for Spam, as one astronaut called his space capsule. Recall what I said about the scorched, still smoldering clump of mesquite within the quadrilateral. And don't forget the vitrified sand and calcined rock. Also, there were the small footprints and ladder impressions. Add to this the stone scraped by one of the landing pods that was flecked with anomalous metallic particles, a scientific analysis of which, unfortunately, got lost because of insider shenanigans that has parallels with other foreign substances that mysteriously went missing – "

"Did anyone ever consider that we had advanced space vehicles before the moon landing," a member of the group blurted out, "and the whole Apollo program was a sham to distract the public from covert space programs? Secret shuttles with anti-gravity bubbles and stuff that would make George Lucas drool."

"I'll take questions after the presentation... and this isn't a conspiracy theory tour, but if the Socorro aerodyne belonged to some secret cabal or black program that flew missions or landed on the moon prior to Apollo 11, why do their astronauts look like children? Cure de nino... or fairytale dwarfs instead of average-sized grownups like yourself?"

"Fair enough, but what about astro-chimps? If they sent monkeys into space, they'd use midgets to pull levers and fire thrusters, too."

"Getting back to the craft's small occupants, these weren't the so-called grays. Not wispy lackeys. Again, they were scaled down humanoids wearing flight-suits. To repeat, these flight-suits seen weren't blowing in the breeze while hanging on Jaunita's clothesline in the middle of a dusty ravine like some skeptics think the officer saw. What were these shorties doing during their extra-vehicular activity before they were spotted and scrambled back into their vehicle? If they weren't inspecting the craft for damage, they might have been searching for something in the area. Maybe they were intergalactic rock hunters looking for some rare sparkly specimen to put in their perky box," he joked. "Okay, Socorro wasn't a crash/retrieval or a soft-landing donation. This time, no ping-pong game was interrupted in the base rec room before the blue berets were mobilized to clean up the scene. No flurry of activity in the impact zone. No lowboys transported a tarp-covered saucer that was later tucked away in an off-limits room. No dead alien bodies had their innards removed before being pickled. None of that stuff happened... this time."

As most of those in the group started to clap, Dalton picked up a piece of poster board that had a red symbol on it.

"Finally, what about the lettering, to use the officer's words, that still causes fist fights among researchers. I'm kidding, but the two camps are divided as to what symbol the police officer saw on the craft. Was it this one?" he asked while holding up a paperboard with a red insignia that looked like an arc over an arrowhead, "or this one?" he said while showing a different red marking on the other side. The second symbol was an inverted V with three parallel horizontal lines beneath it. Dal recognized the insignia as being the same marking in the white ovoid painted on the cave wall, and also on the piece of pottery that he was shown at the curio shop. The owner said it was a Native American symbol for a "Thunderbird track", and Dalton had just mentioned the deafening roar made by the object while ascending into the sky.

"Una V invertido con tres lines debajo... An inverted V with three lines beneath it, as the officer described the lettering to the dispatcher... or the arc over an arrowhead, like the symbol he supposedly drew and signed on a scrap of paper that was found in the Project BlueBook files? Whichever the correct one was, he was told not to divulge it to the public. Questions?"

"Yeah, I just found this inside the quadrangle," a member in the group said as he handed a small rock to Dalton. "It looks like it has shiny particles on it."

After examining it through the magnifying loupe hanging on a string around his neck, Dalton held it up for all to see.

"This, my friends, is a perfect specimen of what rock hunters call Leaverite. Meaning leave 'er right there, because it's an ordinary rock that's not worth keeping."

After Dalton answered a few questions, as the others were milling about the site, looking for traces of charred brush and glassy sand to take photos of, Dal pulled the guide aside.

"I've seen that inverted V symbol before."

"Yeah, both have been printed in many books," Dalton said.

"This was on a ceramic vase that's really old... at least that's what the guy – Bart or Bert – at the Indian trading post said."

"Oh, yeah, I know Bert."

"He told me it was a secret tribal symbol for Thunderbird tracks, so I was thinking – "

"Bert's a wily one," Dalton said with a dismissive smirk. "Did he give you his spiel about the ghost beads or try to sell you any Bisbee turquoise? He has the skinny on what occurred here, and is familiar with both glyphs. Tracks!" He shook his and laughed. "That secret tribal symbol bit... I don't know... but he probably did it himself... painted the symbol to make it look like these things were buzzing around in the sky a long time ago."

* * * * * * * *

Before continuing on his trip early the next morning, Dal backtracked to the Native American trading post. As he walked into the shop, he was greeted by a familiar voice that came from some shadowy corner.

"What you're looking for, it's here," Bert said as he appeared in the haze of burning sage and pinon drifting amongst the cluttered displays. "Oh, you're back. Did you change your mind about the Arizona calibrated trends, or am I the only one in New Mexico that sells grape soda?"

"Well, actually, I was wondering about the vase."

"You're too late. Sold it just after opening this morning. The buyer tried to dicker with me, but I didn't budge with a quality piece. This guy I've known is a local tour guide."

"Was his name Dalton – this tour guide?

"You know him?"

"I was the one who told him about it."

"So, you're hoping for a finder's fee?"

"No, when I mentioned you had it, he told me you were... well, kind of shady, but now I know why he said that. So, it is the real deal. Old, and the symbol was always on it."

"I'm the one that's shady," Bert said with a faint laugh. "He probably didn't tell you that he used to charge people big bucks to see the Los Lunas mystery stone. I don't know if it's a hoax, but that stuff about the inscription on the boulder being pre-Clovis is pretty hard to swallow. The Mormons probably faked those lines of the Ten Commandments. They're the ones who'd have something to gain by a thousand years old Decalogue stone turning up in America."

"Did you know the same symbol on the vase is in some ancient cave art close to here?"

"I know about the pictographs of my ancestors in the cave but I didn't see the same symbol anywhere in the video. Not like that on the vase. Knowing Dalton, he'll link it with flying ships seen way back when. Don't get me wrong. I've been told about the star elders and the crashes in the area. And the tales about the quiet little one that survived."

"Shysie," Dal said.

"These aren't myths – the tales. That must have been brutal… her journey alone in the desert with the sun beating down and elements while being tracked by the military. My people would have helped her, but after some on the rez got sick, they thought she might be a witch. Who knows, she might have came here for a grape soda when this was a gas station. A bottle like that found melted at one of the landing sites."

* * * * * * * *

CHAPTER IV

While stopping to get a takeout deli sandwich in Winslow, Arizona, Dal felt a dull ache around his eyes. He assumed this was caused by smoke that lingered from recent brushfires, but whatever had aggravated his sinuses; he decided to skip the nearby Meteor Crater national landmark. This would mean no space dust from the gift shop. Why he even had it in his mind to buy the dirt after seeing it for sale on the museum's online store he wasn't sure. *Space dust?* He'd had his fill of gas station curios and the kitschy shit in trading posts.

As he continued west on the I-40, the headache persisted. It didn't help that he had to constantly swerve to avoid soaked potholes from the heavy rain that fell near Flagstaff. Equally annoying was hitting the brakes when eighteen-wheelers abruptly switched lanes on the monsoon-slicked stretches that wound through thick forests of Ponderosa pines.

An hour later the road conditions improved and the pressure in his head subsided. The electric blue sky returned and sunlight flooded the cracked asphalt. Having passed a rest area miles ago, he looked for a place to pull over to eat. Exit 157 to Devil Dog Rd looked promising, so long as no shaggy black hellhounds with glowing red eyes and jagged choppers leaped from the shadows to snatch his toasty hoagie.

After parking near a trailhead kiosk on a dirt turn out just off the forest road, an elderly brown-skinned woman riding a black Schwinn mountain bike approached the Jeep. She was wearing a checkered gingham skirt with a matching blouse and a floppy

straw gardening hat. The bicycle's basket was adorned with purplish geraniums and contained a large clear jug in which bright
red ice cubes floated in a cloudy golden-colored liquid.

When he rolled down the window, he could smell the heady
scent of pine that mingled with dust kicked up from the rough
dirt track.

"Yo, banana boy, would you care to buy some red ice cider?"
the woman asked.

"Oh, that's what that is," Dal replied, a bit puzzled by how
she had known that he had a banana in the paper sack with the
deli sandwich that he was just about to peel. As she remained
seated on the bike, he was a bit confused and made uneasy by
her piercing blue eyes.

"It's a palindromic drink – refreshing on a day like this. I'm
Madam Eve, a follower of the teachings of Dr. God. Have you
heard about her?"

"No."

"Dr. God lived on Devil Dog Rd. Do you follow what I'm
saying?"

"Okay."

"She was called the prophetess of Devil Dog Rd. and founded the Palindromic Church of God. Back in the 1920s she had a
cabin near here where she decoded the pronouncements of those
that spoke in tongues."

"You're talking about the babbling when people in the Pentecostal Church are in the spirit?"

"Outsiders still think it is gibberish... even those speaking
it. But, after Dr. God recorded it and played the phonograph
backwards, what she heard was perfectly normal English. She
could understand every word. The incoherent utterances – it's
an inverted language. Do you know why? It's because God is

moving through time in reverse. Everything in our future has already happened for God, who is moving towards our past. Back to the time before the building of the Tower of Bab, when everyone spoke the same language. Dr. God explained how biblical prophecy works. It's because future events have already happened to God. Are you sure you don't want some of my red ice cider?"

"I've already got plenty of drinks. Water, 7up and a couple of Red Bulls. But, here's a small donation," he said while reaching for his wallet. "Yeah, here's a little something," he said while handing her a ten-dollar bill. "Beats spending it on space dust."

* * * * * * *

Twenty miles outside of Kingman, Dal searched for a different radio station. He still hadn't gotten the hang of the touchscreen audio system. When he glanced back up at the road, an almost inconceivable sight jolted him. Directly ahead, taking up two lanes in the middle of the freeway, was a child's swing set. Even more shocking, a little girl with blond pigtails was contently licking an ice cream cone while swinging. With barely time to react, he slammed on the brakes and braced for impact. There was a loud screech as the Jeep fishtailed across the road with the rear end veering towards the shoulder. After fighting to regain control, he skidded to a stop in a plume of dust.

There had been no clash of metal and no airbags had deployed. When he looked back to see if he had somehow managed to avoid the unimaginable, he was startled again by a loud honk as a big rig barreled past him. With a sickening tightness in his stomach and the horn's deafening sound ringing in his ears, he was confused to see that there was no trace of the swing set. A second later, with the smell of burning rubber inside the Jeep, he was even more baffled by what he was seeing.

Though the surroundings were still distinguishable, they were perceived in varying shades of white. Everything had a hueless tone. This white color scheme included the desert terrain, the sky and mountains, the road and passing vehicles, the interior of the Jeep and even Dal, himself. The range of gradients and saturations must have been in the thousands for everything to be clearly defined while essentially decolorized.

As he scanned the immediate surroundings in a bewildered state, darker shaded spots suddenly appeared in a hazy brightness that caused him to recoil back against the seat. When in clearer focus, the blob-like shapes moving in his vision looked more like someone's slender pallid fingers. Panic-stricken, he flickered his eyelids. While doing so, he discerned a ghostly form that was laid over the achromic imagery. The washed-out figure looked like the boy, Lucas, seated at a picnic table with a Mister Potato Head toy. When he inserted its plastic eyeballs, Dal's vision returned to normal.

Feeling a teardrop roll down his cheek, he leaned forward to have a look at his face in the rearview mirror. What he saw alarmed him in that the salty metallic fluid he tasted on his lips was blood that had seeped from the corner of his right eye. With another drop pooling in the same spot, he grabbed a napkin from the lunch sack and daubed it until the bleeding stopped. Though he wasn't sure what had caused this, he guessed that he had suffered a migraine attack that disrupted his vision and caused him to hallucinate. Though he felt no throbbing pain and didn't experience any other symptoms associated with severe migraines, it might explain the white flashes and blind spots, as well as the rapidly moving finger-like shapes that appeared before his eyes. Not wanting to take any chances of having another episode while on the road, he decided to get a room in nearby Kingman instead of driving straight to Las Vegas.

* * * * * * * *

Military tactical lanterns illuminated the windowless interior of a heavy-duty, fully enclosed tent that was similar to a temporary mortuary structure. Inside the shadowy confines, several figures were gathered around a water-resistant wooden chest that had just been unearthed as was evident by the mounds of dirt placed around a cut-open section of the black polyester floor. Among them was Spiller Andrews, the senior-level official of an intel cabal involved in the same ultra-black program that King had been recruited into. Once again the stone-faced higher-up was wearing a rumpled overcoat as rivulets of perspiration trickled down his creased cheeks. King was also there, along with a Native American elder dressed in jeans, a plaid shirt and Arizona D-Backs baseball cap from which long strands of graying dark hair hung.

With the nails having already been removed, King popped the rusty hinges and opened the trunk. Lying inside was a stiff figure clad in a tight-fitting gray flight suit with fuchsia cording. In the glare of the lanterns, the diminutive being's bloated cheeks were visible through its visored headgear. It had off-white colored skin with a slight bluish tinge; scant facial features and slanted glossy black eyes. Both of the creature's exposed hands were badly charred though the fabric its frail body was encased in was not burned.

"I'm not sure what a burnt tennis ball smells like, but this is what I imagined it to be," King said while wincing in reaction to the pungent odor that exuded from the body.

The Native American seemed deeply puzzled by what he saw.

"This child of the Great Spirit looks exactly as it did when we buried it way back when."

"After Tall Cedar, you and another member of the tribe found the body lying beside the odd wreckage," Spiller said as he lifted one of the being's stiff legs to reveal a small metal plate that was attached to the bottom of its matching gray footwear.

The plate was stamped: **PROPERTY OF THE U.S.A.F.** and also contained a series of numbers.

"A make believe trick?" the elder muttered, abashed.

"You see, Charlie, I told you it was government property," Spiller said. "The costume people were dummies. It has a metal skeleton covered with latex skin. That's the rubber-like chemical smell. Add to the mix a little polyethylene. It took you over sixty-five years to do your patriotic duty. Well, at least we didn't ruin a sixteen thousand dollar tent for nothing. Another loose end is tied up and the curator will be happy."

Outside the tent a couple of men in plain clothes loaded the chest into a small U-Haul trailer attached to a nondescript pickup that was parked on a sandy track in an expanse of dry scrubland. Next to the truck was a windowless white van that was covered with powdery dust from the sand spouts that sprung up in the open country and twisted across the rugged terrain. Though the vehicle appeared normal from the outside, it was actually fitted with special materials to prevent data breaches in challenging situations and environments, making it a mobile SCIF container. The safeguards included a biometric scanner that was disguised in the large decal of a splattered Wile E. Coyote cartoon character stuck inside a large dent above the chrome rear bumper.

Inside the secure vault on wheels, Spiller and King were seated at a table that was surrounded by fold-down electronic panels and wall-mounted vertical cabinets.

"What's going to happen to him?" King asked.

"The turkey farm," was Spiller's terse reply after taking a gulp from a glass of scotch.

"Even though he was just a little boy at the time. Why not send him back to his people in Peach Springs… back to Kingman or the Seligman district? Isn't Charlie just another Native American retelling the lore of Star Elders?"

"There are others chasing the story who aren't Haulapai. We'd like to throw them off the scent and don't think make-believe tricks will work. What if he and the others chanced upon more than the escape pod and watched the goings-on from a distance? Even worse, suppose they came into close proximity of the parent craft and fiddled with the scattered debris? What if they took a glimpse through the breach in the composite panel and saw what these demons do to humans? No, we've got to keep digging in our heels."

"I can see how some of that might be telling, though I'm still amazed they didn't have someone watching things before the team arrived back then… no matter how remote the impact site was."

"I've heard that some of the replica pieces weren't replicas… as were other things. The craziest part was a snafu due to predator action. Coyotes got to a cadaver that was made to appear it underwent an autopsy inside the craft and carried if off into the desert. A large chunk of the grisly remains was found near a new housing development. No need for a cover story because police detectives figured the victim had been murdered and dissected by a sicko. Fortunately, they never solved the case because we wouldn't have been able to help the poor SOB they pinned the charges on."

"What's the electric chair if you're doing your patriotic duty," King said with a sardonic smile.

"Any news with your chum?" Spiller asked after downing the scotch.

"He's currently at the Hilton here in Kingman. Well, kind of. It's an upgrade to the last place he stayed, even though he has the money."

"Here? Why stop in Kingman? That's interesting. Makes me nervous – your long leash."

"I'm just doing what I was asked to do."

"I realize you're over-graciously accommodating him for a reason. Gaining his trust is of the upmost importance to the portfolio. The signature data leads us to believe this wasn't just another magic lozenge. They weren't clowning around – that what reached into him. The main objective is a bidirectional exchange. It won't be give-and-take. Not reciprocal, of course, but, hopefully, according to technicians on the team, this biotechnical antenna of his… well, like I said, hopefully, we'll be able to reach back and there will be a bidirectional exchange. Something more than gaining insights into the workings of Humpty Dumpty… or even putting Humpty back together. Yeah, having him handshake with them is one thing, but I'm talking about that critical piece of the puzzle we're missing to view the complete picture."

* * * * * * * *

Dal was wearing swim trunks while seated at the small table in his hotel room. Before going down to the pool, he once again watched the video footage of the ancient rock art from Jix's podcast. As the imagery of dancing figures and abstract symbols was displayed on his smartphone screen, he pressed a bag of True Value Frozen Sweet Peas against his right eye. Though he was feeling better, there was still some swelling and redness.

When the camera focused on the section of the cave mural that included the white ovoid, he was puzzled that the vivid red symbol painted on its sparkly surface was no longer visible. The egg-shaped peculiarity was totally blank, and while pointing it out to her viewers, Jix made a comment about how any markings that might have once been there had been covered by some kind of "super paint."

Though he was confused the first time he heard her say this, this time he was even more at a loss because the glyph that had been glaringly distinct had suddenly vanished as if by magic. Even if it had been digitally removed for some reason, why didn't she notice such an obvious feature while it was being recorded? Maybe it was some kind of test or game she played to see if her viewers would comment on it, he wondered. The only other possibility he could think of was that it was a pop-up graphic that was added later that just happened to be overlaid right in the middle of the ovoid. Since it appeared in the lower right corner, the pop up card explanation did make sense. Perhaps Jix had seen the same piece of pottery in Bert's curio shop and took a photo of the unique symbol.

After taking a dip in the hotel's outdoor pool, he toweled himself off. At dusk it was still over a hundred degrees and he was the only person there besides a man from the cleaning service. He assumed he was the pool guy because he was wearing bright white wranglers that had utility pockets. As the guy paced in front of the sun loungers, he was speaking loudly on his phone about "chlorine" and "working at night when it was cooler." He also mentioned something about "reflective paint." After pulling into Kingman, Dal had seen his share of odd characters and the maintenance guy was no exception. With his long thrice-braided 'Viking' beard and wide-brim pink straw hat with matching neck flaps, he would turn a few heads back in Jaywick.

When he heard him mention the word "chlorine" for the third time, it dawned on him that besides allergens, chemicals in the water might also irritate his eyes. Before heading to the pool he had read on Quora about people living in the Mojave Desert being more prone to allergy attacks due to high concentrations of pollen. The barren landscape wasn't really barren, but, rather, was a breeding ground teeming with microscopic beasties like those visions of tiny organisms that flashed in his head with greater frequency during his travels in the southwest. Again, maybe King was right about him being highly sensitive. The desert was sounding alarms with images of amoeba-like blobs that danced before his eyes. Since allergies could trigger migraines, even clusters of severe headaches, he made a note to get some drops and tablets to combat any foreign matter lurking in the environment. But before going to the Walgreens there was something else on his mind. Finding a place with a good steak.

While waiting for his table in a local chophouse, Dal was having a beer at the upscale bar. Opposite him, a party of three also waiting to be seated at the late hour was sharing a large plate of oysters on the half shell. A middle-aged man with a close-cropped beard was sitting between two attractive women in their mid-40s. All three were sipping murky-looking martinis while engaged in an animated conversation. As he listened in with his eyes fixed down on the polished teak that glimmered in the subdued lighting, he was surprised to hear them talking about an alien spaceship that crashed on the outskirts of Kingman back in the 1950s. It almost seemed like he was trapped in a repeating loop, he smiled while leaning over the stein of pilsner, what with all the farfetched tales involving downed saucers he'd overheard in the past few days. He wasn't going to chime in, until he heard the man mention Jix Black's name.

"Three more the same way," the man said to the bartender, "Ketel One dirty with extra brine."

"And could you put a couple more olives in mine," the woman that Dal took to be the man's wife said, "That blue cheese stuffed inside is simply divine."

"Couldn't help but overhear you mention Jix Black," Dal said. "I've watched her channel. Her show called Black Hours."

"Are you going to see her at the mega-con tomorrow?" the man asked while carefully sliding the empty glasses towards the bartender. "She's doing a live stream."

"She is? Where's that?" Dal asked.

"It's in Mesquite at the Silverado Oasis resort," the man's wife said. Her well-tanned face was framed with wavy dark hair and she was decked out with silvery hoops, a vibrant cabochon turquoise pendant and stacked bracelets that accented her lace tassel beige dress. "Just a few hours drive from here. You go through Vegas and head north."

"You'll see the billboards with sexy blondes beckoning you to the place," the bartender said over the sound of ice rattling in his cocktail shaker, "but when you arrive – surprise – everyone there is on social security. Lots of mobility scooters and portable oxygen tanks," he chuckled as he continued to vigorously shake the pewter container.

"So, a saucer crashed here, too?" Dal asked. "Like in Roswell and Magdalena."

"Roswell, yes, but I'm not sure about Magdalena or Datil," the man replied. "Like the alleged Cape Girardeau incident, both might just be fanciful tales spun by storytelling clubs. Those told at their annual festivals. Seeing how they didn't have procedures in place to maintain secrecy back in 1941, you'd think there'd be more evidence available, but it's actually harder to pin down any details involving the crash scene, so unless something turns up in a field or barn or old photo, there's not much to go on other than a story passed down by the family of a Baptist minister. On the other hand, Sandra, here, is a local historian and curator of the Mojave History Museum," he said while gesturing to the woman with a chin-length bob frosted with lilac streaks. "The museum houses newspaper accounts and microfilm records from the time, and now we've got leaked documents divulged by an intelligence official."

"As you can tell, my husband's an aficionado," his wife said while watching the bartender swirling splashes of vermouth into glasses he removed from a freezer. "He lives and breathes this stuff. We're from Phoenix, going to the conference."

"In 1953, my father took part in Operation Upshot-Knothole at the Nevada Test Site," the man said. "This was a M65 cannon called Atomic Annie that fired an atomic projectile. Some think the payload that wasn't a fizzle and detonated over 500 feet above the ground caused the craft to go down here. Rumors have been swirling for decades and lots of rusty containers of military field rations have been found in the middle of nowhere."

"There's more to this town than a former Route 66 pit stop," the historian added.

"Jix Black broke the story," the man continued. "One of the speakers claims to have smoking gun evidence that he's going to reveal during his presentation tomorrow. Something shocking. The guy's a hardcore researcher, not one of those spouting nonsense about housewives that are celestial lizards. He's smuggling

it into the convention inside something no one would suspect...
like government spooks planted in the crowd pretending to be
new-agey believers. He doesn't want the suits from whatever triple-letter agency to seize it before it's shown to the public."

"If it's not hokey stuff, maybe I'll go," Dal said. "I'm on my
way to Vegas. Moving into a house there."

"Where in Vegas?" the man's wife asked as she reached for
an olive in her glass.

"Babe, leave some room in your tummy for that bloody rib
eye you were craving," her husband joked.

"It's called Summerlin."

"Oh, I hear that's nice," Sandra said. "Near those pretty
red rocks. Did you know it was named after Howard Hughes'
grandmother?"

"Who's that?" Dal asked.

"The eccentric billionaire. He was a business tycoon. Planes.
Hollywood films. Casinos. He purchased lots of land and property
in Vegas. Some back when it was just dusty scrubland. It was later
revealed that he had serious mental problems. Most famously, he
was a clinical germophobe. With bacteria other than his own running amok, he became reclusive. A codeine zombie secluded in
his hotel suite, where he ran his operations while naked except for
Kleenex-box shoes. His staff was squeaky-clean Mormons, who
he communicated with via memos, even giving them instructions
on things like how to thoroughly scrub down cans of peaches before serving them. In the few photos taken before he died, we see
an emaciated figure with long dirty hair. But, he was strongly opposed to nuclear testing in Nevada, so I'll give him kudos for that."

The unkempt appearance of this recluse reminded Dal of
the scruffy fellow with the dingy gray sweatshirt that he vaguely
recalled talking to even though they had never met. Just like the

snatches of conversation with the rancher dude with a droopy mustache and fancy steppers named Toby or something other. He'd read online about the same thing happening to others. They were just dreams. Brain spam. False memories.

"You'd think someone with his background in aviation," the man said, "in engineering and such... and with all his money would have been handpicked to hyper-analyze recovered alien hardware. Who knows, maybe handling off-world materials or examining non-human corpses contributed to both his mental and physical decline? The whole bacteria thing he went to great lengths to protect himself from. And rumor has it that he spent time at a certain ranch that's now a paranormal hotspot. Some even think the place was actually a clandestine research facility. Even more intriguing than the secret lab connection, though, is the Piute folklore of a mysterious object buried in a remote basin in the Nevada desert that's still emitting strange signals."

"I told you he lived and breathed this stuff," his wife said while chewing her third olive. "If the sight of blood doesn't make you squeamish, feel free to join our table when it's ready."

* * * * * * * *

Dal was about to shut the drapes in his hotel room when he noticed a truck pulling a service trailer stop under the lone streetlight in the empty parking area in the back of the building. What caught his attention was the size and shape of the object on the trailer. Though most of it was covered with a tarp, it was obvious from the bulges that the thing being transported was cylindrical in design. Protruding from the middle of the outline of the structure was a gleaming white dome-like appendage. This exposed feature and the oblong contours of whatever it was under the covering brought to mind the stubby white cigar that floated silently through the woods above Sullivan's field.

As he looked on from the upper floor, a couple of men in ordinary clothes climbed out of the truck and walked to the back of a trailer, which was one of those heavy duty haulers with an electric winch, side-panel toolboxes and mounting brackets. When they pulled back the section of dark plastic sheeting secured by tie-down straps that had come loose, a good portion of the object was revealed. There were painted stripes of different colors on the elongated frame that puzzled him until he realized that what he was seeing was the depiction of a giant 'foot long' sub sandwich in profile, with the various layers being Italian cold cuts, lettuce, tomatoes and dressing between two bakery rolls.

While laughing out loud at a dumb thought he had, he suddenly recalled what that lady with her blue steak floating in a pool of blood had said about how the smoking gun evidence was going to be smuggled into the UFO mega-conference in Mesquite, Nevada. In speaking about it being cleverly disguised to thwart any attempts by someone who might try to prevent the truth from being revealed, she said the undeniable proof was going to be "sandwiched" between something ordinary. "Sandwiched" – that was the exact word she used. Was that what was going on here, he wondered? The activity he was observing from his bird's eye view on the upper floor? Admittedly, it seemed crazy, but so did lots of things as of late. After all, he reminded himself, he was only here because a select group of people thought his brain was a fucking antenna to communicate with non-earth bound beings.

Was it possible that the evidence was an actual craft of unearthly origin that was disguised to appear like one of those 1000-gallon above ground propane tanks that owners sometimes painted to resemble flower gardens, watermelons and moss-covered logs? A hot dog would have done the trick, but a hoagie hero was even better.

There was only one way to find out. He'd follow the truck to see if the driver headed in the direction of the resort. What was it called again? He tried to remember what the woman said without having to Google it. *The Silver Bonanza... No, it was the Silverado Oasis,* he recalled as his eyes remained fixed on the Chevy Silverado truck parked below.

He'd already made up his mind about going to the convention to watch Jix Black's live stream, and since he wasn't feeling sleepy, he might as well drive there at night. He didn't want to throw a monkey wrench into the plan, so he'd just watch from a safe distance as they unloaded the secret cargo. Except for a few items in the bathroom, he was already packed. After tossing these into his knapsack, he left the darkened room and hurried down to the side parking lot.

By the time he got to his Jeep, the truck with the hitched trailer had pulled onto the main street. Without hesitating, he climbed inside and started the engine. Leaving the headlights off for the first minute or so, he managed to stay close as the truck headed to a freeway entrance. As he continued to follow it, just as he had anticipated would be the case, the driver got on the I-40 heading west until taking the exit that veered to the right towards Las Vegas.

After only twenty minutes or so with little traffic on HWY 93, Dal was surprised to see the blinker flashing on the transport trailer. The truck slowed at a desolate intersection and turned right onto a dark two lane paved road. The billboard at the turn-off was a garish advertisement for a Wild West ghost town named CHLORIDE. Why were they heading to this off-beat roadside attraction, he wondered. Were they trying to shake him?

After following the pickup for a few miles, a jumble of abandoned wooden shacks and corrugated metal sheds came into view. Among the decayed strata were several habitable rustic dwellings, many of which had front yards of desert scrub that were cluttered with a bizarre collection of colorful junk. Scrap metal statues loomed behind gilded wagon wheel fences and tree branches were festooned with a miscellany of oddments. There were colored bottle trees, paint can trees, tractor parts trees and even creepy dollhead trees. Day-glow toilet seats adorned rotted porch posts and rusted kitchen utensils dangled from sagging tin awnings.

As the dusty lane wound through the wacky spectacle, in the glare of headlights, everywhere he looked discarded items had been cobbled together and transformed into marvels of yard art. Some were quite creative, such as a caterpillar made from a row of bowling balls, old gas pump robots, motorcycle tank tarantulas, metallic wire pink flamingos, copper tubing sausage dogs and peacocks whose tails were rake blades.

Minutes later, the truck stopped in front of a small structure that looked like a classic roadside café, but whose vibrant painted sign read:

GIOIA'S FOOTLONG ITALIAN HOAGIES

What?

Before Dal had a chance to turn around, one of the men in the pickup jumped out and trotted up to the Jeep. Dal rolled down the window to hear what the guy was saying.

"Are you Baz? Here to hook up the tank and check for leaks."

"No," Dal replied. "I'm just checking out the sights. All the junk people have."

"Desert bling." The guy chuckled.

At that moment a service van pulled up alongside the building.

"Okay, that must be the propane guy," the man said.

When the driver got out, Dal recognized the fellow to be the oddball he saw back at the hotel swimming pool with the pink straw hat and 'Viking' beard. Seeing the name AmeriGas on the side panel of the van, he suddenly realized that what he had mistook for "chlorine" was actually "Chloride."

So much for my antenna, Dal, you freakin' dumb ass!

"Well, this is a semi-ghost town," the guy said. "We've been bouncing back. You should come during the day to watch the Old West gun fight in front of the saloon, see the granite rainbow in the canyon and try one of our big ass hoagies."

As Dal was leaving the quirky haven for artsy desert rats, while passing by more of the eye-popping hodgepodge of junk on display, King's black Wagoneer was tucked behind a patch of cacti tinged in moonlight. With varicolored rubbish resembling flowers placed on a weathered tombstone, among the grave's shadowy mourners were mop-wigged mannequins, barbecue grill lids with painted somber faces attached to posts with brass pipe fixture appendages and broken upright vacuum cleaners with dark lampshade veils.

"Not the NHI we're looking for, Dal," King mumbled to himself while checking out an old-fashioned telephone on the headstone. "Where are you taking me next?"

* * * * * * * *

Never had Dal been under such scrutiny and regarded with suspicion, as he'd been the night before while trying to get a room at the Nephi Motel in Mesquite. All the rooms at the Silverado Oasis were booked for the convention and arriving without a reservation after 2:00 am he had little choice but to submit to the barrage of questions asked by the Mormon owner before being given a plastic key.

She didn't want to just know if he smoked, but if he had *ever* had a cigarette? Not whether or not he had a girlie magazine, but if he had *ever* viewed pornography? Did he ever drink alcohol or play the lottery? After being grilled for what seemed like an eternity, the woman, who kept calling him "Dallin", finally relented and allowed him to pay for a room in the fleabag, warning him that the thermostat was stuck at 86 degrees.

But that wasn't the worst of it. During the night, he was awakened by something crawling on his leg. This turned out to be some kind of large insect that he'd never seen or heard of or even imagined existed. The black scorpion-like creature had menacing pincers and something long sprouting from its tail. Talk about a fucking antenna! When he told the woman about it in the morning, she called it "Grampus", like the goddamn thing was part of her family. After doing an online search, he identified Grampus to be a Vinegaroon, another one of the little-known monsters that inhabit the southwest deserts. If agitated, it sprayed a mist of vinegar, hence its name. Dal shuddered at the thought. That's all he needed – to meet Jix Black while smelling like salad dressing.

When he asked if they had a coffee maker, the woman told him that all hot drinks were off limits, including tea and anything that Starbucks sold that ended in "-ccino." Would he like a cup of chokecherry juice instead, she asked, and then began to talk about a star called "Kolob." He wasn't surprised by some of the more bizarre aspects of her religion. Placed inside the cramped room were pamphlets that talked about angels and magic glasses or lenses that a modern-day prophet used to glimpse things that couldn't normally be seen. Absurd beliefs that most people would find laughable, including his mother, he tried to convince himself while squeezing his eyes shut before exiting the lobby.

* * * * * * * *

"Hey, can you please bring me a Lagunitas," Jix Black called out to a cocktail waitress taking orders in the area. "I've already taken my pre-alcohol Z-Biotics and am trying to capture the fabled unicow right now." With her finger, the radiant blonde set in motion cascading reels on the large touchscreen of a flying saucers-themed slot machine called:

INVADERS RETURN FROM THE PLANET MOOLAH

Sci-fi sound effects included an eerie whistling sound as the animations of hovering flying saucers piloted by cows (instead of the ubiquitous green buggers) fired lasers that zapped the rows of pay table symbols, making them disappear when beamed up by the invading herds. "No special cow sighting yet − a very rare enhancement, I've been warned − just lots of earthlings on a farm. Grandpas, chickens, outhouses and stupid mailboxes. Come on, let's collect some wilds," she bubbled, "with bonus spins that re-trigger more free plays, and maybe visit planet Moolah."

Watching Jix streaming live from a corner in the packed casino, Dal noticed her filigree arm tattoo for the first time, though from where he was standing he was unable to truly appreciate the intricate, delicate designs in graphite-colored ink. Behind him and the others standing towards the back, the jubilant cacophony of gaming machines that lined the hallway also made it a little hard to hear what she was saying.

After the noisy blast reels ended, Jix settled back in a chair at the table containing her podcast equipment. She was wearing a black tee with the dubious image of the Sandown Clown ("All Colours, Sam") and a patchwork hippie skirt.

"When not trying to capture the elusive unicow, we're discussing the sequence of events and peripheral bits of the alleged Roswell crash. You know, there are a couple of things that bother me. If he really thought the metal fragments were of otherworldly origin, would the base intelligence officer rush home to show them to his wife and young son before being physically investigated? Wouldn't he have safety concerns about them handling such foreign material? Things like infectious agents. Alien microbes. Also, after the family was done playing with the foil-like scraps, his wife swept the small pieces that were scattered on the kitchen floor out the back door. What! Were they less significant because they were teeny-weeny? And shortly after this, concrete was poured for a new patio. Why hasn't some researcher shown up with a wallet full of cash and jackhammer and sifted through the broken concrete with a fine-toothed comb? They damn near dug up an entire sheep ranch looking for something missed, but couldn't be bothered with a dinky patio."

"If you really want to know what happened," a frail old man in his nineties or beyond seated in a mobility scooter parked on the carpet's kaleidoscopic swirls said, "it's all in this magazine article I have though I don't think I'm supposed to. *Coronet* or *Pageant*? My memory is bad. I'm a centenarian, they tell me. I went on Amazon to get some memory pills but forgot what I was looking for and ordered some toe clippers with long handles. I have a doctor's appointment tomorrow at four... not in the morning, but at night after I have my rice pudding and a glass of

Port. But, if you really want to know what happens when the sky gets torn, I'll send it to you in the mail with stamps."

"Okay, I'll be sure to look for that," Jix said, humoring him, "but if you're not supposed to have this magazine, you better stay out of dark alleys on that thing."

"What can they do to me at my age?"

"Time for one more spin just for funsies before the presentation starts. I'm still waiting for this mythical unicow to appear among the corncob pipe grandpas and mailboxes full of stuff. There will be havoc if one of the saucer's lasers hits the propane tank on that trailer symbol. Hey, who's this new guy in the mix with his redneck livery?"

On her final spin a siren wailed along with a news flash announcement of an alien invasion. After pressing a graphic of a red button on the large display, a darker screen appeared where a number of free plays were awarded.

****

A bear of a man stood behind the lectern in the filled auditorium. Sporting a dark suit jacket, he had a trimmed graying beard and tortoiseshell glasses that had slid down his nose. Using both hands, he held up high for everyone to see a rusty military C-Ration container and foldable P-38 pocket can opener like those used in the field in the 1950s.

"Several of these were found at the Kingman site," he said. "Here we have the P-38 pocket opener, named for its speedy performance when walked around the circumference of a can, or, who knows, maybe because the engineers of the design determined that it took exactly 38 punctures before a soldier in the field could dig into his delectable Pork 'N' Beans entrée."

There was sporadic laughter from the audience.

"Speaking of delish C-Rats, according to one contactee from the time period, the aliens were vexed that we humans labeled the cans that way when the ratio was significantly more beans than pork. Okay, a little levity before I show you what was sent to me in the physical mail by an anonymous person. This is the first time it has been shown to the public. You've already been warned about some of the graphic content in the footage, so, once again, if you are sensitive to autopsy procedures, even frog or grasshopper dissections, you might not want to view certain parts. Just close your eyes until I tell you that it's okay to look. Again, this is how I received the segments. Nothing has been edited."

As the lights in the auditorium dimmed, a video was projected onto a large screen behind the guest speaker. The first images shown were a black and white animated sequence transferred from a 1951 official Civil Defense film that began with a goofy-looking anthropomorphic turtle wearing a bowtie ambling down a country lane. As it sniffed a flower with a carefree expression on its face, a warbling female chorus began singing:

"Deedle-dum dum. Deedle-dum dum.
There was a turtle by the name of Bert
And Bert the turtle was very alert.
When danger threatened him he never got hurt,
He knew just what to do:
He'd duck and cover! Duck and cover!
He did what we all must learn to do,
You, and you, and you, and you,
Duck and cover!"

"Anyone in the room remember seeing this during the red scare in the 50s?" the speaker asked the confused faces in the audience watching the grainy frames that were originally shown to school-aged children in order to demonstrate "Duck and Cover" drills used for survival during an atomic attack. "I like the part where the narrator tells the kiddies that the effects of an atomic flash are worse than a sunburn."

Without warning, a cartoon-looking monkey holding a lit firecracker on the end of a string attacked Bert. This prompted him to stick his head inside his turtle shell. With the close-up on the gray carapace, the scene abruptly cut to high quality color footage of an oval-shaped object with a dull silver finish, whose flat bottom was slightly tilted against a mound of sandy earth around a large gouge where it had plowed into the desert terrain.

With murmurs and louder reactions from the audience, Dal quickly realized what the couple from Phoenix had meant about the "smoking gun evidence" being sandwiched between something ordinary.

All eyes in the room were riveted to the screen as a figure in a yellow whole-body radiation suit scanned the surface of the craft with the 'pancake' probe of a hand-held Geiger counter. As he checked the readout through the dark visor of his mask, behind him two other figures wearing different types of bio-protection suits slowly approached a section of the object where part of the metal skin was pushed out around a gash. The camera angle lowered to show the rubber overboots worn by the men moving between pieces of wreckage scattered amid scorched shrubs, and then widened to capture more twisted chunks of violet-tinged metallic debris glinting in the sparse vegetation. There was no sound with the pictures, which gave the scenes an even eerier quality.

"Okay, you might want to close your eyes for a bit," the speaker said.

The next shot was taken inside the interior of the object. A child's white cowboy hat was lying on the silver floor in the bottom bay. When the camera lifted, it focused on the lifeless body of a young boy reclined inside a horizontal metal cylinder positioned against a curved wall of muted pastel colors. As seen through amber-tinted viewing panes, he was wearing red flannel pajamas that had a cowboy theme, and each hand clenched the handle of matching toy cap pistols. Next, the camera captured something jarringly horrific. While the rosy complexion on the right side of the child's face appeared perfectly normal, all of the skin and facial features had been surgically removed from the left side, exposing nerves, blood vessels and tissue. On the same side, the skull had also been removed, revealing a partly dissected brain. The contrast of this with the neatly combed short, sandy brown hair on the opposite side, along with the boy's hazel retina seemingly full of wonder, was so unsettling that loud gasps of shock from those watching continued even after the image blurred with a glare of white.

As the motion picture cameras continued to roll at the impact site, the frantic movements of a clandestine unit in blue uniforms and matching berets in the foreground gave a sense of scale to the downed object. Amid the flurry of activity, a member of the recovery team puked in some milkweed blossoms, as another appeared to be reciting scripture while in a numb state of disbelief.

"There's a similar reaction from one of the blue boys," the presenter commented, "As you can see, lots of shattered nerves. In reading his lips, we determined he's reciting a verse from Ephesians. A prayer to battle powers of evil."

Along with the military presence in the cordoned-off area, men in plain clothes were observing and taking notes of the confused goings-on. In another close-up, an unblinking stare conveyed the shock of a man looking down at something. The next shot showed a small, thin being wearing a gray-brown flight suit that had a disproportionately large pear-shaped head and vague abstract features lying motionless beside a charred, crushed tumbleweed. Next to the strange creature were glassy fragments, plastic-like material and some kind of small fuchsia-colored box.

Viewed from either a helicopter or low-flying plane, a growing contingent of security personnel fanned out around the object and widespread pieces of shiny debris that fluttered while hung in greasewood bushes in the rugged desert landscape. As they crisscrossed the impact zone, some were holding industrial vacuums.

As the scene switched to night, ground-launched magnesium flares, portable lighting towers mounted on trailers and other remote-area illumination systems had been set up as the clean up process continued. In this battlefield-type "artificial moonlight", canvas-topped military utility trucks, Jeeps and boxy ambulances were parked amid well-guarded storage tents, latrines and a walk-in refrigeration unit. A large tarpaulin was being unfolded next to a lowboy big rig. Watching the night operation, a couple of high-ranking officials with color-coded badges stood next to a black Buick staff car.

"Look closely at what is shown next," the speaker said. "It's from a daytime shot."

While panning the debris strewn about the impact site, the camera paused on a strip of foil that was snagged on a shrub. In an enlarged freeze frame done with video editing software, a tiny paper flag is visible with the word "Hershey's" printed on it.

"This frame was enlarged and enhanced with a computer. Do you see the plume attached to the silver foil? It says Hershey's. It's a wrapper from a Hershey's Kiss. Yes, the candy. I believe there might have been several of these strips with paper flags glued onto them planted among the rest of the foil-like material. Why? Maybe as a test. If each one was accounted for after the site had been sanitized... vacuumed clean by the retrieval team, those in charge of the operation would be more confident that every scrap was collected as the men were instructed to do... and nobody had pocketed a souvenir. You are not going to like this, but the crash near Kingman was a staged event. A training drill or dress rehearsal in which new prospects – those unaware that it was a staged event – were evaluated for things like psychological trauma... their response to stresses and challenges beyond the normal range of human experience, which explains the gut-wrenching condition of the little buckaroo. Had they seen something like this before, with soldiers unable to deal with the situation? The footage is quite telling. Why would they go to all of that trouble and effort if they didn't expect to recover downed alien crafts? It only makes sense if there had been previous crash/retrievals such as Roswell. Those props weren't Russian hardware, and the body didn't look like its name was Ivan. Also, one of the Blue Berets has been identified, which validates the film as being legit."

* * * * * * * *

Inside his hotel room, the dead body of the centenarian that told Jix about the magazine was reclined in a chair with his head slumped down. On the flat screen hanging on the wall an episode of the game show *Jeopardy* was playing.

After seeing the dark spatter on the old man's Terry shower robe, King glanced down at a wine glass that was lying on the carpet by additional purplish stains.

"Their cheapest port," the other man in the room said. It was the guy that once harassed Dal at the "Muddy Boots Tavern" in Jaywick. No longer in his biker guise of goatee, leather vest and tattoos, he was clean-shaven and wearing a casual suit jacket. "Probably a heart attack, which sure makes things easier. I found this in the drawer," he said while handing King the magazine whose red cover featured an illustration of three peppy college cheerleaders doing a routine. "As is usually the case, it's the newsstand issue of *Coronet* dated November 1952. So, no spillage to be concerned about."

"Toxoplasma gondii," King uttered with an assured tone.

"What?"

"The answer to the Jeopardy question. What is Toxoplasma gondii. It's a parasite."

"You'd make a good contestant, King."

"Some say the truth may break in the greatest news story of all time," King quoted from memory a line from the magazine article about the 'Myth or Menace of Flying Saucers.' "Perhaps it will one day, but not at this dog and pony show," he laughed bleakly.

"His Jitterbug has been ringing loudly so there will probably be a wellness check by the hotel staff soon."

"Take what you need to do a follow up. Speaking of damage control, in those clips stitched together from... a sci-fi movie too intense for the time... or whatever they decide to go with, did you notice anything a bit odd?"

"Yes," the man replied with a sly grin. "A fuchsia box that didn't cast a shadow."

"Yes, good eye," King replied with a subtle smile. "How's the kid?"

"My good eye tells me he's infatuated with a tall blonde."

* * * * * * *

While driving at night to Las Vegas after leaving the mega-con, Dal was still kicking himself for not having asked Jix about the symbol he'd seen while watching the podcast. He wished he had at least said hi. With all the stuff others asked her about, he chickened out, and didn't see her again after the live stream.

As a black Escalade whizzed past him, he smiled thinking about what one of the conference-goers said about night drop-off centers at a secret underground facility in a Nevada no-man's land. Identical new black Escalades were lowered into the base, only to re-appear later driven by human clones that were dispatched to various parts of the country where they lived amongst us as spies. The surveillance equipment was contained inside their heads instead of in alien probes orbiting the earth. In a different twist on the same scheme, another person in the audience suggested that espionage by aliens hiding amongst earth's population was a cover story devised and circulated by the government for high-tech monitoring devices *they* implanted in citizens for nefarious reasons.

Then there were the stories of a sprawling complex called "Subtropolis", where 18-wheelers disappeared into the side of a sienna-colored hillside that unfolded, rocks, shrubbery and all, with the big rigs never to be seen again. The evidence for this intricate tunnel system carved out by some advanced stealth civilization living on the planet being that it was a well-known UAP hot spot. That and the great piles of tires set ablaze near the disguised access point.

Strangest of all were the rumors of mental abductions by aliens that used their higher technology to enter peoples' minds and create astonishing illusions to control humans as part of some unknown agenda. A self-proclaimed psychic spy at the conference claimed that this "mind dazzle" scenario was the true solution for what happened at Roswell.

Maybe the idea of implanted visions and false memories, either by aliens, the military or an intelligent species of crypto-terrestrials could account for his own experiences as of late, Dal wondered. Perhaps he should have let that doctor inspect him for alien implants inside the tent set up in the exhibit hall instead of going to the booth that was selling deep-fried Oreos.

As he listened to the guest on a late night talk radio show, whose subject matter was high strangeness, he had to laugh when the guy claimed his screwy ex-girlfriend was a shape-shifting reptoid with an appetite for human flesh.

He was actually laughing at himself while growing tired of unpacking the crazy shit in his head – the constant flip-flopping between simple, rational explanations for his "mental glitches" and more far-out possibilities for the anomalies. Wild ideas bandied about at the convention had gotten him worked up all over again, and the closer he got to Vegas, the more anxious he felt. But, there wasn't going to be a repeat of last night, he assured himself. He wasn't going to avoid what awaited him. As he took another gulp from an energy drink, he hoped the battery of tests would soon begin. He was ready to go through the rat maze.

Glancing to his right, he saw the "Pilot Travel Center", a brightly lit truck stop on the I-15 at Exit 64. From what he had been told, this was the exit for US-93 that was the highway to the famous Area-51 base. He wondered if that's where he'd be taken to for the tests.

* * * * * * *

CHAPTER V

Around midnight it was still over 100 degrees when Dal pulled into the driveway of a single-story house at the end of a cul-de-sac on Desert Bloom. The houses on both sides looked much the same, with similar neutral paint schemes, two-car garages and drought-resistant landscaping of gravelly dirt, rocks and desert shrubs. The porch and interior lights of one were visible, while the other was completely dark and appeared to be unoccupied. Unfenced vacant lots overgrown with white bursage made up the rest of the unfinished cul-de-sac. The house he would be staying at might have been in an affluent section of Las Vegas, but it wasn't the gated community he had expected.

Mercifully, the AC was running, so after turning on some lights and setting his bags down, he peeked inside the Sub-Zero fridge. Surprisingly, it wasn't empty, but what it did contain wasn't too exciting. There were a couple of mushy brown avocados, a container of shriveled blueberries, some plant-based patties and a herbal beverage called Dandy Blend that was a coffee alternative made from an extract of dandelions.

The chef's pantry was equally disappointing, containing only a jar of Moringa Leaf Powder and a box of cocoa wholegrain alphabet cereal.

As he glanced about the kitchen, it was evident that it had been recently upgraded with ceramic tile flooring, custom cabinetry, granite counters and top-tier appliances. Other evidence of remodeling was the smell of wet paint and opened cans of one of Benjamin Moore's gray palette next to the laundry room.

When he stepped inside the master bedroom, along with a fresh coat of paint, he also detected fumes of bleach or some other strong chemical cleaner. Whatever was used, it failed to eliminate traces of something that had rotted. Because of this lingering sickly undertone, he decided to sleep on the couch. Before jumping into the shower he texted King:

> just arrived at the house. what's up with the super food in the fridge? i hope I'm not expected to veganize... leaf powder? thats a hell of a hoop to jump through. besides avocados as brown as the exterior trim lol the place looks nice.

Early the next morning he was awakened by the metallic screeching of birds outside. Checking his phone, he saw that King had replied to his message.

> Kale yes you are! You got a problem with fermented soybeans? Relax, no torture diet. The fridge was supposed to be emptied. I'll stop by in the morn and ditch the stuff.

With no neighbors behind him, the backyard was fairly secluded, even though only partly fenced with a rickety open gate that led to a walking/jogging trail against the backdrop of Red Rock Canyon. From where he stood, he could see sections of the other two houses, having a better view of the one that was occupied.

As with the front yard, it wasn't the manicured oasis he'd imagined, but there was a small swimming pool and pops of greenery (succulents) in gray stone pots. Next to a brick outdoor grill on interlocking pavers in a brownish-red tone that mimicked the desert terrain was a pergola with a picnic table. A couple of mature trees provided some shade, whereas the rest of the yard was mostly sandy loam with a few decorative boulders and an assort-ment of prickly shrubs. In the early morning heat, several birds with long tails hopped about. Glossy black in color with bright yellow eyes, he guessed it was one of these cheery things that welcomed him with a variety of high-pitched whistles before his iPhone alarm clock chimed. Either that or the rusty gate needed a good lubing.

When he walked over in his bare feet to close it, he saw a young girl on the other side. She was bent over a cactus, whose thick spiny joints she appeared to be examining in detail on the vivid screen of her phone. Wearing cargo shorts, a solid crew neck shirt and a tan baseball cap from which hung wavy strands of blonde hair, he guessed she was about ten years old. Next to her was a black cat that seemed to be equally interested in the same specimen of fauna.

"Hello, whatcha looking at there?" Dal asked.

"I thought this might be Blue Diamond Cholla," she replied without taking her eyes off the screen, "but it's not. My phone has a Nanosight magnifier that turns it into a microscope. The spines are silvery. If they were reddish, it would be Buckthorn."

"Oh, yeah, cool, your phone's got a clip-on lens. I just came over to close the gate… to keep the vinegaroons from coming in. Do you live around here, or are you on a nature hike?"

"I live there," she said while pointing to the house next door, "with the pergola painted with Valspar Smoky Quartz."

"Well, then I'm your new neighbor. If you want something really interesting to look at with that thing, you should check out my fridge."

"Oh…"

She paused and closed her hazel eyes for a second while try-ing to decide what to say next.

"It's just some weird food that was left behind," Dal said after realizing that she thought he was being serious.

"Your pergola is sienna colored. Did you have the house blessed by a priest first? Because I saw one sprinkling salt from a little bottle."

"Really? Was he eating popcorn?"

"No, but he fed the pigeons… the real ones."

"What are those shiny birds that make all the racket called?" Dal asked.

"Oh…" Once again she paused and shut here eyes before responding. "The squeaky ones? They're called Grackles. This is Myshadow," she said while gesturing to the cat. "Did you know priests used to be really mean to black cats? He wasn't eating popcorn, but he had a bottle of salt. After he left, I zoomed in on a grain with my magnifier. You could see cube-shaped crystals. Sugar looks different. It has hexagonal pillars. He was also talking funny, so I recorded him from behind a tree. Then I used my translator. It was Latin. Did you know that the devil hates Latin?"

She clicked on the phone's voice recorder and a tinny voice speaking in a foreign language that could have been Latin could be heard. As the man spoke with a pronounced, commanding tone, the girl recited some of his words in English: "I seal this home in the precious blood of Jesus Christ, our Savior…"

"Susie, your breakfast is getting cold," a pretty woman in a pastel jogger set shouted from the patio sliding door of the neighbor's house. "I made you raspberry waffles and those fake nuggs that I don't like."

"But, no avocado toast, mom?" the girl shouted back as she stepped through the gate.

"Yes, and it's getting older, too, so hurry up now."

Dal could see that her mother's gaze was fixed on him. It was the same suspicious glare that the Mormon lady at the motel had given him. This time it was understandable, he reasoned. She didn't know he was the new neighbor or anything about him, and in larger cities like Las Vegas parents were less trusting of strangers than in small rural towns like the one he was from.

"It's Silver Cholla," the girl said while gesturing to the cactus. "And that's a Painted Lady," she said as a butterfly glided over some milkweed. "I have a species identification app that uses AI image recognition. I have to go eat now."

The mother was still intently watching him as her daughter headed towards the house.

"Oh, there's a man standing on your pavers," the girl said while glancing back at Dal.

When he turned towards his house, he saw King standing outside with his arms outstretched in a welcoming gesture.

"I rang the doorbell and knocked," he said as Dal stepped onto the pavers. "It's not the Paseos, but it's private – "

"Ouch, these things are hot," Dal uttered with a wince as he skittered towards a narrow patch of shade by the sliding glass doors. "Say something in Latin."

"Other than the neighbor, who's the prying type," King finished his sentence while stepping aside as Dal hurried into the house.

On a counter in the kitchen was a paper cup of Starbucks coffee and some donuts in a pink box that King had brought. There was also a sealed Manila envelope.

"Blonde roast," King said while gesturing to the coffee, "strong enough to start a busy day beginning by putting on some fucking shoes. Okay, the envelope contains instructions. Follow them... without deviation."

"That donut looks like the poop emoji," Dal said while pointing at a chocolate one in the box that was shaped like a lump of poo with comical icing eyeballs.

"You like to eat crap, don't you? All that processed food. Which reminds me, you're black on supplies."

"Was the person that lived here before me also in the program?"

"He fit the neurological profile," King said flatly.

"So, what happened to him?"

"Let's just say the results were unsatisfactory. Probably due to personal issues, besides a meager diet," King said while emptying the refrigerator and carefully putting the contents into a cardboard box rather that tossing them into the pull-out trash bin.

"Coming from a guy that has popcorn in his pockets," Dal joked.

"Rigid beliefs are also factors. Sometimes, even disciplined recruits can't put away some of the things gleaned by their unique abilities. Unsettling possibilities that aren't part of the typical motifs. And then there are signal overloads, where the most talented assets become overwhelmed during the exchange of what the antenna receives. Not to shake your nerves, but it can be a profound experience to those afforded certain glimpses."

"Projected illusions?"

Ignoring this, King opened the pantry and placed the box of cereal among the other stuff.

"That should do it. Okay, now that you've gained access to the club, go buy some new clothes. Something dressy...stylish, so you don't feel inferior to the others. Your instructions are in the envelope. Follow them to the letter."

Right after King left, Dal got a text from his mother asking if he had finally made it to the house "in the desert." She also let him know that she was worried about Derethia because she had not been to church for a week. A friend had seen her getting gas at Casey's, and her hair was cut really short.

She didn't know why she would do such a thing "to her glory." She didn't respond to her friend's waves and quickly drove off after filling up. Her mom tried calling, but she didn't answer or respond to her texts.

The other news was that the police had visited Pastor Hoburt at his home, but no one knew what this was about. She guessed it might have something to do with a stranger in town who asked lots of questions to members of the congregation about "a religious picture that was seen in the parking lot of the church where it was stuck into the asphalt" before quickly being removed by someone in broken chunks. One of the ladies from the previous cleaning service, who was the first to see the image, believed it was some kind of sign from God, which his mom found plausible "in these days." She ended the text by letting him know that if he didn't like it in the desert he could always come back home.

＊＊＊＊＊＊＊

King was seated at the kitchen table in his condo. While pouring cereal from the box of Nesquik he took from Dal's pantry into a large pile on the tabletop, it didn't take long for him to notice something funny. Finding the same chocolate letters over and over, instead of what should have been the entire alphabet, he began placing the duplicates into smaller piles. When he was done, there were only four letters in total, being C, I, O and P. After positioning these a few different ways, only one arrangement made sense. Seeing how it wasn't a valid

Scrabble word, he figured it must be someone's name. But, who the fuck was Pico?

* * * * * * * *

"There it is," the driver said as he braked in front of several orange cones and pointed to a dark rectangular shape that was barely visible in the shadowy glare of nearby streetlights. Through the window in the back seat, Dal made out a black elevator door that seemed out of place between two huge loading docks with ramps for trucks delivering supplies to one of the newer hotel/casinos on The Strip. After thanking the driver, he climbed out of the town car and nervously glanced about at the dim surroundings in the back of the towering structure that muffled the congestion on Las Vegas Blvd. At eleven at night, there was no activity in the area except for some disheveled person urinating in a dark corner. Even though the delivery bays were unseen by hotel guests, it seemed like a strange location for the entrance to a place that engaged in classified psionic research. But, then again, the contents in the manila folder were equally odd. Attached to a lanyard was a laminated black card that contained a QR code in the form of an 8-rayed energy bolt and a single mini ear bud (that he was to insert prior to entering the building).

The basic instructions were for something called, "DarkSpark", which explained the metallic lightning bolt-like symbol on the PVC card. There was no further information about this code word. Until the vetting process was finished, he figured that's how things would be.

After walking up a short ramp, he pulled out the card and tapped the energy icon against an identical symbol on a sticker on the elevator. A few seconds later, the doors slid open. Once inside, he pressed a glowing button that was embossed with the same vector image. After both doors closed, he felt the elevator rise. The ride was fast and seamless.

When the doors opened, it took a few seconds for his brain to register what he was seeing. He hoped none of the others had seen what must have been quite the dumbfounded small-town boy look on his face. Besides the surprising turn of not being what he expected, what he saw in his first few glimpses was equally confusing. At least he knew why there was no retinal scan or other biometric tech used to control access. Instead of some secret lab facility, he was standing in a spacious ultra-lounge. One that was so exclusive, there weren't even velvet ropes and a muscular door staff.

After a stunning brunette in a sparkly leotard walked past him while sipping champagne from a light-up flute, the first thing he noticed was that the atmosphere of DarkSpark was far more laid back than the heightened energy of other mega-club experiences he'd heard about. Maybe things would be more bangin' on the main dance floor, he thought, dreading the frantic pulse from the decks of top-flight DJs spinning techno beats to sweaty bodies crammed under a chandelier of flashing lasers, but, mercifully, there was no sonic bombardment or kinetic extravaganza at first glance.

As he stepped away from the elevator, a beautiful Asian woman fitted in a liquid metallic bodysuit approached him.

"Welcome to DarkSpark, Dal," a dulcet female voice in his ear bud said. "My name is Lumina, and I am your host for this special night."

There was something about the woman's facial expressions, skin tone and slightly rigid movements (when she tousled her silky lavender hair) that didn't seem right. He wasn't sure if this was some kind of performance art in which the lady was pretending to be a sexy cyborg, or if it actually was an advanced humanoid robot.

"Follow me to your private table, where Kersei will be your server. I can answer any questions you might have about the club, including information about the bottles available, so please don't hesitate to ask."

While following her, he glanced about at the futuristic décor, whose design elements included glowing egg-shaped chairs, bent glass furniture and mirror console tables. Variegated blooms in globular terrariums hung from the ceiling and the interchanging panels on the walls were shimmering with dynamic auroral curtains. The music was a spacey jazz piped through an omnidirectional audio system at an ideal volume.

Women with sleek, toned forms in strapless dresses were seated in intimate corners on white love seats with chrome accents, savoring decadent specialty cocktails while chatting with guys that looked like they just stepped out of the glossy pages of a fashion magazine. Many of the dudes wore crushed velvet button downs and dark jeans, with the majority of women also dressed in a sheeny black fabric to match the vibe, though some had squeezed into sequined ruby, silver and leopard print creations. Most had expensive salon cuts that included glitter-dos, messy bobs and atomic-era pastels.

A girl with a bubble ponytail nibbling on one of the bite-sized appetizers on vibrant Talavera smiled at him before resuming her conversation with another woman taking small sips from the club's signature drink.

"The drink that Elowen is quaffing delicately in a frosted dark glass, whose rim sparkles like the gleam in her eyes, is the DarkSpark martini," the mellifluous voice in his ear bud let him know.

When he was shown to his table, a server (whose name wasn't "Kersei" due to a programming error, he guessed) that had a more natural skin tone and more fluid motions took his drink order. Either "Deryn" wasn't silicon-based or gave a less realistic performance than Lumina's. He thought King might be waiting for him, but the seats in the small room were empty with only a single Evian spritzer on the table. Why did King think he'd be into dancing on a packed floor or socializing with random people, Dal couldn't help but wonder? Was it a nice gesture to welcome him to Las Vegas, or was something else at play?

After the girl returned with his Pacifico, he ventured back into the partygoers. Still feeling out of place, he kept to the edges while soaking up the ambiance. Sure, King had told him to buy something "stylish", but he wasn't about to shell out a ton of money for some trendy Italian shirt just to take a glorified aptitude test.

With his eyes fixed on the gorgeous specimens in diaphanous sheaths that were silhouetted against glowing geometric art, a holographic image of DarkSpark's energy icon floated past him. While being reminded by Lumina about the club's renowned poolside setting, he was all in for a midnight dip before she finished describing some of the luxurious amenities. She had mentioned something about a changing room where swimming trunks could be purchased, and he was about to ask directions from one of the venue staff in dark blazers when he noticed that the opaque glass panes in one of the textured walls of a private room suddenly cleared to reveal a tableau of exotic beauties donning ivory chiffon in seductive poses.

There were no pulsating mixes at the rooftop pool, just eclectic reggae for those dancing under towering palm trees. As another showpiece of the hotel, the tiered watering hole offered unobstructed views of The Strip. Along with the lush foliage around the deco-style pavilion bar and private cabanas, flowering nursery pots created a botanical dream of Japanese painted ferns, violet frangipani and silver dragon leaves.

From his lounger near one of several poolside decks, Dal watched the endless parade of tanned, tatted bodies drinking craft cocktails in the subdued glow of glass patio torches. The swimwear ranged from glamorous dark suits with diamante straps to flashy neon rhinestone bikinis. In contrast, most of the dudes wore the black trunks sold at the venue.

Having bought a pair with the DarkSpark logo himself, Dal finished his beer and waded into the cerulean blue, passing curvaceous 'mermaids' wearing elaborate costumes with golden laminated effects. As they pushed tropical concoctions, in his ear bud, Lumina mentioned the fifteen-dollar minimum at blackjack tables in the swim-up alcoves. Though the audio device was waterproof, he pulled it out and shoved it into the pocket in his trunks. Glancing about, he saw a contrived lagoon fringed by copious dwarf palms. Being that it was close to the infinity edge and less crowded, it looked like a good place to chill. After taking a deep breath, he submerged himself and kicked towards it.

While gliding along near the bottom, he noticed a pair of smooth legs with wiggling toes under some kind of large pool toy. Since he'd been holding his breath for over a minute, instead of swimming beneath it, he surfaced. Brushing the hair from his eyes, he looked up to see a pretty blonde wearing a one-piece black suit sitting on the edge of a floating day bed. Even though the circular white mat with an umbrella at its center was big enough to hold several people, the woman was alone.

"I thought my lily pad was going to be torpedoed," the lady uttered with widened eyes that matched her mock alarm. "Lumina talked about an immersive experience, but, jeez, not into that profuse chlorine."

While taking a closer look at the woman's features, Dal's mouth dropped slightly. He couldn't believe it. If there were any doubt, the delicate necklace she wore had three letters that spelled: JIX.

"Sorry."

"Be careful you don't tumble over the edge of paradise," she joked while tugging one of her mini side braids, both of which were glitzed with sparkle. "You didn't see the sign?" she asked with a carefree chuckle.

"I see you've got a nice party island here all to your self."

"Someone splurged. Don't know whom, and the booking service wouldn't say. I'm not a member of the pool thingy here – Azura – or whatever it's called, but it's definitely over the top like most things in Vegas."

"Sounds like you've got a secret admirer"

"Or someone with a story to tell that changed their mind. I'm a journalist"

"Yeah, I've seen your channel."

"Are you a subscriber?"

"Not yet. I also saw you in Mesquite and wanted to ask a question but didn't get a chance. Oh, I'm Dal."

"Three letters… like mine, Jix. What was your question?"

"It was about one of the symbols in that cave art."

"The wonky ones? Those that I thought were anachronistic. Out of place."

"No, a red one like an upside down V crossed with lines that's the symbol of a Native American Thunderbird. I just thought it was strange because it was centered perfectly over the empty egg-shaped white area, but it was gone when I watched the video again. Did you ever use this symbol as a popup?"

"I don't know what you saw, but it wasn't on our end. I mean, if it wasn't a profile pic or channel icon. Did it last more than a five seconds?"

"Yes."

"Don't know what to tell you, but if you like the channel, I just finished another episode about some guy here in Vegas who claimed he saw a case of a time slip that involved a man trying to order food in a Burger King near the Strip. Yeah, I have my own weird desk. The man was dressed in 1920s clothing and repeatedly asked the poor gal behind the counter if a Whopper was what he called a hamburger. After being convinced that it was, he paid for it with five shiny silver dollars and then told the person in line behind him that where he came from he would only need one and he'd get lots of change back. The man that witnessed this had phone camera footage of the guy vanishing into thin air right after picking up his order. If you want to watch it… and become a subscriber, it's the thumbnail with a title of Whopper Of A Time Dilation Story."

"Did it look real?"

"We had it analyzed. Some thought it was legit, but others detected things… indicators in certain frames that raised concerns. Even if there's no digital trickery, it's probably just the portfolio of some new magician on the Strip. If not the repertoire of a stage illusionist, it could be a marketing stunt… part of some viral campaign for a new movie. Hey, are you hungry? Since my mystery admirer flaked, why waste the goodies this lily pad came with. There are frozen-fruit skewers, chips and spicy dips galore. I can summon Kersei to bring a drink, or flag down one of those Spandex mermaids with pink chucks and gilded bustiers you probably didn't notice, did you."

"A Pacifico sounds good."

"Well, hop up here and let's see what we've got."

When he climbed onto the floating mat, Jix reached behind her and fished out a chilled Pacifico from a well-stocked silver beverage tub.

"Presto," she said with a big smile.

"Nice," Dal said while clapping his hands.

"Can you draw that symbol on a cocktail napkin? Would you believe I forgot my pen, of all things, but remembered my lipstick, of course you did, Jix. What color is best? I've got Coral Bliss and... Walgreens Patisserie."

"What are you wearing now?"

"Coral Bliss."

When she handed him a napkin and tube of lipstick, he carefully drew an inverted V with three horizontal lines.

"A little smudgy, but that's it."

"I should have given you a liner to apply first," she said without a trace of a humor while examining the symbol.

"The same red glyph," Dal explained, "was seen on an egg-shaped object that landed in Socorro, New Mexico. It was white with a metallic shine and since the shape – "

"Which is near the cave – "

"Right, and since the sparkly oblong egg shape was blank, well, that's why I thought it was strange."

"Yeah, and I was wondering at the time why it didn't have any markings since it matched precisely with the cookie cutter removed section, which, itself, I found to be rather odd. Okay, but you said you saw it and then you didn't. No one mentioned it in the comments, so... I don't know. Speaking of things anomalous, what did you think about all the crash/retrieval talk at the con?"

"Not sure. I'm fairly new to all this... taking it all in. They travel all this way only to come in hard? Not to be a buzz kill, but all the stuff might be ours."

"Fair enough. Hey, are you a local, Dal?"

"Yeah, at least for a while. I live in Summerlin."

"That's where I live, too. If you're game, I know a place not far away that was the base of operations for a real crash in the forties."

"What makes you so sure?"

"Burn marks."

* * * * * * *

Dal adjusted the flames on his backyard grill and flipped a couple of sizzling beef franks so that they didn't get any blacker. He should have kept an eye on the gauge, but his thoughts were elsewhere. Having been invited by Jix Black to join her for a drink on her private party island was one thing, but it was what happened shortly after that had distracted him for most of the day and almost ruined his sodium-laden dinner.

The conversation they were having the night before was going well when, rather abruptly, her relaxed demeanor changed. Though he'd been aware that she kept glancing sideways as the two spoke, he assumed she was feeling a little uncomfortable by some fan staring at her, or maybe even just some dude admiring an attractive woman in a swimsuit. With those looks, she was hard to ignore, after all. When she indicated they face the other direction, he realized just how ill at ease she was. It was a man, she told him, but not some obsessed fan or creep leering at her. That wouldn't rattle her, she added with a nervous smile. She had noticed the same guy watching her during her live stream in Mesquite. His hair was darker then, not sandy as it was presently, but she was certain it was the same person. Something about him didn't feel right. Her intuition was telling her that, and her intuition was always right.

When Dal glanced back to see what this man looked like, he was no longer there. He probably realized that she was aware of his presence, Jix said, and disappeared among the throng of partygoers. His keeping tabs on her might have something to do with a piece she was researching for a future podcast. She also hinted that the information she was going to be provided with (by the no show?), if genuine, was highly sensitive. She didn't want him to get mixed up in something that might cause problems and thought it best that he finish his beer and leave. After apologizing for coming off as a drama queen, she took his number and said she would be in touch.

Even though the sun had already set, the heat on his face was becoming intolerable. It was like he turned on an oven inside an oven. The smell of burnt flesh was making him nauseous, but having not eaten anything all day, he pronged a couple of the charred Nathans that were less crispy than the others and cradled them in the couple of buns that he hadn't ripped to pieces and scattered over the pavers. The reason for tearing apart the others was that he was also feeling paranoid about being watched. Not by a person, but by the bright orange eyes of a pigeon that was fixated on the backyard while perched under a slight roof overhang on the house.

Having noticed the peculiar manner in which its head bobbed while the rest of the body remained perfectly still; he wondered what might be under its feathery mesh. The bread was a test to see if it would swoop down to gobble up the scraps like any true scavenger would. Somewhat to his surprise, the cozy fucker didn't budge from the ledge, even after he split open one of the blackened, shriveled franks and tossed it onto the ground. Instead, it repeatedly nodded at him with the same unvarying motion that initially roused his suspicions. As he contemplated buying a ladder and ripping the damn thing open to see if its fillings were artificial and contained a camera of some kind, from the corner of his eye he saw a luminous orange sphere floating near the partially opened gate to the jogging trail.

Whatever the bright orb was, it seemed to be performing tricks as it silently darted about. After soaring high above the fence, it descended in a controlled manner. Instead of touching the ground, it hung motionless for a moment before continuing in a playful manner, zig-zagging over shrubs in the gravelly loam while flashing a vibrant spectrum of colors.

As Dal walked towards it, it glided behind a tree before making a beeline towards the gate. There, it vanished from his view, only to reappear seconds later, performing similar aerial maneuvers. Making a faint whirling sound that at first he didn't hear over the clatter of the air conditioning unit, the object was about the size of a softball that emitted a multicolored glow. Before he could get a better look at it, once again it squeezed through the space in the gate as if precisely directed to do so. When he followed it to the other side, he watched as the dazzling globe was caught in mid-flight by the curled fingers of his ten-year-old neighbor, Susie.

"It's in the boomerang mode," she said. "I closed the gate most of the way to keep the vinegaroons out."

"I didn't know what it was. So, it's a mini-drone? Sucker goes pretty high for a toy."

"It does more tricks than other hoverballs on Amazon I've seen at glow parties, but it can't go through walls and stuff like the one at your house. My cat won't chase it after seeing that. It also makes a pretty good personal fan."

"Really, right through walls?" he humored her. "Well, I haven't seen anything zipping about."

She flicked her wrists, activating the toy with a small drone-like motor encased in a plastic shell before launching it. After moving swiftly though the gate, the flying spinner remained aloft for a few seconds before returning towards her opened hand.

"Oh," she paused. "Maybe the kids came back to get it."

"Kids. What kids?"

"The kids that came here inside an igloo. They don't like to be called Eskimos. They're Inuit. Indigenous people from Greenland. They eat dried cod, not pigs-in-a-blanket. Is that beyond sausage you were making? My mom says a veggie mash doesn't snap."

"No, they're real cow eyeballs and assholes— elbows, I mean. So, these people from Greenland were here in the backyard?"

"There were three kids dressed funny."

"Funny, how? You don't mean like snow-shoes – not in this hellscape."

"No, they had parkas. They were just thinking. And two of them had Etch-A-Sketches. Red ones, not drawing pads with color touch screens."

"You mean those things that you make doodles with? What were they drawing?"

"I couldn't see what they were sketching while they were thinking. Not from Eagle Eye. Maybe some cool graphics – "

"Eagle Eye?"

"That's the tree fort by the house on the other side with the Adobe Beige pergola. I watched them through my Helius Sight-Night Vision glasses."

"And they came here in an Igloo," Dal laughed. "Made of blocks of ice."

"No," she paused before answering. "Oh, the white container one of the kids went into looked kind of like an igloo. Or like one of those plastic boxes you see where new houses are being built."

"You mean a porta-potty?"

"Maybe, but the kid with the eye mask was in there for over an hour… until the glowing ball came down to play. It jiggled and bobbed like it was dancing before it took turns hovering above the other two kids' heads."

* * * * * * * *

"Where's the mustard, it's asking," King joked in response to the loud shrieks of a Grackle pecking at the remains of a burnt frank on the pavers in Dal's backyard. "You'll attract coyotes with those scraps. Okay, since you've had a chance to settle in… and had some fun, it's time to take those scans. Buckle up, kiddo, things are about to get wild."

"It's gone," Dal said while shielding his eyes from the glare of sunlight reflecting off the tiles near the empty nook under the roof overhang. "I guess the thing was real."

"No, you were right about the mechanized precision. That was very observant of you, Dal. It probably just flew to the nearest recharging station," he deadpanned. "It has an induction charging coil. Sorry, I forgot to mention some of the security features here. But, if you're worried about it watching you with a hot date back here, frankly, I'd be more concerned about your neighbor – what's her name, Cindy? – spying on you from her tree fort perch than some government pigeon-drone with suboptimal components."

"Her name is Susie – "

"Right, now what's this about Eskimos with Etch-A-Sketches and seals balancing cosmic fireballs on their noses?"

* * * * * * * *

Sensors dotted the electric fence line of a sprawling facility, whose white facades wavered mirage-like against the surrounding desert. Situated on the outskirts of Las Vegas, the private company called BELFIORE AEROSPACE designed modules for orbiting space stations, as well as essential systems for a sustainable lunar base. Structural concepts of these prototype habitations included inflatable domes and geometric erectables. Patrolled by black armored Lexus SUVs, rumors swirled in UFO circles of more exotic materials than pre-fab composites and shielding geo-synthetics being analyzed in the complex's hangar-sized structures and smaller out buildings. Formidable access control features added to these dark suspicions.

On the drive, King had filled Dal in on the mysterious place. Besides manufacturing various space platforms and conducting multi-modal research in a simulated space environment, the company's offbeat billionaire owner publicly stated a deep interest in psychic phenomena, UFOs and paranormal occurrences. Along with the various science modules, there was a medical laboratory on the premises with next-generation equipment, including an MRI with faster scanning times, improved image quality and analysis technology. In touting the machine's higher magnetic fields, increased signal-to-noise ratios, advanced coil designs and amplified contrast for detecting brain abnormalities, King almost forgot to mention that it was also designed for minimal discomfort. More to the reason for Dal's visit, he also spoke of an array of assessment tools that determined psionic strength.

Guards with black berets waved King's car through a side gate in the steel weld mesh barrier, where a couple of sedans were parked in a dusty lot next to a warehouse dock. There was also a windowless white van that Dal noticed had a large decal of the cartoon character, Wile E. Coyote comically flattened above the rear bumper.

A couple of hours later, King was sitting at the table inside the mobile SCIF with one of the senior members of the project, Spiller Andrews.

"Why send him to a signaling camp?" King raised his voice. "He doesn't have the training or the knack for that stuff. Not to mention his frat house diet. You know the psychometrics tests were a sham. With what he was fitted with, we might be able to open a direct line to engage with the guys upstairs. A bidirectional exchange, as you, yourself, said, with something other than fucking celestial blobs, sentient or not."

"Look," Spiller said while tightening his grip on a glass of scotch, "I have my own issues with these contract workers thinking they're expanding the aperture and triggering encounters with NHI. Reeling them in with focused thoughts alone. Sure, something's reacting to external stimuli, but most likely these shape-shifting light bursts are the result of scientists monkeying with a dynamic energetic medium. They're setting the sky ablaze with self-replicating plasmoids that appear to display the behavior of conscious entities, but are actually directed energy weapons adjusted to the individual. They're playing on our pre-conceived notions of creatures of fantasy. Case in point is how the interaction with them is giving the lachrymal glands of Special Forces honchos a good workout. God help us if those most capable become soft. Soldiers laying down their weapons while overcome with emotions in close proximity to what they think is the Blessed Virgin out for a joyride. Whether beautiful, terrible or enigmatic, close-range exposure to these lab-created specters… it's a game changer. But, my reason for taking your chum to a signals outing isn't to get lovey-dovey over luminous clutter, it's to see if any of the field workers are able to pick up on what's inside his head."

"That seems risky to me, Spiller, potentially exposing such a valuable asset. Unless there's some other reason that I don't have a need to know, I suggest we stick with the game plan. We've a distinct advantage with him."

"Call it desperation if you want. The pot is boiling over. With the Internet the truth isn't so strange anymore that it discredits itself. The mainstream media is talking about trans-dimensional beings. Congress is looking into black budget stagecraft. Dark money. With hyper-spectral cameras, we can no longer try to explain these parades of orbs as cotton puffballs that floated in from...wherever. The disinformation apparatus is overloaded and when you factor learning algorithms into the mix... Those who are complicit have become like proverbial rats fleeing a sinking ship, with private industry that have the hottest material from our toy box trying to return the stuff so they won't be held accountable."

After downing his scotch with a large gulp, Spiller eased forward in his chair. In doing so, the deep creases on his forehead and purplish bags under his rheumy eyes became more pronounced.

"This thing in Jaywick wasn't invited – "

"Well, maybe it was," King cut in. "Have you listened to those sermons evoking the presence of the spirit to transform lukewarm members, or calling upon angels to appear in their time of need? Besides that, there is an interesting backstory with Dal that I'm still looking into – "

"He wasn't implanted with that optics package to take Polaroids of fucking cornfields," Spiller uttered while tapping his empty glass on the table. Reaching for the bottle, he quickly regained his composure and poured another finger.

"It was for a specific purpose. Why did the kids cross the Rubicon, risking so much to do so? There are still those gaps keeping us from seeing the big picture. After all these years, and the toll it's taken, I… we need that revelation that leaves *my* jaw hanging. Need to grasp it before our adversaries do because of some mistake made in the battle to the finish line."

"Even if there's a friendly wave?" King asked while recalling what a stranger had said after he approached the booth that both of them were seated at in the PIT STOP sports bar and pointed to a faded photograph of a blue race car hanging on the cluttered walls.

"There is something that I wanted to tell you," King said after waiting for a reply that never came, "something that he saw, or thinks he saw."

"Now, you have my full attention."

* * * * * * * *

Dal was drinking a 7up from the well-stocked fridge in the break room. He was glad to be done with the MRI and various other tests, even though there had been "nothing to sweat", as King had reassured him. The worse part was the odor of the adhesive gel, whose strong acetone fumes still lingered in his nostrils. In fact, most of the tests were so routine and repetitive that at one point he might have dozed off, which would account for the gap when he checked the room's wall clock.

He was also a bit disappointed that he hadn't seen anything exotic. While being escorted down a long corridor, he had passed some workshops that contained domes and cylindrical shells with minimalist designs on skids that King thought might be mock-up lunar habitats. In another area he glimpsed some pod-like structures made of glossy polymers that he guessed were also modular shelters. The bio domes with their foam membranes and translucent hydroponic bubbles looked futuristic, but not on par with the sleek alien reproduction vehicles rumored to be housed there.

As he waited for King, a man walked into the room. He was middle-aged and handsome, with sharp, russet-brown eyes and slicked-back dark hair. Impeccably dressed, it wasn't the luster of his designer silk suit that stood out to Dal, but the man's stiff clerical collar.

"I take it you are the new guy," he said with an Italian accent that was deep and slightly raspy. "I am Father Ferrata. Call me Emilano or Emilio if that's easier."

"Hello, I'm Dal. Sorry about the smell. The EEG glue came with the Frankenstein bolts."

"From Indiana, I understand. I am from Bologna, Italia. Where there aren't as many pigeons in the main square compared to your parking lots here in Las Vegas. And the take-out-pizza isn't as good, even with our crazy sausage. I am visiting with his Excellency, Archbishop Falconieri. Xavier and I just came from the observatory in Arizona where we beheld the echoes of God's creation. *Grandissimo!* We are here for the Vatican's upcoming conference on astrobiology. I am a presenter. I understand you are also looking for signs in the heavens. Not celestial portents – I am referring to visitors from higher worlds... from the fiery gulfs... perhaps arriving in wondrous vessels. If you do not mind, may I ask if you have any concerns about evoking such unknowns?"

"I take it you think it's a bunch of baloney?"

"On the contrary, it is my personal belief that we humans inhabiting this humble planet in a multiverse are but a few leaves fallen in a forest. In charismatic circles, angels are routinely summoned, and, yet, at the same time these priests are casting out the baddies."

"No one's laid their hands on my head," Dal said. "Only some electrodes."

"Yes, but my question is – if it is not known what these beings are, how do you know what you will get?"

"I don't think I'll be calling anything. Just listening."

"But, you are an intuitive communicator, no?"

King arrived and acknowledged the Father with an unctuous grin.

"I see you've met Dal – a man of few words, and Dal you've met Monsignor Ferrata. Looking quite suave in his viscose blazer. Is that Kiton? – the finest in Roma. *Figata*, if I'm saying that right."

"Needed for the discotecca here," the Father said with a cheerful acceptance of what he perceived to be a backhanded compliment.

"He and his Excellency have business here," King said while pouring a cup of coffee. "They're recalibrating. Not just with the sparking expansion revealed by VATT, but their employer has a vested interest in things they've been observing for centuries, going back to the baroque optics in the old tower, little comfort to Galileo with his own scientific lens. Yeah, everything from luminous dots energetically active among the fixed stars to huge Spielbergian bling hanging in the night sky. Having descriptive texts in their secret – excuse me – private archives, they set the standard for the mechanisms of concealment long before Uncle Sam's minefield, but anticipating disclosure, they don't want to have to do a lot of running to catch up, am I right, Father?"

"As our friend Lieutenant Colonel Mockenhaupt knows, the Church's stance is one of openness to a new interpretation of the ancient narrative… a more nuanced understanding, even when that involves using psionic components for making contact with those seen as a glorious extension of the divinity of divine creation… but not haphazardly – what do you say, willy-nilly. The Church has long been waging war against an internal invasion."

"Well, that makes us good partners. I'll worry about infected bait, while your department is deluded souls. Now, Dal, here, needs to re-take an EEG. The last one wasn't about sleep patterns."

Moments later, Dal was informed that there wasn't going to be another EEG. Instead, he would be taking an additional test in another building where the security was even more stringent. While sensing his unease in the elevator ride down, King tried to settle his nerves. "Relax, you're not a fucking guinea-pig. There's lots of biologic security, including a keen filtering system. It's been well scrubbed by decontamination procedures. No infective agents. No space bugs, so chill out," he chuckled to lighten the mood as they continued to descend. "You don't need a protective suit, but if you want one – head-to-toe shit – let me know. I'll be with you, unshielded as well."

After getting off the elevator, they walked down a stark hallway that was brightly lit.

"You're lucky this walk doesn't require goggles. The special ones with split lenses that only show what's in front of those paper shoes they make you wear. No Draconian measures, today. Now, don't worry about touching anything in there. I want you to feel the thing and describe any images that form in your head. No matter how faint the impressions might be. Any feelings, Dal, any thoughts or reaction."

After armed security personnel opened a large steel door, Dal followed King into a spacious gray room. Rather than the white ovoid object that he half expected to be gaping at, he was confused to see an old-fashioned station (or delivery) wagon, whose vibrant white paint gleamed against the concrete walls and cast a reflection on the polished gray flooring. With its walnut panel siding on the rear corners, red wheels with moon hubcaps, shiny chrome bumpers and trim, he guessed it was from the late 1940s or early 50s. Despite its age, it looked brand new parked beneath the fluorescent lighting.

Both doors were open so that he could see the dark brown interior. As he leaned inside and pressed his hand against the dashboard, he didn't experience any kind of sensation like King thought he might. Same when he touched the round gauges and chrome Motorola radio with its red knobs above the manufacturer's plaque. While softly drumming his fingers on the steering wheel, he started to feel stupid, but continued to touch the interior components at King's request.

"Sorry to disappoint you, but I'm not picking up any vibes," Dal said with the faintest gleam of amusement in his eyes while rubbing the pigskin seats with his palm.

"Okay, before we put it on Craigslist, try the rear compartment," he heard King say.

When Dal walked to the back of the vehicle and ran his fingers over the bubble taillights, he still didn't receive any impressions. With no response from the "lux-lamps", he opened the fold-down gate and ducked his head inside. Even with the persistent smell of the EEG paste, he was struck by an overpowering odor that was more foreign than unpleasant. The phantom emanation he'd gotten a whiff of in Magdalena was similar, but not as concentrated as what was now overwhelming his senses. Due to its strangeness, his reaction was to step back. As he did so, his throat tickled and his skin began prickling. This was followed by a sense of awareness that others were moving around him. Turning his head, he caught a glimpse of a woman standing on a sandy track alongside the station wagon. She was wearing a dark blue dress with a white apron. With the cap on her wavy hair, it looked like a nurse's uniform. One that was outdated.

She appeared to be in a state of shock as she shouted at someone.

"Where are its parents?" he heard her ask as the image became distorted, wavering like a mirage or one of his ocular migraines. "Oh, my God! Where are they?"

"I don't think they have parents," a male voice responded in the dusty haze.

"What do you mean?" the woman uttered.

The way her image rippled and flickered in the glare of sunlight on the desert vegetation made Dal dizzy. With whiffs of burnt desert sage mingled with that queer pungence he couldn't identify, he braced himself against the lowered tailgate and sucked back the nausea in his throat.

"Yes, they do," he said. "You're wrong. They have parents."

******* *

CHAPTER VI

Why wouldn't the smell go away? Dal grimaced as he washed his hands again, more thoroughly than he did fifteen minutes ago. He'd been scrubbing them with a strong odor neutralizing soap for three days, but could still detect that peculiar smell over the lemon and eucalyptus fragrance. The odor wasn't that offensive, he'd convinced himself – nothing like skunk acid – just extremely odd, so much so that he repeatedly sniffed his fingers.

Also on his mind was the latest news from his mother. There was still no sign of Derethia, but the police believed she had left town of her own accord and weren't investigating the matter as a missing person case. Her other update was that town folk were asking more questions about strange events that occurred during a church service that a cleaning lady had related to a "busybody reporter." Some wondered if Pastor Hoburt staged an event using puppets made to look like demons that appeared to float about in a spotlight operated by an accomplice as part of some misguided attempt to attract new members. Though his mother doubted any of this was true, Derethia had once confided to her something the pastor said about a vintage children's doll that she found to be creepy. So much so, it caused her to have bad dreams. Her mom wondered if the rumors surrounding Hoburt might have had anything to do with why those three men in suits that visited her (and poked fun at her for using canned peaches in her cobbler) asked questions about people in the congregation wearing funny masks. Before ending the call, she asked Dal if he might have been involved in some kind of trick like the one where he made those "devil signs" appear on a banana?

"Do I have to touch anything?" Dal asked as he rinsed his sudsy hands off.

"No, there's nothing to touch this time," King said with a re-assuring tone. "No assigned duties. Just observe their meditative exercises, that's all."

It didn't take King long to realize why the thought of touching something seemed to be Dal's only concern when he suggested that he tag along with him to observe the psionic team at a signals camp. He had stopped by the house to drop off a laminated badge and to share the results of the MRI. Though he'd only been there for a short while, he noticed that Dal had washed his hands several times. When he wasn't holding them under the running faucet, he was either fidgeting with them or grabbing some Nilla Wafers that he held in his reddened fingers for a while before eating them.

From discreet glances, King determined that the rash wasn't that bad. The hands were a little irritated, but nothing like contact dermatitis that needed to be treated with some topical cream. He hoped the frequent washing due to a phantom smell didn't become an obsession. There were stories he'd heard about medics that handled the bodies from crash/retrievals that went to extreme lengths to rid themselves of the horrible stink that remained with them long after the event.

Besides burning their uniforms, they washed their hands until the skin became raw. Some literally scrubbed the flesh to the bone. Of course, they were dealing with actual bodies and possible infectious agents, not olfactory hallucinations like Dal was experiencing.

On the positive side, the odor that Dal had tried to describe wasn't sulfurous in nature. Not something like thioethanol that was part of the formula sprinkled about during psyops involving simulated alien encounters. The reasons for such elaborate ploys varied, but the idea of a secretive unit carrying out an abduction scenario involving gray entities or other alien caricatures to spread a new social contagion worked in the favor of unsanctioned SAPs to discredit legitimate reports. It was the same type of task force that paid Dal a visit the night of his encounter at the church. They had been given strict orders to get scans of the foreign device with a portable imaging system, but to leave everything in place. The team was stealthy, quick and efficient, like the dark helicopter they arrived in. As the blue-skinned trolls (depending on which costumes were packed in their duffle bags) did their thing, the operation had gone so smoothly that Dal wasn't even aware of a strange presence in his bedroom. And though the unit often tagged their victims with biochips, he wasn't a test-subject so monitoring devices weren't inserted at that time. Not having the need to know the source of the targeted implant, the men were left to guess. The non-sulfurous smell meant that Dal's perception was from an actual occurrence as opposed to him merely parroting tabloid accounts or telling King what he thought he wanted to hear. What he picked up on was real, and this was a good start for things to come.

When they sat down to discuss the test results, King focused on the morphological differences in Dal's brain – such as the higher connectivity of neurons – instead of addressing the damage to tissue revealed by the scans. Along with experiencers of the phenomenon, similar physiological effects also showed up in the MRI pictures of those overexposed to ionizing radiation. The abnormal scarring in Dal's case was most likely the result of the hyper-optics device installed along with the extra touches that he was wired with, but might have occurred from an earlier encounter with the gray automata programmed by off-worlders. Things were getting crowded in his head, to be sure, including the recent device that King had authorized for tracking and security reasons, but for the time being divulging this, whether our own stuff or bionics implanted by cerebral lab meat doing the dirty work for what he referred to as the parallel folk, might be too much to digest.

After giving him the medical data, King circled back to the subject of the signaling camp. There would be other neuro-divergent people there, he explained, those genetically compatible to interact with the phenomenon. What he didn't mention, however, was that he, himself, didn't focus much of his energy on the intuitive communicators (ICs). It was part of the program, but mainly served as his cover – the requisite black program shield devised to protect the deeper project from prying eyes.

Not to say that some of the comms weren't interesting. Mainly those from the Inuit kids using their natural, inborn tools (unless part of some hybridization process?) rather than the results from the highly-trained specialists that attempted to summon anomalous vehicles, whether controlled by a non-physical intelligence, thus making the crafts living machines, or by organic packages using brain interfaces.

There were plenty of potential targets, but the problem was to sort them out. Many of the glowing spheroids that morphed and changed shape were plasma manifestations, radiating magnetic bubbles that could possibly be nascent lifeforms. Most of the unknowns, however, were courtesy of DARPA as energetic configurations designed for military applications. With the addition of these weapon systems appearing in the skies, things were getting even more confusing. The unique appearance and characteristics of either natural plasmoids or those modified in laboratories resembled the techno-signatures of energized gates involving theorized exotic transport systems, including portals associated with quantum tunneling of much larger objects.

The other problem was that our foreign adversaries had their own collection platforms. Some were neuro-meditators with taught skill-sets while others were computer hackers that gained access to sensitive material. Which was why King favored the indigenous types using non-electronic pads like old-fashioned Etch-A-Sketches to record the comms they received in the secure zone of their own minds.

But overriding all – the natives of Greenland and those in the analytic tradecraft – was the hope that Dal's presence among the ICs would circumvent most of these issues in interacting with the parallel folk. Though, as both he and his boss were aware, it was really *their* project.

After getting Dal to sign some routine forms and handing him an envelope with cash, King asked him if he had any questions or concerns about the signals exercise other than touching something still haunted by an incident that happened many years in the past.

"What that guy from the church said about visitors from outer space – do you think he's really okay with the idea?"

"The dapper Monsignor? Imagine having browsing privileges to over fifty miles of shelved documents; many so old they're blanketed with a purple fungus. Then imagine the hidden truths contained within them. The Church has their own covert programs to protect their doctrines, but they realize we're at an inflexion point. They, too, hear the constant drip drip drip pounding in their ears. They've been tracking the crescendo of mysterious signs in the heavens. So, they need to respond. Engage in dialogue. Offer a greater transparency, before dest-

abilizing revelations force them to. What some call catastroph-
ic disclosure. It's no coincidence that a Monastery of nuns was
founded in Roswell shortly after the incident in 1947 and remains
there to this day. But, they can adapt, as they've done in the past,
and even teach the Gospel to advanced beings in the unlimited
worlds of God," he said with a look of amused incredulity.

"Or, they might claim the sightings of these craft further val-
idate certain truths in the Bible they've expounded all along. For
example, your phantosmia, the smell in your head," he said with
an uneasy glance at Dal as he continued to wriggle his fingers, "a
perfume that no breeze disperses befitting of the glorious presences arriving in shining vessels."

"Yeah, I get it. They're in a tight spot, but if they don't have a
problem with ETs, why did one of them sprinkle salt around this
place to make it safe from demons? The little girl neighbor said
she saw a priest doing this."

"Wearing a Roman collar? And this happened before you
arrived?"

"You didn't see him on pigeon vision?"

"No... no, I didn't, but maybe there is more than calcium in
that box of cereal."

"What?"

* * * * * * * *

Having just returned from a walk on the trail behind the house,
Dal was slouched on the couch, cooling off from the afternoon
heat. Since the smell on his hands had finally gone away, his
thoughts returned to Jix. As he watched her latest podcast, he
wondered if she'd ever get in touch with him about going to
that place she mentioned where some kind of crash happened.

Though he had his doubts, seeing how their lifestyles were so different, he thought it was quite a coincidence that the show was about people using their psychic abilities to contact aliens.

"There's nothing new about human-initiated contact to engage with the phenomenon. To communicate with chatty spirits or aliens without call blocking," she said while seated in her home studio. Wearing a black V-neck blouse, her face was framed by blonde curtain bangs. As usual, she wore minimal makeup that didn't mask the appealing aspects. It was just the right amount, Dal thought. "Instead of laser pointers and mental signals, back in the 1950s, they used flashlights, Ouija boards and clunky radios. And, if we're to believe the contactees of the time, galactic brethren with names like Valiant Thor, Orthon and Aura Rhanes responded to save wicked humanity from the atomic bugaboo with earfuls of platitudes that also included anti-tobacco sermons. With their jeweled eyes singing this cosmic spiel, who's worried about microbes from Uranus?"

After saying this, she made a funny face that was one of her engaging traits.

With his attention focused on her quirky mannerisms, Dal almost didn't notice that the old-fashioned clock hanging on the wall behind her had 17 numbers for 17 hours of day and night.

"What are we to make of this drama? The space friends that emerged from silver contraptions in tight-fitting jumpsuits that shimmered against the bland expanses? It seems comical. The cans of instant coffee and motor oil described by the saucer ride boys, but should we snicker at aliens dressed in uniforms that resembled those of Greyhound bus drivers? Not Aura Rhanes, of course – the captain from the planet Clarion had style with that celestial do of hers," she said as she adjusted her microphone. "The whole idea of light exchanges and brain workings to vector in off-worlders by people standing in a circle in some farmer's field or seated on a blanket with a box of fried chicken. There's a new name, but that's all that's new with the sky-watchers of old, other than duller beacons and hormone-free drumsticks. Are psionics a disinfo strategy as some claim? Tried and true tactics of triple-letter agencies reaching into and pulling out old schemes from their bag of tricks?"

As he continued to watch the podcast, he found himself nodding off. The hike in the extreme weather had taken more out of him than he realized. At one point he thought he heard Jix calling his name from the screen. Still in a dazed state, he glanced at the screen of the pad on the coffee table, confused that she was now dressed differently. When he heard a series of loud knocks, he realized that he was seeing her on the doorbell camera. She was standing out front in what looked like a motorcycle vest.

"Are you there? Dal, it's Jix."

He got up and shuffled to the door. When he opened it, she was pacing about.

"I was in the neighborhood and came by to see if you wanted to get a ghost burger?"

She was indeed sporting a biker look, wearing a leather crop vest over a pink tee shirt, with faded Wranglers tucked into pull-on boots. Her hair was disheveled, and she was holding a matte black helmet, whose aerodynamic shell was aggressively styled.

"You ride," Dal said while eyeing the Harley-Davidson Sportster that was gleaming in the bright sunlight on the driveway. "Very cool. So, what do I need to put on to go to this place?" he asked while glancing down at his cargo shorts and frayed sandals.

"For this place, you're overdressed. Just grab some shoes and I've got a spare brain bucket."

As Jix revved the engine while pulling out of the driveway, the neighbor Susie passed by on a Razor scooter, launching her multicolored hoverball as she did so.

* * * * * * * *

"These are the burn marks I told you about," Jix said while pointing to several black notches on a cherry-wood bar top. "They're from cigars smoked by the actor Clark Gable in 1942 as he waited here for several days for news about the fate of his wife. She was among those on a plane that crashed nearby. Sadly, everyone died. But, as to the reason the saloon is said to be haunted and they have delish ghost burgers, is cheating during a poker game... maybe the swamp cooler wasn't working... and the bullet holes are still in the wall."

After getting a couple of beers from the bartender, they passed by an old potbelly stove in the wooden decor and grabbed a table in a corner. In the late afternoon, the rustic confines of the oldest bar in southern Nevada were crowded with locals, tourists, history buffs and weekend warriors.

Once seated, Jix pulled out a photo and handed it to Dal. It showed a research facility in the early 1960s. On the security gate was a sign that said: ASTROPOWER, with the company logo beneath it being a red insignia shaped like an inverted-V.

"I found this in an old engineering journal. Astropower was a propulsion R&D firm based in California. Maybe what landed in New Mexico back in 1964 was a prototype lunar thingy with their logo?"

"Pretty close," Dal said, "But piloted by kids? That doesn't make sense."

"True," Jix said while running her fingers through her tangled locks. "Not to mention there was plenty of desert where the company was located to perform tests. Speaking of the desert, while doing research about the flying saucer contactees of the 1950s – "

"Yeah, I watched part of that – "

"I came across lots of crazy stuff and just figured the downshift nature of the space brothers landing in craft with surfaces of pressed-tin like the walls of this saloon were mind games to deflect the truth. That or ratfuckery by the commies to get us to scrap the bomb."

"Is that why that clock was there?"

"Yeah, it was a homage to the absurdity, you know, the plumbing fixtures, bunk beds and instrument dials like a Buick dashboard that the contactees saw inside the saucers, looking like props from a terrible sci-fi film. But, as to the crackpots, some tried to establish contact from ham radio shacks. The replies they got sound like galactic prank calls, like boiling a pot of water helps with the signals, Another said to pay close attention to something in a Bugs Bunny cartoon from 1952. Oh, did you know that rabbits don't really eat carrots and the only reason Bugs chomps on them is because of a scene in a movie by our friend here that couldn't be bothered to use an ash tray, Clark Gable... Where was I? Oh, anyway, I was having some fun with my subscribers when I got a message asking if I was aware of the three vanishing stars in 1952 as shown by consecutive exposures taken from the Palomar Observatory. The suggestion was that these bright point sources very close to one another weren't stars, but something else lurking in our solar system and possibly orbiting the earth.

The kicker is that these sub-hour triple transients were followed by the famous UFO wave over Washington D.C. that started on the very next day."

"Whoa."

"Tell me about it… and it gets even stranger. The message in the Bugs Bunny cartoon about flying saucers that was released around the same time in 1952 – the one that our attention was directed to – that was supposed to be funny at the time was a resignation letter from the director of Palomar stating that when he starts seeing things like this, it was time to quit and take up turkey farming. Some viewers joked that it was a whopper that didn't cost five silver dollars, but others who saw the cartoon back in the day said the letter part was edited out for some reason. I'm still looking into all this, trying to connect the dots with the time-line and such."

After the server brought the ghost burgers and a couple more beers to the table, Jix took a bite followed by a quick gulp from the bottle as if her mouth was on fire.

"Later that same night, I get a message from a person that wants to remain anonymous. It said that no matter how far-fetched it seemed, the contactee puzzle shouldn't be ignored. Those that weren't dreamt up by con artists looking to make a buck or staged as part of some test, or as psyops by enemy agents or our own. It's not what people think, or could ever have imagined. It involved the earlier crash/retrievals and those stranded on this terrestrial plane. He then quoted from a letter by an informant that visited the Muroc facility."

After taking another drink, she read the notes on her phone:

"In some instances I could not stifle a wave of pity as I watched the pathetic bewilderment of rather brilliant minds struggling to make some sort of rational explanation which would enable them to retain their familiar theories and concepts. The complete collapse and confusion of things that beggar description turned out to be the toys of the little guys. Toys so advanced they baffled our best minds at the time. There is a lot more to the story, but that's for another time. That's how the message ended. Talk about dangling a carrot on a stick."

"Maybe other kids came later," Dal said while still chewing, "like those the cop saw in Socorro before the vertical take off... all looking for someone or something."

"You think what he said is true?"

"It's possible, isn't it?"

When they were finished eating, before leaving, Dal was leaning against the rustic bartop, waiting for Jix to return from the restroom. While checking out some of the faded historic photos pinned to the wall, he noticed a traditional old clock hastily attached by silver duct tape that looked exactly like the one she used in her podcast. Unlike the prop in her studio, however, its second hand was moving erratically around the face, sticking at times and speeding up at others. Watching the broken pointer, he had an uneasy feeling that something was about to happen. He hoped it wasn't the onset of a migraine, but whatever it was, he was quickly losing control of the situation. As the surroundings took on a vivid, dreamlike quality, his first thought was to keep from drifting into a freaky episode in front of Jix, one where the people and objects around him became detached from reality, things like that goofy clock on the wall.

He was suddenly aware of someone watching him. Turning slightly to his right, he saw that the man seated on a barstool looked more like a bizarro comic book figure than an actual biker. His swarthy complexion was too smooth to be natural and the whisker stubble had obviously been drawn with a dark marker. Though he was wearing mirror sunglasses, with his toupee of thinning gray hair, Dal recognized him to be one of the men that had visited his mother. *Had he seen him again after that?* His sweatshirt had a yellow smiley face with a bleeding bullet hole between the eyes. The rest of the biker get-up looked like a cheap Wal-Mart costume that came complete with a tattoo arm sleeve, and the fabric of the black vest exuded a chemical smell like leather cologne. The only 'colors' was a red iron-on patch that read:

HELLO, AND MY NAME IS TROUBLE

"Oh, for fuck's sake," Dal uttered. "Not this again."

The man grinned broadly as he stiffly lifted his hands from a plate that was squeaky clean other than a pickle spear. Both fists were tightly clenched as if he was holding an imaginary hamburger that he pretended to take a bite from before wiping his mouth with a paper napkin.

"This ghost burger is good," he said with a deep flat tone.

"Okay, turn it off. The stuff works, but makes my eyes hurt. Turn it off," Dal pleaded to whoever might be listening.

"I am waiting for Doctor Pepper to join me if you need to have someone look at that eye?" the man said in the same monotone voice with odd spacing between the words. "We are the ringmasters of this shit show. Hanging around here talking like that is a bad decision. Do you really want to wear a straight jacket and be over-dressed for this place? Not if her hole is your goal, you don't," he cackled while chewing nothing at all.

"Boil a pot of water, boys," Dal muttered, "Because your signal's fading."

Feeling a hand touch his shoulder, he turned to his left where a slender figure in western-style clothing was standing. With sun-creased features and a bushy mustache, Dal recognized the ranch hand as being a friendly sort that had appeared in recurring dreams.

"Howdy, pard," he said with a gentle voice while doffing his straw cowboy hat. "Name's Toppy. Don't give much mind to that feller bugging you. Airin' the lungs like that in those silly duds. Though he's wobblin' his jaws at you, it's *me* that he wants to lasso so that I don't cross any boundaries. He's the tin star from my parts, but don't let that keep you off any trails here – "

"Keep honking, I will be reloading," the hostile specter uttered; his stilted, repetitive speech in contrast to the cowpoke's convincing intonation. "I will be reloading. Keep honking."

"I'd be much obliged if you stepped inside Magdalena again, friend," the rancher said with expressive eyes while stroking his mustache. "This time take a closer look and you might be surprised by what you find. And tell that pretty thing," he winked, "Toppy said them ain't hen scratchins."

"Where's the fucking rescue squad?" Dal uttered as he glanced about the crowded bar, realizing that one of the dramatis personae of these surreal occurrences was missing.

"You already heard what I had today," a voice in his head said flatly.

"So long for now, I need to eat some smoke," the biker-type said. "Be very careful."

From the corner of his eye he saw Jix walking quickly towards him.

"Would you believe he followed me here! Time to go," she uttered with a sense of urgency.

With the sound of her voice, both of the talkative oddities at the bar vanished and everything became normal. Though visibly shaken by the shocking nature of their vibrant presences, he didn't have time to deal with it at the moment.

"Who followed you?" Dal asked. "Where? Into the bathroom?"

"That man I told you about. He's on the patio. When I came out of the ladies room, someone that watched the last show waved me over to tell me something about a contactee that talked about giant lunar potatoes made to be a laughing stock by the press. That's when I saw him sitting at a table by the stage where the band plays."

"What's he wearing?"

"He just looks like a casual biker type. Has sandy hair," she said while trying to remain calm.

After gesturing for her to take a seat at the bar, Dal walked out onto the patio to have a look. The man that matched her description was talking to a woman and didn't see him. He was wearing a "City Moto" t-shirt. He had seen it and him before. *Where?* And then it hit him. Instead of confronting him, he walked back into the bar area.

"Did you see him?" Jix asked.

"Yep, I did, but he might be following me, not you."

"Why would he be following you?"

"Because he once ordered an IPA at this place I worked at called the Muddy Boots Tavern. Since he was being an asshole, I poured him a nonny instead."

After a brief pause, she pursed her lips in a subtle frown and nodded.

"Well, that explains everything."

* * * * * * * *

"The whisper campaign had already started," King said while glancing sidelong at Dal on the drive through the high desert. "I can't shadow you by myself, and we didn't want to chip you like some lady's fucking Cocker Spaniel. Funny how that gal thought she was being watched," he said with the faintest gleam of amusement in his eye. "What for? Shows like hers are a dime a dozen. Funny, also, my associate was at that place on his own dime. He didn't even know you were there. Okay, tell her you are under surveillance as part of a background investigation to get a security clearance – "

"You mean, tell her what I'm doing?"

"No. Say you're being vetted for a job at a private aerospace company. Tell her you're a glorified screw turner. You're not a technician... not a propulsion engineer. She might be gullible, but if you tell a Syracuse grad you're a geospatial analyst, see how far that goes," he said with a bleak laugh. "It's a less sensitive job, but they still want to know how much alcohol you consume and the kind of things you might say to impress a lady. Part of the package to access your character. Now, do you need me to tie your shoes?"

While heading to a site adjacent to the Tonopah Test Range designated on old government maps as "Area 52", plumes of dust whipped across the ribbon of asphalt that wavered in the blistering heat. Along the way, the monotony of sand and sparse desert vegetation was broken by roadside bar-cafes, brothels and jerky shacks. There were also a few abandoned ranches with decrepit windmills and junked vehicles. On one dusty main street, they saw more burros than people on the boardwalk of a historic saloon.

"You were visited shortly after weren't you? Had tangential non-veridical perceptions... that crazy shit that more often than not follows a brush with the phenomenon."

In Dal's head the answer was a resounding "yes." Unlike those hazy episodes in the past that left a nagging feeling of something that needed to be acted upon, this time he clearly recalled the exchange between what he imagined to be an external manifestation involving semi-tangible projections of something implanted in his mind during his encounter with an anomalous object (though, at times, the dialogue of the curious portrayals needed subtitles!). If he understood it correctly, the message involved a being of unknown origin searching for their missing child. *Was it still alive after all these years?*

If clues were to be found in the sleepy town of Magdalena, as the rancher type had inferred, albeit in an oblique way, he wondered if it was the "odd child" called Shysie that someone was hoping to be reunited with, either to rescue or return its remains. Certain things were beginning to make sense, such as the vision he perceived of a delicately featured humanoid during his visit to the village and the more recent incident involving the old station wagon that had been used as an ambulance in response to a downed object in the desert that he 'observed' using his psionic abilities. With this sudden urge to assist in discovering the whereabouts of one of the victims of the ill-fated craft, taking into account the walk-on avatars at the haunted saloon, the empath had less concern about the sinister intent of one of the figures than the heartfelt request of the other.

* * * * * * * *

"Eeny, Meeny, Miny Moe, catch an unknown by the toe," King muttered absently as he adjusted the dials on a field communication device. Both he and Dal were seated at a folding table near the edge of a helipad, whose green perimeter lighting tinged part of the surrounding desert scrub. As King saw to some prepatory tasks, Dal's eyes were glued on the sparkling night sky. Now, he realized why Tonopah was a stargazer's dream.

An Inuk boy had his hands on the knobs of an old-fashioned Etch-A-Sketch toy that was placed on the table behind King. From the blank expression on his face, it was evident that he was already engaged in his meditative exercises. Also in close proximity to the landing area were three portable pods called QuietCubes. Blackout curtains and red indicator lights meant that the other kids from the Greenlandic Inuit tribe were also sending mental signals from their focus rooms.

"Instead of the intended target being a curious ethership, how about a bevy of buxom space nymphs, beacon people," King joked as he sprinkled his Southwest Dust seasoning into a bag of popcorn. "I'm certainly open to receiving that," he chuckled while jabbing Dal with his elbow. "Hopefully not cloaked, or disembodied floozies, either. Flirty aerial sylphs, what do you say, beacon people?"

"Sir, you're coming in loud and clear on the VHA-H. Over," a crackly voice snickered in the speaker of a handheld unit.

"Copy that, the overwatch didn't mean to disrupt those currently engaged in psychoenergetics," King replied, barely managing to suppress a laugh. "Neutralize thought-obstacles," he said with a serious tone. "Maintain clean intention, beacons."

"Hard to scrub personal touches from the system, boss. Over," a static-laden voice replied.

After a half an hour passed without any unusual activity in the sky, King picked at the few remaining kernels in the bag and sloshed the ice water in his thermos bottle.

"Where's the weird stuff, boys? The night's popcorn tricks. Bait 'em with a salt fish hack, Katjuk."

"That a plane?" Dal casually asked King while pointing to a single bright light moving against the stars. "Or a helicopter. What is that?" As he leaned forward, his voice became more animated. "A large drone, maybe?"

"There's not supposed to be anything out here tonight," King said while reaching for his night vision binoculars. "That's restricted air space. It's not the Hoverfly, because that's tethered behind us."

Whatever the pulsating blob was, it emitted a vivid amber glow that was getting more intense as it slowly descended over a rock-strewn mesa, whose jagged outline was discernable against the boundless stars.

"There's definitely something in our neighborhood," King said softly into his tactical radio unit. "Mentalgram received, boys. Gotcha, sucker. We're in the observable phase," he added after checking a computer monitor that was placed among the electronic terminals on the crowded table. "According to the dialogue box, the object's been touched on all sides."

"Why are they so trusting?" Dal uttered in hushed tones, aware of the 'quiet mind' behind him.

"Maybe because you've graced us with your presence," King said with a faint smile while reaching for his binoculars.

While switching from the digital infrared setting into the white-light mode, the UAP appeared to be a coherent structure that was spinning rapidly with a luminous fluidity. When he adjusted the focus, he could see that it had an elongated ovoid shape that discharged radiant filaments in multiple colors, with the most prominent being magenta.

"Stay in place, Zeke. Don't move. This is safe ground, buddy."

While gliding slowly over the tufted shadows of a shallow arroyo, it suddenly darted quickly from one spot to another, morphing into a flatter shape with sparkly eruptions and fiery tentacles that seemed to be exploring the desert terrain.

"Did you see that?" Dal asked with an excited whisper.

"Having a toroidal moment. That's one curious plasmoid or floating alien brain... or something with interesting vehicle morphology. We didn't snag a sexy sylph, but at least it's not Old Grumpy."

168

The words had barely left King's lips when the energized bubble briefly flashed with an intense peacock blue corona.

"Oops, spoke too soon."

As the refulgent orb continued to float playfully over the sage-dotted sand, King glanced back at the Inuk kid's vapid stare. Curious to see what was on the Etch-A-Sketch, he got up to look at the screen. Along with a sequence of numbers, that included lat/longs, there was a faint drawing of something. Straining to make out the image in the anti-glare gooseneck lamp, he did a double take.

"What's going on in that head of yours, Gordon?"

"Be advised, there's something on the range," a team member said over the radio. "You're not going to believe this – the size of it. What did those leg-pullers draw down?"

"Say again. Come in. Over," King said on his radio.

"Check out your Panasonic. If you're not receiving the images from the UAS, just turn around. It's right behind the touchdown zone. What the fuck is that!"

"Looks like a cattle drive," another voice blurted out. "I just hope they don't stampede. Over."

"Roger that," a calmer voice said. "The alert systems have been triggered and both the Spectre and ground based sensors are picking up a thermal signature."

"You have a visual that's not the UAP?" King asked. "Come in. Over."

"Affirmative. Turn around to have a look if it's not showing up on your Toughbox."

Both King and Dal turned their heads at the same time, each recoiling in shock before jumping from their seats, unable to understand what they were seeing.

It was the same faint picture that King had seen seconds ago, only now the size of the projection of the drawing looming in the distance was impossible to grasp. Not only was the depiction of a cattle drive enormous in scale, the entire scene appeared to be moving. A doodle of a horse-drawn prairie schooner dwarfed the natural desert features and blotted out much of the starry horizon as its wood-spoke wheels rolled slowly amongst the phantom herd of cows. Everything in the lively overlay had an indistinct silver-gray color that matched the aluminum powder stylus on the glass screen of an Etch-A-Sketch.

"Wait until the data analysts see this," a giddy voice crackled over King's radio. "The project officer wanted popcorn tricks. Well, you've got them."

Before King could respond, the ghostly images flickered before dissolving like the ephemeral display in a hand shaken Etch-A-Sketch. In the same instant, on the opposite side, the electric blue discharge of the shape-shifting orb imploded before the plasmoid entity vanished without a trace.

"Be advised unknowns are now coming out of the north – heading towards your operations," a voice on King's handheld radio said. "Looks like three and they're descending rather quickly. Over."

"Roger that," King replied while raising his night vision glasses to zoom in on one of several dark shapes flying silently over the sandy wash. "What happened to a heads up from the Hoverfly? Over."

"Ghosting. Over."

"What are they?" Dal asked. "More plasma nugs?"

"They're anything but luminous, as you can see, and its not a fucking Etch-A-Sketch doodle come to life," he said while trying to make sense of what he was seeing. "Large gyroplanes maybe, or robotic platforms. DARPA bucks at work."

In the night vision mode, the object King had the glasses trained on looked like a flying Humvee. In addition to the familiar rugged, boxy frame, he could make out the rotor system, ailerons, stabilizers and other radical design features protruding from the carbon-fiber composite armor. The crew compartment had a darkened windshield, so he couldn't tell if the multi-purpose combat vehicle was manned.

"Bi-modal tactical vehicles. VTOL Hummers. And, hopefully ours."

As the flying Humvees swooped down near the helipad, powerful white beams from their undersides swayed across the desert terrain before illuminating the QuietCubes.

While tilting slightly and landing vertically on reinforced tires, dry branches snapped from the crushed vegetation. Dal shielded his eyes and ducked as the prop wash churned up sand, gravel and bits of creosote bushes that stung his cheeks. In the blinding glare of spotlights, he could hear doors open and the crunch of boots hitting the ground. A figure with a dark bandana covering most of his face aimed a barrel at him and after seeing a brief shaft of intense light everything went blank.

Seconds before a thin beam with an orange tint struck his head, King had the presence of mind to set his smartphone down and use his foot to cover it with sand.

When he came to his senses shortly later, several grim-faced security personnel were at the scene. While checking with flashlights to make sure everyone was okay, they roused the Inuk boy who was slumped forward in his chair with his head sunk towards his chest. As the kid slowly opened his eyes, King noticed that his Etch-A-Sketch had been taken.

"Don't suppose anyone got a license plate," King asked while rubbing his eyes.

"Don't ask me," Dal said, still feeling a bit fuzzy after being knocked out.

"I didn't," King snapped.

"We don't know who they were, sir. Heavy hitters, that's for sure. They didn't get those spiffy rides off a local showroom floor."

"Top tier action right out of a comic book," another guy added. "Non-lethal pulses. Maybe a rapid response drill or un-announced test of sorts – "

"Let me stop you before you say or just for the fun of it," King said with an annoyed look while raising his palm.

"Anything missing that you can tell?" one of the guards asked.

"Besides part of my brain, just a chuck wagon," King said tautly. "And some coordinates… Maybe of the trail's end?"

"They sure were in a hurry during your nap."

"Yeah, and hopefully any shaking erased the screen. The poor man's encryption protocols," he said while picking up his phone and brushing the sand away. "Like this technique. What about the others?" he asked while gesturing to the pods.

Instead of glowing bright red, the strip lights on the Quiet-Cubes were a steady green.

When King, Dal and a member of the security detail entered the first workstation, the limp figure at the fold down computer table didn't appear to be seriously injured, but his drawing toy was also missing.

"Nasty customers," King grimaced.

"What did they want?"

"Materials to make thermite," King replied with a crooked smile.

* * * * * * * *

On the drive back to Vegas, King stopped to get gas and have breakfast at a roadside diner that was similar to others Dal had seen in the middle of nowhere, except that this greasy spoon had a brothel attached to it. Half of the stucco facade was lime green with other side being hot pink, a color scheme that was probably designed so as not to confuse a family of tourists as opposed to a lonely trucker, King joked while standing at the pumps.

The retro décor was also typical: a checkered floor, bold colors with chrome accents. Alien-themed novelties were for sale, displayed along with the usual kitschy stuff. Glancing at the tacky displays while grabbing a booth, Dal was amazed that there was no sign of Elvis among the other iconic figures of the era, even more so no 'King in his flashy jumpsuit floating in the glowing beam from a flying saucer' merch.

At the early hour the place was nearly empty. Other than a cook and waitress, the only other 'customers' were a scruffy desert rat hunched over the Formica counter, possibly asleep, and a woman that was probably one of the sex workers, dealing with banking issues on her cell phone.

King was still in the restroom when the food arrived. A side of hash browns and Red Bull for Dal, with a club sandwich and black coffee for King. While taking a long drink, hoping to snap out of the brain fog he was still experiencing from whatever had incapacitated him and other team members, he happened to glance up at the flat screen hanging on the wall to his left. With the volume turned off, a pretty blond weather girl in a sexy outfit was giving her forecast while stepping in front of the myriad of stars that were projected as part of a night sky used as a backdrop for the graphics. While watching her, he noticed that a vivid point of golden-amber light appeared in the star field. When it began moving erratically in the otherwise static projection, he wondered if the pulsating orb was one of the studio technician's ideas of a joke.

As the glowing sphere intensified, it suddenly plunged from the weather graphics and bounced onto the tabletop, having transitioned from the television screen into the physical realm within the diner by some impossible means. Startled by this astonishing trick, Dal recoiled against the vinyl upholstery, watching as the radiant bubble flashed an electric blue color. After assuming a different shape, the floating jelly-like blob lifted the saltshaker, turned it upside down, and carried it across the length of the table, sprinkling a powdery white line before releasing the container from its energetic grasp.

Emitting a peculiar electrical odor, the sparkling globe descended onto the floor and rolled silently across the diagonal tiles. Seconds later, it slowly rose onto the table across from where Dal was sitting and squeezed through a mini jukebox, causing a silly 1950s tune to start playing before it emerged from the other end, tearing the glued wallpaper as it climbed over the booth. Both the Mojave rat and cathouse gal seemed to be oblivious to its antics as it glided the length of the counter, playfully circling and bobbing over a cake dome, napkin dispenser and coffee maker. As it dipped momentarily behind the counter, the bland-faced cook peeked from the kitchen. When he turned back to the grill, the living radiance flared in a vintage Coca-Cola mirror, cracking the reflective surface before darting into *and fusing with the brushstrokes on the framed canvas* that depicted a lonely stretch of road in a barren desert setting. Drifting over the moonlit 'rolling' tumbleweed in the painting's foreground, the bluish ball rapidly accelerated, streaking across the vibrant composition before vanishing on the starry horizon. It was if an invisible artist's hand had live-painted its trajectory with a rapidly dissolving pigment.

"Hey, the water in your mop bucket is boiling," the drifter said nonchalantly.

If the mischief-maker wasn't some kind of after-image from the earlier incident, maybe it was one of those "hitchhikers" that King had warned him about, Dal winced inside.

"You should see pudgy Elvis on the crapper in there with big black alien eyes," King chuckled while sliding into the booth.

* * * * * * * *

"Like I told the lieutenant colonel, I saw the show and listened to the comments, which were all over the place to explain what is clearly shamanic activity and a record of ancient traditions," the anthropologist from Jix's podcast about the cave pictograms said as he led King and his partner into the dark recesses of the abandoned mine.

"We appreciate your expertise," King said while negotiating rotting beams, ore carts and mining cables in the flickering glow of flashlights, "but have our own jobs to do, and that is to investigate the intel we receive, in this case, from an elderly gentleman with a notable background that also watched the show."

Hearing himself, he couldn't suppress a smile. He didn't have the time or energy to concoct a better story and didn't really care. There were bigger things to worry about.

Having plotted the coordinates in the photos he'd taken of the Etch-A-Sketch screen, he located the vicinity of the defunct mine. Convinced it was Dal's antenna that received the lat/longs in reply to the mentalgram sent by his ICs at the signaling camp, not to mention the nudge of the cattle drive that wasn't an overblown ad for green chili cheeseburgers, he pursued the matter further. An Internet search took him to the episode of "Black Hours" that featured the secret cave in the mining district near Magdalena.

While watching the video footage, there was something about the sparkly texture of the blank ovoid that raised his brows. Ditto with the unusual bluish glyphs that everyone agreed didn't bear any resemblance to pre-contact symbols. Using a data platform, he contacted Chayton and arranged to view the pictographs under the pretense of it being a sensitive government matter that he couldn't discuss over the phone.

The legwork had been done without informing his superior of the plan. He hadn't exactly gone rogue, but after the recent raid he was starting to wonder if there might be separate factions with conflicting agendas within the program. In violating security protocols, the most serious breach was an item that he borrowed from the inventory of the "ToyBox."

"It's routine stuff we've done a hundred and one times," King said, "but it's always nice to go on a fieldtrip and get away from the wan monotony of the workplace, even if that involves startling snoozing rattlers. Look, nobody's ready to invoke eminent domain here. It should only take a couple of minutes. If there's nothing of interest, we'll be on our merry way and leave you to your totem figures and rain dances."

"What exactly is it that you're looking for?" Chayton asked with a knowing grin. "Something other than ritualistic language, I'm guessing."

"Call it territorial markings."

When they reached the opening in the false wall that was the entrance to the circular chamber that contained the cave paintings, King motioned for both men to stop.

"I know what I'm looking for, so I'll go in alone."

After entering the ceremonial space, King stood back to take in the entire mural. In the widened beam of his bright tactical flashlight, he visually compared the more common renderings composed from mineral pigments with those graphic devices that displayed blatant stylistic differences. He then focused his attention solely on the oddities.

After putting on a surgical glove, he pulled from his pocket a shaker bottle of Southwestern Dust. Reaching into the seasoning powder, he removed a thin piece of metal that he had managed to smuggle from its place of safekeeping with his wearable and a little ingenuity. He held the fragment up to the blank surface of the whitish-silver egg-shaped feature, careful not to hold it too close so that it didn't escape his grasp and meld into the lustrous sheen of the ovoid. He'd heard the stories from the C/R debris field where this type of structural 'healing' had occurred when pieces from the same object came into close proximity of one another. After confirming that the materials, both of which didn't reflect his light source, matched perfectly, he hid the scrap inside the bottle.

Thoughts raced through his mind. Who placed a piece of the metallic skin of a craft not made on this earth on the wall of a cave? And how had they managed to attach it in such a seamless manner?

Was it done by a person that somehow acquired the debris and was trying to hide it, or was it the work of one of the parallel folk that left it there as a signal to fellow off-worlders? And what about the missing piece of the cave surface that was the same shape and size. It had obviously been removed with a precision cutting tool. But, for what purpose? The answer, he believed, lay in Dal's head.

* * * * * * * *

Dal was getting his "Fix of Jix" while eating a bowl of cereal on the couch. It was the earlier episode of the cave art that he'd seen dozens of times. While adding some slices of avocado to his cornflakes, his eyes nearly popped out of his head upon seeing the red symbol inside the usually blank ovoid in the lower corner. This time it looked slightly different. Instead of the inverted V with three horizontal lines, there was a red arc over an arrowhead shape above a shorter horizontal line.

"There you are," he uttered while leaning forward. "Astropower logo, my ass. This thing is talking."

While watching to see if the glyph might change shape again, the doorbell rang. Instead of checking the Skybell system, he got up and went to open it. When he did, he was surprised to see the Italian priest standing there. *But why was the priest surprised to see him?* With a shocked look on his face, the monsignor quickly averted his eyes. Thinking it might be the Navajo ghost beads he was wearing that caused this reaction, Dal grasped one of the juniper shells to show him that the necklace was just a common trinket from a Native American trading post.

"They're just juniper berries," Dal reassured the priest. "They're supposed to offer protection from shit lurking about... or floating about. It's Emilano, right?"

"Si, I have my own beads that I use for reflection," he said shakily.

Though still taken aback by what he'd got a glimpse of, fleeting as the disturbing sight was, he managed a faint smile while tugging at his tab collar. As before, Father Ferrata was stylishly dressed, this time wearing a short sleeve black clergy shirt with tailored trousers that had a gold Versace brand logo on each side of the belt loop.

"Buongiorno, Mister Gordon. Did the lieutenant colonel call you about the password?"

"Password?"

"Si, or signal," he struggled to find the right word while rubbing the styling gel in his combed back hair. "The pass required for the discotecca that I wish to borrow."

"Oh, you mean the card for DarkSpark. No, he must have forgot. But, let me get it. Sorry about the Indian beads. You looked like you saw a ghost."

****

CHAPTER VII

King was viewing MRI scans on his computer that appeared to show damaged brain tissue. The affected area of the basal ganglia in the detailed images were from one of his Inuit psionic assets, whose concentration had been distracted during the recent summoning process. As he looked over the photos, his concern was that the sudden interruption in the linkage between the boy and the target was responsible for the lesions. When those behind the incursion were identified, he would bring the scans into evidence.

After taking some notes, he clicked on the footage of the orb that had appeared during the exchange with his IC team (or was attracted by Dal's presence). When seen in slow motion and captured in single frames, the energetic blob assumed a limbed hourglass shape with a radiant toroid-like halo. Noting how similar the images were to the typical trapezoidal bodies seen in panels of ancient rock art, the connection made by some between the composite figures with angelic entities described in religious texts seemed perfectly feasible. In trying to connect the dots, the question in his mind was: were these heaven-spanning discharges the interface between earthly beings and the parallel folk? Self-replicating carriers? He recalled a Biblical account about such celestial messengers: *Don't forget to show hospitality to strangers, for thereby some have entertained angels unawares.*

When he was finished comparing the images in the video footage with photos of the abstractions in the pictographs, he pulled up an encrypted file of the members in the program that were Vatican insiders. The first document concerned an essay penned by Monsignor Ferrata.

What caught his attention was a color microfilm image that showed the intricate decorations on the vellum leaf of a 15th-century illuminated manuscript that was one of only a few surviving examples of a variation of the Book of Hours commissioned to have pages that were stained black and, hence, given the name, "Black Hours." Along with the lavish rubrication and miniature paintings in the prayer book, columns of devotional text were written in gilded Gothic minuscule script on a dark midnight blue background.

The second page on King's screen was a magnification of the front matter, enlarged for clarity of the hand-written marginalia that extended into the dyed black borders, and also to better reveal the annotations beneath landscapes composed of somber coloration.

Ferrata's notes focused on these additions: *A copy of Black Hours preserved in an inaccessible archive labeled miscellanea that required three separate permits to view. This devotional book to the Holy Mother popular in the Late Middle Ages contains puzzling notations in text that includes the calendar of canonical hours, psalms, suffrages and Gospel sequences. These personalized touches are in three different hands with embellished initials and gilt flourishes. Those having the audacity to make such changes claim the work contains the numbers of a secret calendar. In addition to the footnotes in the text elements, the stark terrain in the miniatures is composed with somber colors in contrast to the abundant foliage in vibrant pigments more befitting of Our Lady. Those behind the scribbling on the pertinent pages hint that this unique copy of The Book of Hours contains the true key to heaven. When taken as a whole, the work thus becomes a master clock to reveal specific times when the key can be turned to open the gate. However, to those of faith, the withering of florid decoration and alterations to prayers said at regular intervals sound a warning note. The mournful palette suggests traffic with spirits as darkly stained as the soaked vellum might be responsible for such an elaborate deviation. The key may turn, but to where does one enter?*

When he was done reading Ferrata's comments, he clicked on his voice recorder: "Question: What is this precisely-timed event shining through in the liturgical calendar of the copy of Black Hours and why does it interest Ferrata more than other moldering texts of forbidden knowledge?"

Scrolling down, he came to a more recent essay written by the monsignor. This concerned a magical experiment known as "The Amalantrah Working" that was performed by the British occultist Aleister Crowley in 1918. The visions perceived via the mediums in the various sessions that were of interest to Ferrata were listed in a column:

"I see an egg with one end broken and [a] hand inside."
"An egg placed in oblong on a pylon."
"Whose egg is this?"
"Egg is symbol of some new knowledge, isn't it?"
"How are we to get this new knowledge?"
"It's all in the egg."

A note stated that at the same time Crowley established contact with a being that arose from The Amalantrah Working, and that a portrait that he drew of this entity shows a large, pear-shaped head with vestigial facial features and exaggerated slanted eyes that is a dead ringer for the modern depiction of a "Gray" extraterrestrial. Today, the drawing of the entity functions as a gateway for occultists to channel forces from other dimensions. It further stated that The Beast 666, which Crowley called himself, created the Abbey of Thelema in Italy as an anti-monastery for magical activity.

And then there was the curious matter of a series of rituals performed by one of Crowley's disciples that were designed to create a portal and allow extra-dimensional intelligences into the terrestrial zone. This operation, designed to produce a *child mightier than all kings on the earth*, was carried out in the Mojave Desert in 1946. Many consider the result of the Working to be the famous incident that occurred near Roswell, New Mexico in 1947.

When he was done reading all of the relevant passages in the essays, King once again switched on his voice recorder. "What's behind curtain number one? Assessment of Ferrata: Using intuitive communicators to invite unknowns down is a double-edged sword. A powerful doorway is opened, but what steps through? Clearly, as reflected by his words, the good Father leans more towards a demonic presence."

* * * * * * *

"Not bad, huh, wildlife fifteen minutes from a slot machine," Jix said while pulling out a couple of cans of hard seltzer from a cooler.

"Yeah, I can almost see my house… and look, there's a Painted Lady flying over a Blue Diamond Cholla," Dal said with a smug look.

"Really?" Jix responded with an impressed nod that didn't seem a hundred percent sincere. "Do you want passionfruit or citrus lime?"

"I'll go with the lime one to start."

The two were sitting alone at a picnic table in Red Rock Canyon, a nature reserve in the Mojave Desert just outside of Las Vegas. As the sun was setting over a red sandstone cliff, ancient pictographs at the base were visible between some juniper trees.

"And there's peach salsa, watermelon, a cracker crust tomato pie from a recipe that I've never tried and cheesecake cookies for whenever. Yeah, the pictographs of hand stencils might have been done for funsies because they're not six-fingered, but it seems like gorgeous orbs with Boltzmann brains impressed the indigenous people here. That's what I call them. Anasazi isn't PC."

"How come?"

"They might have been chaos cannibals. Researchers found a human protein in their coprolite that shouldn't have been there."

"What's that?"

"Something you didn't want to step in back then. Not with these leopard patterned Nikes," she said while lifting her foot to show Dal her new sneakers. The leopard print added a tinge of color to her beige sweatpants and matching slouchy pullover.

"You know," Dal said after taking a gulp of the boozy seltzer, "I don't think the Indians made the drawings. Those weird stick figures you guys think are blogs of things they saw in the night sky like orbs and glowing stuff were actually made by the crazy things themselves. They're selfies. Plasmoid selfies."

"Ha-ha."

"I'm not kidding."

"How goes the vetting protocols? Any news yet on your clearance? Maybe that guy checking the porta-potty with a color-coded badge was really checking on you."

"No, but I've got my handy screwdriver at the ready."

"Ready to reverse-engineer something."

"What's that?" he said while taking a bite of a cookie.

"I forgot you're not the chief scientist."

"Not yet. Maybe after my six month review if I get the job."

"So, before your dad left, he didn't talk about trying to replicate something so exotic that the screws only turned by using the mind... by though-transference?"

"Why would he say that... and how did you know he left us?"

"Oh, shit, I thought you told me he did. Sorry, that must have been someone else. Maybe a guest." *Way to almost kick over the rice bowl, Jixy.* "Sometimes I think the whole crashed UFO thingy is just an elaborate psyop to send the spies from adversarial nations on a wild goose chase. The more unknowns the better, so they keep the rumors coming, stacking imaginary saucers into imaginary hangars. All the warehoused crafts and dead alien bodies and shadowy gatekeepers and new whistleblowers are fabricated to mislead, and the mind games are still ongoing, with those playing their various roles being pieces of the deceptive mosaic. It's the scenario that makes the most sense."

"Did your new source say anything else about why the three stars were gone and Bugs Bunny was edited? Because he sure seemed to think the little guys were real."

"Not yet."

"Jix, you make all these podcasts about strange events, but has anything strange ever happened to you?"

"Hmm... Okay. I've never talked about it, but I have a clear memory of being in this diner when I was really young. As my mother and I were finishing eating, I saw a glass container of pink fudge on the counter. I really wanted a piece, but when the pretty waitress went to get me a chunk, we saw that most of them were covered with a swarm of ants. That was the end of that. When I brought this up in my teens, my mom wigged out. She said it happened, but I wasn't born yet. She was pregnant with me at the time."

"That's pretty cray."

"She never told me about it, but the memory somehow got passed on. The pre-natal aspect wasn't the weirdest part, though.

She told me that she was driving on a lonely stretch of road at night when she saw the bright lights of the diner with nothing else around it for miles. After what I told you happened in the place with the ants, on the return trip she noticed that the diner was gone, and there was no indication of the place having ever been there. She'd always been dumbfounded by the event, but my memory of being there with her caused even more befuddlement. That's the story... and don't dare ask me how the food was. Okay, now it's your turn."

He thought about telling her that he'd seen the red glyph again. That it was in the same spot as before, but this time it had changed shape. Since no one else saw it the first time, he came to realize that it might only be visible to his eyes, similar to some of the other phenomena associated with his encounter. Because he wasn't sure how she would react to this (other than to include him as a guest on her show), and that he needed to discuss it with King first, he came up with a different reply.

"The strangest thing? Hmm... Okay, here goes. I once got asked by this lady to join her for a picnic at sunset, even though there were plenty of other guys that would have loved to be invited to enjoy her company and gaze at her beauty as she shared private memories. This was something hard to explain, like the diner, but that I will always remember."

"Don't forget the part about the kiss," she said while leaning forward and kissing him softly on the lips.

The wetness of her tongue against his was more of a thrilling sensation than he imaged it would be. When she pulled back with an inviting smile, he gently touched her hair and kissed her again, this time longer and more passionate.

"Is that Coral Bliss?" he asked while catching his breath.

186

"Patisserie. Maybe try again and you won't want another cookie."

* * * * * * *

Wire-framed glasses rested on the aquiline nose of Archbishop Xavier Falconieri. Wearing a traditional black cassock and purple round head covering called a *zucchetto*, his fingers remained interlocked as he sat at the table in the mobile SCIF, listening to Spiller and King's heated exchange with serene detachment.

"I don't consider my team to be biological equipment like the TELES system," King exclaimed angrily to his superior. "They're not just frequency whistles, so what's being done to find those responsible?"

"The purity of your intentions is quite evident, as are your rigid standards," Spiller replied with more than a trace of sarcasm.

"I've found a little levity eases my axillary personnel when confronted with things that challenge what they were taught in Sunday school," King retorted with his face still flushed with anger.

"TELES?" the archbishop mumbled with a questioning look on his dignified countenance. "Ahh, *Sirena. Macchina psichica*," he said before the others had a chance to reply. "Electro-mechanical signaling."

"We're looking into it. Giving it high priority."

"Does anyone come to mind? I recall something about a race."

"Obviously, someone taking a close interest to what you're doing. It could even be a matter of certain actions being reflected back at you. The phenomena shape-shifts and mimics does it not? Besides letting me know that the Greenland kids – excuse me – your calibrated psionacists, aren't merely dog whistles, what was your other concern?"

"Monsignor Ferrata," King said. "I need to know from his Excellency that the diocesan priest isn't obsessed by the notion that what we're inviting – that every radiant organism in the night sky – is some maleficent deity. Can you say with high confidence, Xavier, his thinking isn't that we're resorting to magicians for salvation, and that he doesn't harbor desires to throw a wrench into the summoning process."

"What makes you think he does?" Spiller asked.

"His thoughts on the occult in general, as well as taking seriously the gibberish in this Black Hours book he pulled from the bowels of the private archives."

"Lieutenant Colonel Mockenhaupt," the archbishop said after taking a drink from a glass of artesian water, "Emilano's engaging curiosity with such a work stems from the delight he takes in reading the tabloid press. As a leisurely pursuit, he discovered in a dusty attic in the private archives a collection of *avvisi* bound in volumes. Such ephemera could have easily been pulped during Napoleon's reign, but instead of being turned into wrapping paper for butcher shops and fishing stalls they were returned to the Vatican repository. As it is today, petty gossip and rumor was popular in the 16th century. Some sources for these early journalists – called the *menanti* – were reliable while the specialty of others was scandal. Either way, it was a dangerous profession and the punishment both to the *avvisi*-writer and reader that possessed such illicit material was strict. It was while perusing these dispatches that he first came across the foreign word, *lekjaz*."

"What's that?" King asked.

"The *lekjaz* speaks magic words. He was a storyteller. According to the scandal sheets, many children were enchanted by a tale about a piece of the heaven-worlds that was located somewhere on the earth. It was said to be one of the many rooms in the Father's house. The magic words caused these children to disobey their guardians. Like music from the Piped Piper, they were lured and went in search of it never to be seen again. But to return to the heretical book, it also promises the key to an unseen world that can be found here on the earth. With painted prayers that show a *deserto* with cacti instead of greener slopes, one might think that this is simply the New World. After all, there were other depictions at the time of maize, pumpkins and squash. But what about the heavy emphasis placed on time? One doesn't just need to be punctual as with the fixed times of prayer during the day. Exact timing is required as determined by the mystery clock in the altered copy of the Black Hours. And here is something right up your alley, lieutenant colonel. In the early 1930s, the book was once in the possession of an intellectual salon in Milan until their esoteric ideas were banned by Mussolini's fascist regime. Hearing about the object that Pope Pius XII helped the American forces obtain from northern Italy after the troubled times, Pico wondered if this piece of heaven was something similar. One of the phantom fliers that went down centuries earlier. An object that was invisible except during certain timed phases when it wasn't cloaked."

Spiller gestured with a raised hand that let the archbishop know that he should not continue any further.

"What he wants to know is if he is an exorcist?" Spiller asked.

"Pico?" the archbishop replied.

"What did you call him?" King asked.

"Pico. It is Emilano's nickname, though I couldn't tell you why. But, to answer the question, he is not. He has a degree in astrobiology from Sapienza University in Rome."

After the archbishop left the SCIF, Spiller poured himself a glass of scotch and offered King some.

"I wonder if the monsignor factored in Joshua's missing day," King chuckled, "Backward shadow and all. Talk about a sandy foundation, pun fucking intended."

"How did you manage to smuggle it out of the Toy Box?" Spiller asked with an unsettling gaze. "A piece of the general's furniture."

"How?" King said, unable to hide his surprise that Spiller knew he had borrowed the fragment of exotic material. "The same way someone took one of the little fuchsia boxes from the playthings to use as a prop in the dry-run of a C/R."

"Fair enough. For what purpose?"

"To see if my guy could tell us more about it. Why else? If the outer skin knows some of the other functions of the craft from the biology injected into its structural makeup, then maybe it could tell us the purpose of the boxes, seeing how they defy all of our detection sources."

"We're shutting down the psionic aspect of the program," Spiller said bluntly. "Shifting our focus in another direction that you're currently not read into."

"You're pulling me from the program?"

"We're transitioning into another phase. Take a vacation."

"Trying a new approach? Seems rather abrupt."

"Go on vacation. Somewhere that's not so damn hot."

* * * * * * * *

Dal was checking out Jix's home studio as she fiddled with some equipment. It was the same set that he saw while watching her podcast about the early flying saucer contactees. The backdrop included silver wallpaper with glued on dials, buttons, gauges and switches that looked like props from a campy sci-fi film set.

Avoiding the funny wall clock as best as he could, he pointed to a rusty coffee can placed on an outdated instrument panel with blinking light bulbs.

"What's that all about?" Dal asked.

"M-J-B. It's the brand an officer from the Galactic Council served Smitty. The coffee was percolated by the same free energy device that powered the scout craft the Nazi crew buzzed about in, though it leaked smelly oil, go figure. Just another bonkers story from the contactee era. And that control by the can is one of my banana hair clips. Hey, just for funsies, and to test my levels, sit down and let me interview you."

After sitting down across from her, he put on the headphones she handed him.

"I'm here with Dal Gordon, who's got an interesting story involving high strangeness. First of all, thanks for sharing your experience. Start at the beginning and tell us what happened? What do you remember, Dal?"

"Do you mean besides you asking me out on a date?"

"Was that a date? Maybe it could be considered one, but when I think of a date, it's more like what we're doing tonight. Dinner and a play. No, just make up something."

"Okay, well, this cleaning lady saw me being taken by a flying bus that had a Jack in the Box antenna ball. While my mind was in a park where black Frisbees were being thrown by people that tossed them at your eyes if they thought you saw too much, those in the bus put something in my head so I could see a fly crawling on a blueberry ice cream cone from a long distance. Yeah, go figure. With the add-ons I can sometimes see these people that can appear at anytime. One of these walk-ins wants me to search for this missing child... a quiet little one that stole a wig from a thrift store and lived on green crackers back in the

1940s. The other warns me not to search for the child, maybe because of what it was looking for. There's something important there... in the Dreamy Dust Gulch...I don't know what. Maybe... violet crumbs."

When he took off the headphones, Jix pressed the stop button.

"What the fuck are violet crumbs?" she asked. "That was quite a brain-drain."

"You told me to make up something."

Though his intention had been to play along with the pretend interview, he suddenly found himself saying things he wasn't planning to tell her yet, so she wouldn't think he was off the rails like some of the nut jobs that left unhinged comments during her podcasts. The stream of thoughts just poured out, though he had no idea why. The mentioning of fragmented memories of being taken away in a flying church bus and strange manifestations of walk-ins seen with magic eye pieces were crazy enough to be made up on the spot, but what would she think about those things he hadn't fully recalled until now, such as the park where black Frisbees were used as mental blocks to shutdown one's awareness of anomalous events and the magnified view of a fly on a child's ice cream cone? Would she believe he just pulled them out of his ass?

Seeing her perplexed look, he quickly changed the subject.

"So, what's this show we're going to tomorrow about again? "You said it was supposed to be shocking."

"Yeah, it's a reinvented version of Le Grand Guignol. This was horror theater popular in Paris in the early 1900s. It was about shock value. On-stage performances, whose macabre themes were billed as not for the faint hearted. There was even a doctor in the theater to treat those that passed out from all the gore. You're not squeamish, are you?"

"Not with fake blood, I'm not."

One of the plays was about a brain surgeon that operates on the man having an affair with his wife. To get revenge, he brutally mutilates him. So, yeah, splatter-fests like that in a back alley playhouse. One of the short plays tonight is about demonic activity during the Middle Ages. I don't want to give the plot away, but the carnal desire of the gray-skinned incubi gliding about in a woman's bedchamber isn't what it seemed to the archaic mindset when taken in a modern context."

"Sounds pretty wild for a play even today."

"It's off the Strip. Not at Caesars or the Bellagio."

When he got up from the chair facing Jix, he noticed a stack of mail on a table. One of the manila envelopes had been opened, with a vintage magazine called *Coronet* placed next to it. Dated November 1952, its red cover had an illustration of three college cheerleaders doing a routine.

"Why'd someone mail you that?"

"I think it was sent by this really old man in the audience at the conference in Mesquite. The return address just said, CODGER."

"Yeah, I was there. I think I remember the old codger."

"He was like a hundred years old and probably suffering from dementia, the poor guy. He said it had an article that was a smoking gun for flying saucers. I haven't read it yet, but I checked online and there are lots of copies for sale – on eBay and Etsy and others – so there's nothing special about it. I'm sure it's the usual shit about saucer flaps causing mass hysteria that was only weather balloons, Venus, or radar ghosts. I'll check it out later, but tomorrow should be a hoot. Unless people in the audience start tossing black Frisbees at our eyes to block out our sight."

* * * * * * *

King was wearing a Hawaiian shirt while stirring a well-garnished tropical drink in a ceramic mug. He and his partner were seated at a bamboo table draped in artificial palm leaves that faced a thatch-roofed bar, behind which a large movie screen featured surfers gliding on waves in the sparkling Pacific Ocean. Other screens showed scratchy footage of drag races, clambakes and the beach lifestyle of the 1960s. Designed to look like a darkly lit cave, the popular Vegas Tiki bar was decorated to the hilt, with colorful string lights festooned over nautical details, hanging parrots, carved masks, paper flower garlands and other island kitsch.

"A great place to come to after a mistake, don't you think," King raised his voice to be heard over the reverb-drenched surf music while removing the fuchsia paper parasol from the fruity cocktail and stirring the floater of dark rum with his index finger.

"If it really was an error in judgment on your part," his partner replied after taking a sip from his own iced tropical potion.

"Inside chatter tells me something's going down," King said. "Just in case the lions are smelling blood, here's something you should think about. The incident in Lombardy in 1933 wasn't a reactive component to psionic contact modalities, per se, with the craft lured into proximity by female mediums with long horsetail hair acting as cosmic antennas. No one flipped a switch. Consider that the occupant may have been attracted, however, by something. Suppose this was arcane knowledge. We're stepping into difficult terrain here with talk of the occult sciences, but it is at least plausible that dark mythos engendered a search by those from elsewhere. Which means, there's no methodical approach on their part to make their presence known. There's no scrutiny to us tribal animals about our destructive ways. They came here looking for something that might have been here for a very long time. What this is – is the big question. The Catholic bunch might be close to the answer, but don't trust them, especially Ferrata. One thing's for sure, though, if it's found and the public gets wind of it, the ontological shock people speak of will be multi-pronged. A Hydra-headed monster."

"Ignore the symbolic connection of the magenta shade with a nuclear blast cloud and keep an eye on the bead-rattlers?"

"Affirmative."

"On a related subject. There was a lot of legwork involved," his partner said, "but as it turns out, that fellow that ruined the carpet in his hotel room with the spilled port was part of the program damn near from its inception. His specialty was misleading others."

"We found the magazine in his room. No mention of astro-planes."

"True, but what if he deeked us? Gave us a bum steer."

"Maybe I should pay the lady a visit."

"While you're on vacation? Let me take care of this, King."

"No, she's made you. Besides, I'm the one with his finger in the Piranha Punch."

* * * * * * *

Dal was trying to decide what to wear to the theater when Jix called to tell him about a change of plans. There was excitement in her voice as she apologized for "breaking the date" before explaining the "reason for flaking." After he had left yesterday, she had checked out the magazine sent anonymously. There was an article about a flying saucer incident and parts of it were so mind-blowing that she wanted to do further research for an upcoming podcast. She said the jaw-dropping part was about a "strange mechanical plane" that was recovered in Italy in 1933. There were no occupants, but the craft was taken to a nearby facility and secretly studied before the papal authorities made arrangements in the wake of World War II to hand it over to the Americans. It was put on a military transport and taken to an Army Air Force technical base.

When she checked all the archived copies of the same date (issue #33, she added), the contents were exactly the same *except* for that one article, leading her to believe it was recalled just after being issued. After gathering up the few sold copies they replaced it with a sanitized version. There was a lot more to it, which she would tell him later.

Whoever ordered the pizza that was delivered to Dal knew just what he liked. Thin crust with ground beef, onions and banana peppers. He wondered if it was Jix, though he was pretty sure he never mentioned his favorite toppings, as the topic never came up.

As he chewed on a slice at this late hour, glancing out the dining room window, he noticed that some lights had switched on by the gate to the jogging trail. His first thought was that Susie was playing with her luminous hoverball or some new flying spinner toy even though it was way past her bedtime. Walking over to the sliding glass door to get a better look, what he saw didn't make sense. It looked like an old movie marquee, whose glowing letters were blurred. Stepping outside onto the warm pavers to investigate, he saw flashlights bobbing about in the same area, though the dark figures waving them were indistinct in the bright glare.

The only sound he could hear as he moved closer was the crunch of his beat-up sneakers on the gravelly sand. Adding to his confusion about the garish display, several security guards in black clothing were standing behind red velvet roping that had polished silver balls on the top of the stanchions. Above the rickety gate, a string of floating amber lights read:

THEATRE du GRAND-GUIGNOL

Seeing this, he felt a mental tingling. With an increased awareness that the stage was set for an inexplicable occurrence, he tried to settle his mind. Maybe Jix had planned the whole thing as an elaborate surprise, he tried to rationalize before a sense of panic set in. When he saw the neighbor lady show up in her silk pajamas, he was a bit relieved.

"Hi Cynthia. Where's Susie?"

"She's having a sleepover with one of her friends in the tree house," she said with a puzzled look.

"Have your tickets ready," one of the security guards uttered.

At the same time Dal received a text from Jix:

grab the seats. i'm in the lobby getting us some wine and s'mores tarts.

"Put anything in your pockets that's metal in the container," one of the men said to Dal after scanning the app on his digital wallet. "Sorry, ma'am, there's dress code," he told Cynthia. "Even back alley thrill-peddlers have their standards."

"The show's about to start," another man said as Dal emptied his pockets and stepped through the gate. There were three attached movie seats of modern design in the desert scrub that faced the outline of the red cliffs. Though their presence on the sandy loam was completely absurd, he felt a strange compulsion to take a seat and wait for Jix. As he eased back, the night sky suddenly filled with more stars than he'd ever seen. When he blinked, most of the celestial objects winked out, with only the normal smattering of stars remaining visible due to the ambient light of Las Vegas.

He tried to get up from his seat but was glued to the spot.

"You can go back to sleep," a uniformed maintenance worker with a lobby broom and dustpan chuckled. "The show's over. Next one's in forty five minutes," he said while kicking up puffs of sand as he swept the desert floor.

"What was in those banana peppers?" Dal asked before blacking out.

When his eyes slowly opened, he had a panoramic view of a starry sky viewed through a multi-window configuration inside a domed structure. Through the optical quality Plexiglas cupola in this observatory module, he also saw a large array of solar panels and other outer features on an integrated truss structure.

How had he been taken into outer space?

A flood of sensations surged through him, above all total incomprehension of the situation. Strapped into a futuristic recliner, he shifted his gaze in the windowed workstation. On either side of him were high-tech Nomex spacesuits that had attached helmets with glossy dark visors. On the sleeves and fabric panels were triangular crew patches with embroidered Marian crosses.

After unfastening the straps, he found himself floating above the seat. Reaching for a tube that ran along the wall of the cluttered module, he clung to it to keep from drifting off. Not sure what to do while experiencing weightlessness, he moved freely from point to point, grabbing hold of fixed scientific instruments to tether himself.

As he glided over some cargo pallets, he caught glimpses of the cramped interiors of crew quarters where sleeping bags were fixed to the walls along with screen control panels and personal mementos. In a slightly larger module, he was surprised to see that the walls were covered with frescos of religious themes. Along with mosaic panels of dramatic imagery, plaster statues of saints associated with the celestial realm flanked vividly colored bas-reliefs depicting winged cherubs. Beneath a circular overhead window surrounded by a host of painted angels, a covered altar and liturgical paraphernalia were illuminated by the flickering glow of electric candelabras.

Strangest of all was the book on the lectern. It was an ancient manuscript, whose vellum pages of devotional text were written in gilded Latin script against a monochromatic blue background with black borders.

The darkly ornate 15th-century "Book of Hours" was opened to show a miniature painting that featured a columnar cactus that was banded and crested with a tessellated, fan-shaped appendage that had a dark pink flowerhead. Beneath the curious botanical illustration, a single word was written with a modern marker.

IMPOSTORE

Suddenly, the hatch opened and several armed figures wearing camo fatigues floated into the module. They appeared to be members of some elite Special Forces unit with mission specific layers of tactical gear that included chest rigs, M4s and mag pouches.

"You buggin' out?" one asked with a faint smile. "Could really go for a corned-beef sandwich right now couldn't you?"

"What's going on here?" Dal uttered. "I'm not hungry. Just want to go home."

"That was a joke. I take it you're not familiar with a little NASA mischief. The bread crumbs chaos."

"Do you guys have some water in those?" Dal asked while gesturing to a canteen.

"That would be quite the spectacle in microgravity," the man replied with a dry laugh.

"What the fuck do you think he was just joking about," a black guy shouted. "You don't watch the Simpsons, bruh? The preserved contraband is now in Indiana if you don't get rambunctious on me and live long enough to buy a ticket for twenty bucks."

Right after he asked for a drink, a cube-shaped robot floated into the compartment holding a green pouch that was labeled: Pellegrino water.

"Hoity-toity water," another guy said. "That's some ritzy shit that astrobee's got. These Italians sure travel in style."

"I work with the lieutenant colonel," Dal said.

"I don't give a golden hemorrhoid who you work with, simp," the black guy uttered. "Your new job is a turkey farmer, turkey. Did you think you were going to float around in this techie crib looking for Ezekiel shit while booking faster than some Guido's Lambor-fucking-ghini. Seven sunrises every day – bruh– that's seven doings per day."

"What my polysyllabic-cursing friend here is trying to say is that you're going on another ride. With a 77, 500 mile per hour speed limit we're bouncing from this can of God-fearing snatch before another glorious sunset pops up. And before leaving the simulator you're going to have to put on an eye covering."

"Comply, bruh, or I'll smoke your ass," the black guy said with a menacing wink.

* * * * * * *

CHAPTER VIII

The shrill whistling of a grackle awakened Dal. At first he didn't know where he was, but as he glanced about the room, he recalled the guy in camo fatigues and duty gear switching on the antique brass table lamp with a tatty shade and gesturing to a couple of Andes mints placed on a pillow in the Victorian bed frame, whose iron posts were draped with lace. After drawing the damask curtains to block out the morning twilight, the man left the room, closing the door softly behind him.

Having only gotten a few hours of sleep, Dal climbed out of the bed still wearing his clothes and opened the curtain. As the sun streamed in through the dirty, cracked glass, he could see the slanted porches of a couple of weathered shacks surrounded by jagged ridgelines against a cloudless blue sky.

With each minute that passed, details about the night before became clearer. He had arrived in an armored Humvee shortly before dawn, and the three soldiers without rank tabs that took him there referred to the place as a semi-ghost town, though they weren't at liberty to discuss the nature of the small desert community or disclose its exact location. Seeing part of what looked like the conveyer belt of a rusty apparatus, he figured the decrepit structures might have been the remnants of an abandoned mining camp. Though the rugged terrain looked similar to other scrubby hillsides in Nevada, having estimated the drive time to be about four hours, he sensed the place was somewhere in the vicinity of the signals camp near the restricted military range in Tonopah.

On the drive, he was informed that he was being taken to a remote location for his own protection. His former boss had been dismissed from his duties during an ongoing schism in the program. It was members of the opposing faction that were responsible for the raid by commandos of the lieutenant colonel's ICs. While in the temporary safe haven, he would be contacted by his new boss and asked to participate in a few more experiments. Having been provided sparse information about this new development by the Special Forces honchos, the only thing he was sure of was that after being drugged and taken from his house, he had been placed inside a simulator for what was to be a manned space station operated by the Vatican. Even though he had been forced to wear a blindfold, he was able to recognize stamped markings on the painted concrete floor that matched those in the private aerospace company that designed and built space platforms. It was the same facility where he had been introduced to Monsignor Ferrata. What he wasn't sure of was if those that came to his aid were on the same team as those that abducted him?

He wanted to contact King to get his take, but they had confiscated his phone, telling him it would be returned after their chief geek scanned it for tracking devices. As he tried to sort things out, he heard a woman's muffled voice speaking to someone in another room. Thinking she might have some answers, he opened the door to see what was going on.

In the living room, he saw a woman seated behind a polished demilune table with an erased blackboard behind her. Matronly looking with puffy cheeks and coffee-stained teeth; her intense cobalt blue hair was braided close to the scalp in distinctive zigzags.

She was wearing an old-fashioned olive drab uniform decked out with a ceremonial golden aiguillette, colorful ribbons, phony medals and esoteric badges.

Without acknowledging his presence, she continued to speak to the otherwise empty room, pausing only to take a bite from a slice of pizza (topped with ground beef, onions and banana peppers, he noticed) or to run her fingers over the bright blue coils on her pate.

"As I mentioned earlier in today's lesson, when discussing craft that operate on wishful thinking, there was an interesting footnote that I picked up from some thought-speak at the recent conclave concerning one of the concepts for a classic looking flying saucer that was printed in the 1960s. According to an astute Michelin Man-type, the various components in the cutaway diagram are actually coded allusions to the events surrounding the assassination of former American President Kennedy. Terms like disruptors, equidistant-spaced poppers, gravity shields and negators all have double meanings. Even peripheral furnishings in the sectional view such as internal washers are ciphers for the conspirators of the plot. Okay, enough about these absurdities being a facade. When discussing the perilous visits by those to our home planet – even if they had good intentions in chasing a fable – most researchers don't take into consideration just how much damage and misery was caused by their disobedience. Which is why such visits, regardless of the motives, were prohibited by the kids' parents."

Dal jumped up from a cushioned settee when a faint rumbling sound caused the furnishings to shake. For a minute, he thought the old grandfather clock with the flaking enamel dial might tumble over.

"That's just the train," the woman said.

Moments later a HO-scale model train raced along on a track layout that he hadn't noticed on the worn carpet. As the engine, flatbeds, tankers, boxcars and caboose passed by a stand of miniature Ponderosa pines and plaster forestry workers before disappearing through a crude tunnel-like gap in the ornate baseboard molding, the woman continued:

"Let's look at the mysterious circumstances of untimely deaths after Kennedy's ideas became too problematic for the constellation of unauthorized special access programs. He ordered direct cooperation between the adversaries to share highly sensitive information about the otherworld visitations so that a clear distinction could be made between the knowns and unknowns. This so that each country's advanced aircraft weren't mistaken as behaving provocatively, leading up to a deadly confrontation in those bomb-happy days. With intelligence agencies like the CIA caught in a pickle, the result of the tension this caused was that Lancer – the Secret Service's codename for Kennedy – had to get wet. And then came the revelations of pillow talk and a little red diary. Those entangled in the leaking of outer space matters became collateral damage. The list is long. No, the visitors didn't point the gun barrels or inject the barbiturates, but they created the mess by being where they didn't belong. The calamity of the past brings us to the present. A member of the alliance has thought-spoke concerns to the galactic panel about the possibility of another incursion involving the same off-worlders and same legendary tale. Only this time, it's not kids with toys, but their guardians in their grown-up crafts."

Hearing a commotion outside, Dal went to see what was going on. As two elderly men were kneeling over something, he got a better look at the bleak surroundings.

In the glaring sunlight, clusters of ramshackle structures that resembled shantytowns he'd seen in photos were perched on a hillside, whose surrounding ridges were dotted with the usual parched brush. From his vantage point, the desert hideaway appeared to be nestled within the browned cliffs of a larger canyon.

The acrid smell of creosote resin lingered in the air, causing him to have a gagging reflex in the stifling heat. In all directions, patches of burro-weed had been cleared for the placement of ground foam on which the tracks of an elaborate model railroad layout had been assembled. Instead of a hobbyist's bench work, the mainline on the sandy floor branched off with complex switching into contrived openings in the run-down trailers and snaked through corrugated metal shacks.

The argument he heard appeared to be about a tarantula that had been struck by the same train that just passed through the living room. The dark brown arachnid remained motionless on the tight loop of flextrack, partly stuck under a Lionel diesel locomotive.

As the dispute continued he heard the sound of someone playing a piano. Glancing at the adjacent structure, through a collapsed wall he saw a man with long snowy white hair playing a battered upright while completely in the nude. Adding to the bizarreness of his sunburnt presence, a dozen Grackles were gathered around the piano, taking turns vocalizing with high-pitched whistles that were in tune and time with the tinkling melody.

"That was purely by chance," a gaunt, bearded figure said to the elderly figure wearing a dingy baseball cap with the logo of the Area 51 softball team named the 8-Ballers. "It doesn't matter that neither of us saw it happen. It's on the tracks where it was struck, so pay up, Bill."

"I'll give you a tiny piece of the green cracker, as was the actual bet we had," the old timer holding a wireless remote control said somewhat reluctantly. "I'll bring it to you after I remove the carcass and get this train back on schedule. I've got coal hoppers on their way from the transfer zone."

"That's acceptable to me, Bill."

"Would you mind keeping it down!" the naked pianist uttered in an irritated tone.

"A hawk carried off my last flutist and its replacement is having a tough go with triplet scales. And try convincing a common blackbird basic concepts – like how percussion is supposed to be felt, not heard, or how oboes are always slightly out of tune to a proud female mimicking double reeds, poor darling."

"Apologies, Nils," Bill said. "We know you're busy with the symphony."

"A diverse repertoire of guttural shrieks does not equate to expressive woodwind accents," the pianist chided one of the chattering birds as it retreated behind a threadbare recliner.

"At least there were no passenger cars among the rolling stock," the man in the 8-Ballers cap said while scratching his chin stubble. "Did you see it happen?" he asked Dal.

"No, I just got here. I was listening to that whacko woman when I heard you guys."

"The lady in full dress with all the chest candy? She arrived in a hot air balloon a couple of days ago. Not sure why the guards didn't shoot it down? I found some of her talk interesting, like the time they crated up a Babylonian stargate from Saddam's summer palace and took it to Bulgaria, but then she went off on a tangent about how little dinosauroids are hard to potty train."

Having enough of this madness, Dal returned to the house. Inside, the space cadet was still talking from behind the polished table.

"By the way, our Arcturian visitor to the class today is quite the shy sort and will remain cloaked when called to list the known crash/retrievals. All you will see is a shadowy form and the piece of chalk squeaking against the blackboard."

After quickly eating a slice of cold pizza from the blank card-board box, Dal checked the noisy avocado-green refrigerator. Seeing some bottles of water in the stained interior, he tossed a couple of them into a plastic grocery bag along with an orange and headed toward the front door.

Without any idea of which way to go, he passed a couple of tumbledown shacks and started down a rough sandy trail. After a few feet, he once again felt the ground shake, pausing at the flashing red lights on a HO-scale signal crossing that lowered its gate.

"That caused that?" he wondered while gazing down at a model military train with a desert sand color scheme that passed by a prop water tank placed amid the actual shriveled flora.

As a flatbed with a searchlight and shipping containers was followed by a big army cannon launch platform car, he stepped over the track, cursing out loud for having to be mindful of the miniature world spread out all around him.

Looking around at the expanse of barren desert, he realized just how isolated the tiny population was. Determined to see if there was a road or signs indicating the closest town, he continued, quickly losing his footing and sliding down a rock-strewn mound.

As he stood up and checked the scratches on his arm, a wailing siren echoed off a canyon wall. Shading his eyes while looking up, out of the blinding sun there appeared a large-scale model of a World War II-era Nazi dive-bomber. Highly detailed with swastikas on its carbon-fiber frame and inverted 7-foot wingspan, the remote control Junkers Stuka performed an acrobatic maneuver before suddenly swooping down over the rugged terrain. More alarming than the ear-piercing "Jericho's Trumpet" prop-driven siren was the bright white flash of guns firing from the canted wings as the plane strafed the withered scrub on a nearby hillock.

While seeking cover under a craggy outcrop, a camo dune buggy came into sight and skid to a stop in a plume of dust. The 1980s militarized sand rail was fitted with a bristling array of modifications that included a mounted 50-cal gun. Grabbing onto the roll cage, the black Special Forces commando with full tactical gear lifted himself out of the patrol vehicle and unbuckled his tan helmet while pointing an XM7 assault rifle at Dal.

"Where's your permission slip, Flash?" he asked as the roar of the Stuka faded in the distance. "Here, I've got my fingers on my gangsta grips ready to make waste to some Pleiadian wimp trying to escape on the cosmic tide and it's your bones they'd be picking out of the sand. One motherfucking day here and you're already acting rambunctious in this blistering shit. Now, get your alabaster-skinned ass back up there with them little choo choos and wait for further orders."

* * * * * * *

King parked his Jeep Wagoneer by the curb in a residential area. Picking up the manila envelope on the passenger seat, he glanced at the word CODGER scrawled beneath the postal stamps before pulling out the vintage *Coronet* magazine that had an illustration of three college cheerleaders on its red background. Opening it to the page with an article about flying saucers in the 1950s, after skimming the text, he shook his head and smirked. Shoving it back into the envelope, he called his partner.

"Her copy of *Coronet* has the usual bare bones article. No Magenta stuff."

"Good. Did you have any trouble getting it?"

"None. She seemed nervous looking at my well-tailored dark suit and ID with a foggy photo. Guess I do a pretty good job of impersonating a cleaner. Glad I didn't shave my eyebrows or show up with floppy pink bunny ears."

"She just handed it over?"

"Pretty much."

"Like you said, King, she's no dummy."

"Meaning?"

"I don't mean to be dispiriting while you're on vacation, but if it were me and I was given something impossible to find that the powers that be would take a great interest in, the first thing I would do is go online and buy a couple of easy to obtain copies of the same magazine as a security measure in case someone came calling."

"You think she outsmarted me? No... no, you're overthinking this... yet again, but if that were the case we could sure use her on our team."

"You're probably right. I'm just covering all the bases. Anyway, I've got lots of news thanks to that nosey little girl, Susie. Not only does she confirm the salt-shaking priest, she has a photo of Ferrata taken in the act. And at the time of the Desert Bloom blitz she was in her tree fort sipping Starbuck's dark roast and watched – get this – as some of those manly cars landed behind the houses – "

"Humvees – militarized –"

"Yep, that once on the ground moved like a crab... diagonally, the little brainiac made a point to let me know. And then soldiers poured out and entered Dal's house. Minutes later she saw them carrying him on a stretcher, which they placed inside one of the vehicles. So much for the pigeon some crackshot took out with our little techie on the scene. And here's the best part. Shortly before Dal was snatched, she took color night vision footage from her Eagle Eye of an Xpsilon parked out front."

"What's that – some kind of spaceship I don't know about?"

"It's an Italian car. A Lancia Xpsilon painted Ardesia Black, she informed me along with some details about the car's hexagonal headlights… you've got to love her. I felt bad about stepping on her cat's tail. The driver, who I'll bet was Ferrata, handed a guy pretending to be with DoorDash or Grubhub a pizza box. Another bet I'd take is that this pizza was tampered with."

"Narcotized."

"Then the mother showed up and asked me what I wanted."

"What did you tell her – that you were investigating the latest cult to set up shop in Vegas?"

"No, that I was investigating an alien that escaped from Area 51 and was last seen hiding on her cul-de-sac. I told her that if she saw a tall white being to call the police."

"And?"

"She actually seemed relieved and said it explained lots of strange things that happened as of late."

* * * * * * *

Seated at a rough-hewn table in the scarlet twilight, Dal was drinking a can of seltzer as a colony of bats wheeled overhead. When he returned from being scolded by the black security patrol guy, he was surprised to find a suitcase with some of his clothes, toiletries and personal items, but not his wallet or smartphone. Also, the fridge and cabinets were stocked. The lady with the blue braids was gone, but the train continued to pass through the living room at intervals. When it stopped amid the pine tree scenery, among the rolling stock was a postal coach that had a Post-it note affixed to its roof. Written on it was:

GORDON 116 SHADY GLADE.

"Until I'm convinced it wasn't already immobilized and placed on the tracks, you're not going to get a piece of my green cracker," the elderly fellow wearing the 8-Ballers cap told the bearded guy. "I'm having the stiff remains dissected for traces of wasp venom like from those my eye-witness saw buzzing about… and they're hard to miss."

"I didn't take you for a welcher, Bill," the guy said disappointedly.

As the men continued to bicker, the naked man on the piano was critiquing the performance of one of the Grackles during a rehearsal:

"Once again I find myself wallowing in a foul sewer of despair due to the vacuity of a simple worm picker. You're too brazen… overpowering. A trill shouldn't sound like a painful dentist's drill. Continue to do so, and we'll soon behold the epitaph of the obbligato flute section. I need a delicate, lyrical tone that shimmers like a wonderful night of stars."

"Hey, where's 116 Shady Glade?" Dal asked Bill.

"It's behind the old mining works," he replied. "When you get a chance, tell the teach to be on the lookout for a raspberry syrup tanker for her wonderful muffins."

Dal was looking for the address on an old house with a leaning porch when a man quickly rounded a corner carrying a badminton racket. With his eyes trained on the high wooden fence at the edge of the sandy yard, he quickly picked up his pace, running as a small glowing orb soared over the weather-beaten posts in a high arc and dropped sharply in front of him. Showing quick reactions, the man whacked it hard with a nice backhand return that caused the orange sphere to flare even brighter while barely clearing the fence and disappearing on the other side.

"I'm getting too old for this game," he said out of breath.

Though he had cleaned up his scraggy appearance, with his silver hair cut short and chin stubble shaved, Dal recognized the stained gray sweatshirt with a yellow smiley face.

"At least it's not a black Frisbee," Dal said with a twisted grin.

"You don't have to worry about that," the guy replied while repeatedly glancing at the fence.

"I'm not worried about anything. I could blink my eyes and you'd be gone."

"Really? Is that right? Be my guest, sport. Go ahead. C'mon, focus."

Dal's best try had no affect.

"Yeah, it doesn't work on my home turf."

"You're here for real?" Dal asked with a puzzled look. "How were you in my head?"

Before he could reply, the shimmering globe speedily returned from the other side of the fence. As the man was about to smack it with his racket, it swerved at the last second and shot straight up into the starry night sky, where it moved in an erratic manner before winking out.

"Good thing I don't keep score, because you can never beat the damn things. They don't even give you a chance, the poor sports are always popping back up to the sky pretending to be Chinese lanterns or space detritus."

At that instant, a tactical dune buggy with two crewmen squeaked to a stop in front of the house. The driver shone a hand-held spotlight on the cluttered porch.

"Gentlemen you see anything out of the ordinary in the neighborhood?" he asked.

"Which one of our bipedal friends got away this time?" the man asked while dropping his racket. "A Loveland Frog or Hopkinsville goblin?"

"If it were in that nutso menagerie," the black soldier said, "it would probably end up on your grill with that other nasty shit."

"Smoke the good stuff. That reminds me, did you bring me any scrapings?"

"Yeah, a flat possum with a sparkling candle in its ass."

Having a good laugh, the men sped away.

"You missed a great dinner, but how about a glass of el cheapo wine? Better yet, care to join me for some whiskey – I know a well-equipped canteen."

"There's a bar here?"

"Not on the main drag."

"What's your name? You already know mine."

"You can call me Flash like the others do."

* * * * * * * *

Upon entering the guy's bedroom, the first thing Dal noticed was a hanging plaque with a bible verse that read:

THERE ARE MANY ROOMS IN THE
FATHER'S HOUSE.

As he glanced about, a low rumbling sound caused flaking plaster to rain down from an exposed ceiling beam. With heavily curtained windows, the dark furnishings included a messy bed, chest-o-drawers and antique piecrust table with several cans of orange seltzer.

"Your place on Cactus Kiss is nicer, but I've got an above ground pool out back with a sand filter."

Inside the walk-in closet, the guy lifted a pair of bowling shoes placed on top of their cardboard box. Inside the shoebox was an early Indentimat scanning system. After pressing the prompt button, a bright beam of white light shone down on the shiny finger-shaped grooves on the device.

"It's an early hand geometry recognition system that's synced with my wearable."

When he pressed his hand against the grooves, a green button flashed before a hinged wall in the closet swung open to reveal the door of an elevator.

There was a faint smile on Dal's face as he wondered if that was the sole meaning of the sign with the biblical verse.

"It only goes one way," the man joked. "Has a fingerprint scanner for verification. More crapola biometrics. Blisters on my fingers from my grip on the badminton racket sometimes confound it, so we'll see if I'm allowed access."

When the door slid open and they stepped inside, the ride down was smoother than Dal expected. After coming to a stop, they walked out into the eerie fluorescent shadows on a sidewalk in a corridor covered with beige ceramic tiles. Their skin appeared jaundiced in the artificial lighting as they waited by the tracks of a narrow-gauge rail system.

"That's what causes the shaking," Dal said. "I didn't think it was the little Lionels."

"Next to creosote in my boogers, worrying about stepping on a Taco Bell or knocking over a coal trestle is the most annoying thing about living on the turkey farm. But the diorama makes for a good cover in a secret facility that houses an otherworld toy box. This part of Subtropolis has been a ghost town for some time. A ghost town with an earlier maglev transport system that runs 24/7. No iris algorithms or vascular recognition here either. Just outdated hand-key devices, but back in the day it might as well been magic. Now you know why ashtrays in military jets cost over six-hundred dollars and other bloated costs paid from funds siphoned off a generous budget."

"I heard about this crashed disk that was so large it couldn't be moved so they just buried it where it came down."

"There's a little truth in every good lie."

Momentarily, a passenger shuttle approached and stopped at an empty guard shack. Walking through the opened door, they sat down on a plastic bench as the transport continued further into the underground facility. After a minute or so, the train stopped in front of some conference rooms with papered-over windows. There was also a barbershop with an iconic striped pole in front, a storefront for an ice-cream parlor/five-and-dime combo and a night club with a glitzy faux facade, whose vibrant marquee read:

SUBTROPICANA

"This is our stop."

After getting off the shuttle, they headed towards the club. Before entering, Dal stopped to check out a newspaper vending machine on the sidewalk that was filled with copies of the *Las Vegas Review Journal* dated late November 1963.

"It was deserted that long ago?" Dal asked.

"Yep, and the lights are still on. Bubbler works, too," he said while gesturing to a drinking fountain. "They used to say this place had the best entertainment under the Sands and the Dunes," the guy joked as they entered the enlisted club with its pool tables, jukebox and carousel of slot machines. Surrounding a small dance floor were booths and tables. On one of the tables was a copy of the *Review Journal* whose bold headline read:

JFK DEAD

Picking up the newspaper, Dal took a seat on a stool as the man walked behind the well-stocked bar.

"Kennedy and his dalliances. If you take that as a souvenir, those dudes in their fast attack Chenowths will know we were down here. What's your preference – Eagle Rare bourbon or Four Roses blended?"

"Whatever you're having," Dal said as he carefully folded the paper.

"You didn't drink whiskey in your past life?" the guy asked as he poured some Eagle Rare into a couple of glasses. "Not enough regulars tonight to take roll call but happy birthday to me," he said while raising his glass for a toast.

"Mom said I might run into you in Vegas," Dal said as the glasses clinked.

"Was it my birthday or the color of my eyes?"

"Only us Hoosiers call it a bubbler," Dal quipped. "What happened to you, Dad?"

"What happened to Dane Gordon, the elite special forces guy that suffered PTSD? I wanted to protect Corina – your mother and you, but so much for that. The Tier 1 Unit stuff became a cover for my real task of playing with the toys here. One of our ancestors named Elbert picked the wrong day to go coon hunting and they've targeted the family ever since. It took a while – with the inner block – but I finally started to recall what happened. Corina and I were having a picnic near Sullivan's field. She was pregnant with you at the time of the encounter. Suddenly, the sun became brighter than it should be... and much hotter. I couldn't look up... neither of us could and for some reason we laid down flat in the grass. That's when I saw these three little guys coming towards us. It looked like they were hopping about in some kind of funny shoes. I couldn't figure out what they wanted because we had already eaten our basket of food and there were all these ants crawling on Corina's pink fudge – "

"Pink fudge? That's weird."

"Your mother became hysterical… and I didn't have my rifle, so I aimed my index finger at them like it was a pistol and started firing, picking them off one by one. They fell down on the ground, so I thought I killed them all… but I guess I didn't. Since they're not supposed to be here, they wanted to use my eyes to find something – "

"Maybe it's a little girl they call Shysie?"

"We call her SSHHAA, but that didn't work too well, so because of a parent's grief, as ironic as that is, all these years later they're back trying it again with you, hoping the soulless proxies in the oblate spheroid don't botch it this time around. Fast forward. I scored high with some tests and racked up more points than anyone on an arcade game so they invited me into a special program. But, I couldn't make heads nor tails with the flurries of tiny symbols in my head to try and gain access to any of their flying toys… toys more advanced than our current tech. Hell, we can't even determine the color of the things. After being taken inside a protective enclosure they showed me her second skin. What we call a flight suit. When I touched it I couldn't feel anything… there was no tactile sensation to the material… but later it really messed with my head. When the nightmares got worse, they put me in the muck dump, with all its rustic charm."

"These beings that visit us – do you know where they come from?"

"Behind the scenery."

"No other idea?"

There are certain things that cannot be conveyed to a finite intellect. Hang in there, son, until I can figure a way to get you out of this. Hell, the way things are heading, with internal conflicts over the chain of custody of the recovered material… those that want disclosure and pushbacks to this, and the schism over religious beliefs, that might not be long in coming as things continue to unravel."

"I don't want to leave until I find out what it is they're looking for."

"Toppy is one persuasive caballero. Earlier, you asked about our group text. Your mom's in it, too. Back then she blotted most of it out, but some things seeped through."

"She goes to church now."

"Yeah, I know."

"The rancher-type is looking for his kid," Dal said, "but also for what his kid was looking for."

"What that might be is unclear, but the notion of the bona fides that were downed being gifts with different parts of the whole scattered over different countries so the various nations have to come together and cooperate with one another if they want to reap the benefits of the technology is plumb wrong."

Before he could say another word, an alarm sounded. Along with the high-pitched wail that sounded like an air raid siren, mechanical bells rang on the bank of slot machines, followed by the clank of coins in the payout trays.

"Shit", Dane uttered while setting his glass down. "Shit!"

"What's going on?" Dal asked. "An emergency alarm?"

A red piece of candy called an "atomic fireball" rolled across the dance floor trailing a shower of bright sparks. As Dal watched the jawbreaker head straight towards the legs on his bar stool, there was a powerful white flash that blinded him for a second. When his vision returned, standing in front of him was the strangest thing he'd ever seen.

The lanky creature had a humanoid form with a globe-like head of whitish skin made from a 'living' polymer, though at quick intervals the synthetic facial tissue took on subtle rainbow sheens. The eyes were glossy black triangles. It had a silver dot for a nose and yellow lips that were firmly fixed in a circle. Orbiting the globous head was a convincing 3-D projection of a tiny lambent moon that went through the various phases with each revolution. At the center of its kaleidoscopic suit was a panel with minuscule unintelligible symbols. Shapes on its pantaloons danced amid unvarying tinselly frills. Jeweled shoes that left behind swirling colorful tracks completed the bizarre costume.

"Gadzooks," Dane said while gazing at the variegated buffoon. "Another paint factory must have exploded. Now, turn that racket off."

"Zibbles and Zubbles, it's confetti-poppin' time," the robot clown said with a warbling voice that had a distinct chime. After putting a slender white finger to its unmoving lips, the piercing siren stopped.

Accompanied by the tooting of a steam calliope, it began to sing an unusual rendition of the happy birthday song. As it did so, inside its right triangular eye, the avatar of a fairytale baker with an apron and chef's hat appeared holding a cake with unlit candles. As the figure with the confection moved towards the edge of the eye, it disappeared for a second, only to re-appear in the left eye with the candles now ablaze. After finishing the song, the zany thing told Dane to blow into the wedge-shaped eye socket that had suddenly sprouted a bushy brow. When Dane blew out the candles, a stream of smoke poured from the clown's mouth, with the other visual gag being the eyebrow catching on fire. As the hairs frizzled, a silk string appeared out of nowhere and remained suspended in midair. Feigning panic, the cosmic jester asked Dal to pull the "dingle-dangle." After giving the string a quick tug, a cartoonish cloud appeared above the clown's round head and began to sprinkle rain that quickly extinguished the flames.

"Take a bow," Dane said while clapping his hands. "This is my son, Dal."

"Lad?" it asked. Before Dane could respond, the clown's head rotated counter-clockwise in a full circle. "Dal!"

Next, the jokester pulled from a pocket a tin palette of watercolors.

"Pocketing stuff from the five-and dime again?" Dane asked.

Holding a blank piece of paper against its chest, it dipped a wet brush into the half pans, and started painting. Seconds later it placed on the bar top a caricature of Dal and Dane that was extremely odd, though the sketch was rendered with impressive draftsmanship.

"Thanks for the present, Gadzooks, but aren't you going to sign it," Dane asked while handing the clown a ballpoint pen.

When it reached out to grasp the pen, Dal noticed that its fingertips had tiny suction cup-like protrusions in various geometric shapes. There was no trick that caused the Government Issue Skilcraft pen to leak, but with blue ink stains now on the digits of its robotic fingers, the watercolor portrayal became smudged with a disorderly array of strange glyphs scattered across the paper.

"Now, you'd better hightail it back to the Toy Box," Dane said. "The guards will soon be here with their battle rattle."

"Dare I dither, Dane?"

"No."

"I know," the clown replied.

* * * * * * *

When King broke into Jix's house he found the living room in disarray. Pads and throw pillows from the modular sofa were scattered about, drawers in the entertainment center had been rifled through and left open and a rubber plant ripped from its jardinière left dirt on the carpet. As he ran his finger over a wall outlet, he thought he heard a noise in the kitchen. Pulling out his Glock handgun, he went to check it out.

When he opened the doors to the large pantry, he was startled to find his assistant hiding in there with his own Glock at the ready.

"Just let yourself in, did you," King said. "The lady's trying to prettify the place and you make a mess like that."

"That was our friend Ferrata's doing. When I arrived his Xpsilon was parked down the street. I watched him return but he didn't have the Ra Ra Ra as far as I could tell. I had better luck. Found a copy of *Coronet* in the freezer – stuffed inside a Salisbury steak frozen dinner box. I checked it out, but it was the same as the others, so I placed it back in the box if you want to have a look."

"This is getting ridiculous," King laughed. "There's nothing behind any of the curtains."

"I also checked the online auction house and several copies going for around ten bucks each were purchased on the same day, so there might be another one or two hidden in the house for someone to find."

"Yeah, maybe inside the vacuum cleaner bag, which is why Ferrata didn't bother to clean up his mess."

* * * * * * *

"Gadzooks wasn't always an entertainer," Bill said as he wiped the perspiration from his forehead with his worn-out 8-Ballers cap. "That toy was someone's companion. But, it adapted to our ways after being stranded. The engineers still tinker with it every so often, but they're just left amused by its tricks."

The former Area 51 employee was sitting at a picnic table under the starry vastness in Dane's backyard. Along with Dane and Dal he was eating a bowl of elk stew and sipping a beer. The quietness of a particularly hot summer's night was only broken by the *readle-eak eak* of a few Grackles vocalizing in the distance.

"Nils doesn't know what he's missing," Bill said, "but he's stressed about getting the brass section in shape. With their fits and bursts you'd think that would be the birds' strong point."

"With the right seasonings, I could make a dirty combat boot palatable," Dane said as he took a swig of whiskey. "Speaking of Gadzooks and its silly antics, back-engineering itself can have comical outcomes."

"Talk about playing a tuba in a bathtub. You've probably heard about the crashed B29 bomber of ours that the Soviets recovered and duplicated. The engineers were told to copy every aspect exactly, right down to the fucking screws used. Well, the bird had flak damage, so when they displayed their shiny new clone, it included three bullet holes the engineers drilled. Now, that's just a myth, our boys poking fun at the knock off, but in another carbon copy I heard about an ashtray that was scrutinized and replicated without the slightest deviation. Even though the Russky pilots weren't allowed to smoke. Same with a thermos bottle found inside a downed American plane. Something similar occurred with a piece of the New Mexico debris back when the Watertown Strip Ballers ruled in slow-pitch softball. The object was a small cylinder made of some composite material that we couldn't make a pinhole puncture in. No one could figure out what the thing was until a small amount of purple liquid was extracted from the top. The ultra-thinly bonded metametals contained bilayers like human skin. Both impermeable and porous, having a controllable porosity."

"Did you ever find out what it was – the purple liquid inside?" Dal asked.

"Yeah, it was grape soda. Nehi grape soda, to be precise. The object was a thermos, and a damn good one. Companies today would kill to know how it works. It's kept the soda chilled and carbonated for nearly 80 years. It sure would help if we knew how to dismantle the stuff. Like those little boxes – the fuchsia colored ones that don't cast shadows – that might be something like our ashtrays, or possibly something of great consequence. We might never know because of the extreme measures taken so that those in the basements can't collaborate with others."

"The stumbling blocks are intentional," Dane said.

"You might be onto something," Bill joked.

He held his next thought as the same two security guards approached in camo fatigues and duty gear.

"Take a look at the resort-style living back here, Gil," the black guy said to his partner. "A galvanized pool, swanky couch and breathtaking views. Perks from covert appropriation and nothing to do but sip leisurely cocktails and play badminton with other guests. We should all live so well. You got any of that rattlesnake watermelon left, Flash?"

"Just the rind. Not much flavor," Dane deadpanned.

"The indulgence is over for someone," the other guard said. "We've got orders to transport your son to another facility and to get him there on the double."

"The Toy Box?" Dane asked.

"Might be the place," the guy replied. "Somewhere a Greyhound doesn't go."

"I don't want to miss the symphony," Dal said.

"You won't be gone that long," Dane said with a reassuring gaze.

"Grab a few things and do it pronto. It's going to be a bumpy ride and you'll be given foggers this time."

"You can ditch them once inside," the black guard said, "so you don't step in any vomit the reptilian janitorial crew hasn't mopped up. And take heed, you don't want to get rambunctious on the other side, trust me boy."

"You'll be fine, sport," Dane said with a calm demeanor, though his finger drumming on the table betrayed his earlier assured expression. "They just want you to look at something as they stand around scratching their noggins. Just don't take any contraband like a birthday present," he said with a discreet wink.

"Hey, click-clack," the black guy said, "on the way here we saw a doozy of a spider dead on the tracks that you might want to extricate. It's by the junction."

"By the oil derricks and stock pen?" Bill asked.

"Not that junction," the guard uttered with a strident tone that expressed impatience. "We accidently flattened those this morning when the sun was glaring in our fucking eyeballs. The junction with those aggravating platform figures that I hope a heavy monsoon washes away. Lets go, Flash. Don't be taking your slow on my shift."

* * * * * * * *

After ringing the bell of Ferrara's condo numerous times, King turned the knob and opened the door. Making sure no one was home, he checked a couple of rooms before walking into the monsignor's darkened office. He'd only taken a step or two before an overpowering odor accosted his nostrils. It was the putrid stench of rotting flesh. While trying to keep from gagging, he discerned the back of the head of someone seated in a chair at a desk. When he called Ferrata's name, the figure remained still. Turning the swivel chair, he recoiled at the site of the grotesque rendering of a life-sized doll wearing a Catholic priest's stiff collar.

Patches of clothing and animal entrails had been cobbled together to fashion the monstrosity. Seaweed, moss, clay and clotted blood were also incorporated into the makings of the effigy.

Walrus tusks protruded from a hideous face that was, itself, a strange farrago of mollusk shell eyes, a crow's beak for a nose and pink margarite lips with a lolling tongue of twitching worms. Plopped on the head was a dark wig that glistened with styling gel.

Old mittens covering its hands were placed on the computer keyboard along with crystal rosary beads. In an opened notebook on the desk were the Latin names of various species of cacti. Underneath the list were the words:

Cactus poacher from Europe named Lucketti

* * * * * * * *

CHAPTER IX

"The payback's a bitch," King said to his partner as the two strolled on a paved walkway that wound through the largest public cactus garden in Nevada. "Talk about gagging a maggot, with that mishmash of animal guts, moss and bloodied fur."

"I can only imagine," his partner said before popping a piece of satin crème chocolate into his mouth. "Knock a buzzard off a shit-wagon," he said as he chewed.

"I don't know who sent this tupilak, as Greenlanders call the effigy, but those Inuit kids don't have it in them. It must have been one of their parents or someone in the community that had a grievance with him and went to lengths with this nasty business to avenge a wrong-doing."

"We know what that was."

"To their way of thinking, in the least case scenario, an act of witchcraft is a prophylactic to ward off any further meddling in their affairs. In any event, the monsignor is going to need a good deodorizing agent."

"A message has been sent – that's for sure."

"Now for Ferrata's notes. Without map coordinates – I think its fair to assume – he's enlisted the help of Europe's number one cacti smuggler. This Mister Lucketti only traffics in the rarest species," King said while glancing about at the prolific collection of desert-adapted plants native to the southwest along the winding path, "to supply overseas nurseries and collectors for their prized live-forevers. Many of these are endangered. Ferrata made a comprehensive list to exclude the so-called imposter illustrated in the copy of Black Hours from the Middle Ages. Safe to say, this species grows in the middle of nowhere and possibly remains undiscovered – "

"You mean un-rediscovered," his partner interjected.

"If not extinct, it is in such a localized area that it only grows on the side of one hill, and by one hill I mean it can only be found on one hillside in this part of the Chihuahuan desert, where it has no business being in the first place. What I'm thinking is that to pinpoint its exact location we need to find our own expert, someone local to that specific region in New Mexico. Hopefully, this expert isn't a poacher, but a protector and knows of our imposter. We convince him or her that developers are eyeing their next subdivision complete with an eighteen-hole golf course. Try to get them to save it before it's wiped out. Some of these guys are so concerned about poachers that they won't reveal a new find, even to other specialists in the cacti community. So, it won't be easy. Okay, back to the big picture. With the date on their secret calendar fast approaching, they don't have much time before another window closes. The opportunity for cosmic scavenging on a much greater scale than the retrieval of inferior toys."

"When you say *they* – we know Ferrata's gone rogue – but what about the boss?"

"Spiller? There are too many zigs and zags – like this path we're walking on – to know for sure. At this point, I'm not sure what's black or what's white. Hell, maybe I've gone rogue."

"What about Dal?"

"He was scooped from the range and taken to a certain unmentionable DUMB, where he is currently probably lost for words while wearing a wrinkled tee-shirt."

* * * * * * *

Wearing an aluminized Rayon surgical gown, complete with mask and gloves, Dal was standing inside the sterile environment of an enclosed circular structure that resembled an operating theater having tiered seating behind partitions of laminated glass.

As Spiller, Ferrata and a couple of other figures observed him from behind the sanitized windows, he hesitantly inched closer to a medical treatment table on which was placed a cylindrical pod. Pausing for a second, he saw that the translucent casing had a metal logo emblem and brand name that said:

SAMSONITE

The glinting lid with its view-ports had been raised to display the artifact within.

When Dal leaned over the pod, what he saw was a spread out, creaseless metallic garment that was a yellowish-tan shade, though the exact color was hard to determine. He had been told that the extra-vehicular mobility suit consisted of an ultra-light material, whose metallic micro-lattice contained unique optical properties that created this confusing effect. Where a person's face would normally be in the faintly glowing hooded unit was an opaque tear-shaped visor.

As with the other recovered NHI bodies in their possession, the exosuits or "second-skin" had been spun onto the beings and couldn't be removed, even with high-tech cutting tools because the cleaved fabric instantly re-bonded itself. What the engineers were most interested in was getting his impressions of the foot coverings, as the skin-suit had its own "body accelerator." The cloaking mechanism and self-cleaning feature were damaged, but the fast-moving travelator was in perfect working condition. Evidence for the former could be seen on the bottom side of the accelerators' alumina gel-like material, both coated with dust or some powdery substance that had a faint purplish tinge.

As Dal ran his gloved fingers over these foot coverings, the living fabric of the exosuit reacted by suddenly lifting itself from a horizontal position. While doing so, a dark circle containing several unknown symbols appeared in the chest area of the shimmery meta-material. With lightning-fast speed, the limp garment arose from its 'suitcase' and began silently gliding about the room in an erratic manner. After zigzagging the length of the room a couple of times, it pressed itself flatly against a glass partition where it remained perfectly still.

"I didn't pick up squat," Dal shouted to the scientist in a conference room. "Except for it warning me not to touch it. I'm done. I'm not going to wear that wig or put on those ugly sunglasses you found. Why can't you guys scratching your heads figure this shit out?"

"Just have a seat and wait to be debriefed," the man said.

"Dude, I'm not in the Army. When do I go back to Vegas?"

The words barely escaped his lips when he found himself staring at the colorful blur of spinning digital reels on the large screen of a modern slot machine. When the spools came to a stop, he saw a series of cartoonish symbols that included fuchsia boxes, jagged metallic strips, camo dune buggies with guards, a floating exosuit and a vintage white station wagon. The sound of crickets indicated that there were no winning lines.

"May I have your damn attention," a female voice with a warm timbre said over a crackling speaker. "Seating is now available for Black Regret in the Poker Zone. Thank you."

Glancing about, he appeared to be inside some post-apocalyptic casino. Through the haze of tobacco smoke he could make out a wild disarray of scavenged gaming machines eagerly being played. Neon signs that buzzed and flickered under plastic sheeting as water leaked from the concrete ceiling dimly lighted makeshift bars and stalls. The rattle of coin-operated fruit slots echoed off the soot-darkened, graffiti-covered tunnel walls, against which were placed frayed poker and blackjack tables. The carpeting was a shabby patchwork of bedizening remnants, on which a parade of cocktail servers in trashy lingerie moved through the unsightly maze, carrying booze and Styrofoam cups.

"Wild ass punch," one uttered, ignoring a darting rat. "Wild ass punch."

The boxy machines on either side of Dal were the creation of a depraved mind. The electronics of their previous incarnation had been gutted and replaced by a diorama of the Las Vegas Strip that was visible behind tempered glass. Scurrying about the detailed miniature mockup (constructed of a flame retardant material) were live cockroaches of various sizes. As a digital clock ticked, the glassy-eyed players squeezed the trigger of an attached squirt gun that shot a stream of flammable liquid at the cityscape, with the goal being to torch as many of the insects as they could before the session timed out.

"Cook, bitch!" one of the players uttered as a roach set ablaze scuttled over a yellow taxi. "Got one big enough to have a social security number trying to cop a heel. A cruel necessity," he said to a tatted waitress in flashy undies that passed by.

Trying not to be distracted by the ingenuity of noble apes, Dal focused on his own machine. His second spin wasn't a winner either, though a couple of different symbols appeared in the frames. One was a pear-shaped face of a non-human entity, with the other being a 'scatter' graphic of a rancher with a droopy mustache and straw cowboy hat.

There were a few winning combinations with his next spins, but all of them having small payouts. Before pressing the play button again, he checked the paytable. Good hits included what he called the 'Shysie' symbol and 'exosuit' graphic, with a frame filled with five 'Fuchsia boxes' being the jackpot. A number of 'Toppy' scatter symbols triggered a bonus feature that included a virtual assistant named "Sindy." After selecting multiple line payouts (zig zags), he continued to play, scoring a couple of diagonal winners with small values, but mostly he heard the sound of crickets.

"Yo, mofos," a male voice sounded over the distorted speakers. "Will the ass-clown that owns a shopping cart with pink floater rims please contact the tunnel captain."

"I can cook these quivering fucks all day," the guy playing the "Gotcha Cucaracha" game said with his gaze fixed on the diorama, "but can't find a single match to light a blunt."

After a few more losing spins, and his credits getting low, five scatters showed up on a frame with majestic orchestra strikes. The parade of imagery on the screen exploded with a vortex of colors that was quickly replaced with a new display. Instead of the animated cartoonish illustrations, a dozen blank ovoid-shaped graphics appeared against a background that was a grainy photograph of a downed egg-shaped object surrounded by scattered debris in a rugged desert setting tinted with green, steely blue and amber tones. Seconds later, a lively 'Toppy' icon popped up, tipping his straw cowboy hat.

"And here I was fixin' to hang up the fiddle, pard! Choose five, but only one is ace-high."

Before Dal could make his choice, the virtual helper appeared on the screen. Instead of the sultry graphic he expected, Sindy looked more like the neighbor girl, Susie.

"You would think the red Thunderbird symbols pay, but that's not what you want... Oh, it's the ovoid with different pictographs that you want."

"Tarnation!" Toppy uttered jubilantly.

Dal pressed his fingers on the screen, selecting five of the ovoids in rapid succession. All of them contained the red Thunderbird glyph, though he didn't receive additional credits.

The bonus screen went black for a moment and returned with a darker contrast. The only image was the comically intimidating man with the ambiguous complexion and ridiculous toupee who had manifested several times previously, making demands (to the point of absurdity) while claiming to be "the highest authority" looking into the "crossing of boundaries." When Dal had told Jix about the shadowy figure's strange behavior and vague threats, she found it interesting that an entity whose ludicrous characteristics were consistent with the Men in Black types of UFO lore was investigating the mysterious visitors themselves, as opposed to an experiencer – a twist that Toppy also acknowledged in an oblique manner.

The man was wearing a loud 'Vegas' button-up shirt emblazoned with poker symbols, dice and gaming chips in every color of the rainbow. As he looked directly at Dal, he stuck a fork into his specialty cocktail.

"Bust. Where are the tokes?" he asked with a deep monotone. You've been hornswoggled. I am the eye in the sky in this sawdust joint, and, again, I ask, where are the tokes? Bust."

Getting up from the machine, Dal looked for a way out of the place. Moving quickly through an extensive labyrinth of slot carousels and baize tabletops featuring Mouse Roulette, Chicken Shit Bingo, Devil's Numbers and Scorpion Keno, he veered to avoid the flood control tunnel dwellers and gamblers waiting in line at a row of vending pushcarts that made up the casino's buffet.

After pausing to check out the twinkling party bulbs on the facade for "Velveetas" restaurant, he continued along the jumble of
busy carpets into the Sportsbook. Having a large odds, scores and
betting lines board with plastic colored letters, the space included rusty mechanical horseracing games on tin tabletop spinners,
live-action tortoises inching along in rivulets of urine on a painted
track and caged street fighters with shirtless, bloodied physiques.

Reaching the tunnel opening where valets were attending
to bicycles, scooters and shopping carts, he picked up his pace
while negotiating a homeless encampment of tents, plywood and
cardboard shelters.

The moon was shining as he scrambled up a sandy embank-
ment strewn with pallets, junked electronics and rubbish. While
moving quickly in the desert vegetation, he suddenly felt his body
detaching from the surroundings. As the scenery shifted, he glanced
about disoriented. With nauseating vertigo, he struggled to regain
his equilibrium under the throbbing brilliance of the night sky.

Scanning the gravelly loam, he caught sight of a small tactical vehicle that was partly concealed by a clump of moonlit
bursage. Seeing the toy, he breathed a sigh of relief, thinking he
was close to the turkey farm. While taking a step towards it, he
heard a grating voice shout, "Do not move."

He would quickly realize that his mad dash had actually only
been a few yards from one of the disguised access points to the
secret underground facility, where he had earlier been escorted
to by security personnel in order to get some fresh air. The small
autonomous vehicle was anything but a toy. It and others like it
were part of the layered approach of cutting edge surveillance
technology to protect the highly restricted area.

* * * * * * *

"Everything is honky-dory," said Dal in a raised voice while addressing those inside the briefing room. "If it's such a clean zone, how'd I get that crud – what do you call it, violet crumbs – on the bottom of its shoes into my lungs?"

"Where'd you hear that?" Spiller asked after he and Falconieri exchanged furtive glances. The senior official, Falconieri and monsignor Ferrata were seated at an oval table in the room. All of their faces were pale, having a yellowish cast with bluish undertones in the artificial lightning. Around them were interactive white boards and other presentation systems.

"Those protective gloves," Dal said while looking squarely at Ferrata. "Do you also go around poking holes in condoms?"

"Now, let's not get silly, Dal," Ferrata replied. "Listen, I don't know what caused the mental manipulation you experienced, but it wasn't from ineffective gloves. The thing wanted to show you something. Was it speaking to societal decay, a nuclear holocaust, climate change or some other global disaster like a solar outburst? Perhaps a nightmarish scenario from a comet that dwells in the darkness. I don't have the answer, but any help using your perceptive apparatus is greatly appreciated."

"You mentioned something about a symbol," Spiller said. "What is this Thunderbird track, and where did you see it?"

"It's the same symbol that was on that craft in the Socorro landing, and the other one looks almost the same."

"Other one." Spiller's brows raised.

"I saw it on the wall of a cave in a video... on the Black Hours podcast, but Jix doesn't know anything about it. She and no one else, as far as I know, are able to see it. Sometimes it's there, and at other times it isn't."

"Black Hours," Ferrata said. "Interesting title."

"Do you know what either of them mean?" Spiller asked.

"Have no clue."

Dal and the others in the briefing room were watching the cave mural footage on a high-resolution screen. As the camera panned the figurative renderings of the ancient Puebloans, the stylistic contrast of the vivid bluish glyphs with the more familiar composite figures and geometric designs caught Spiller's attention.

"I'll be damned," he uttered with his eyes glued to their unique shapes.

The archbishop also seemed to take an intense interest in these markings that resembled modern math symbols.

When the camera paused for a close-up of the blank feature with egg-like symmetry and a non-reflective metallic finish, Dal turned to the others while pointing to it.

"Do any of you see it – the red symbol?"

Instead of responding, all three appeared to be stunned by what they were seeing, albeit to varying degrees. In their protracted silence, it was Ferrata's expression that conveyed the most shocking reaction at the sight of Dal's glossy black eye coverings. He thought he'd glimpsed something odd once before, but to see the full dark membrane was jarring.

* * * * * * * *

In looking for the closest Catholic Church from the range in Tonopah, Ferrata was pleasantly surprised by the Italianate architecture of St. Patrick's. The handcrafted Gothic revival carvings on the confessional were also to his liking, right down to the traces of woodworm rot. Though he wasn't sure of the identity of the priest in the central compartment, as the penitent, he spoke softly into the partition with its latticed opening.

"Father, forgive me for my sins in the past, and that which I am contemplating, for the heart has its reasons. Where some see cold indifference, through my lens, I see infiltration, and have direct evidence of this from those clothed with clouds, but that can manifest in any form. Of those masquerading as cosmic guardians in a clever ploy to undermine the Bible and divert believers from the one true spiritual path, the devil places more barriers around the book – plants with thorns. Of this living energy, the blood of angels in fiery chariots, there is no light. These lying wonders are my dilemma – what I wrestle with when the hour cometh… in the final trump when everything changes. In John 20:17, Jesus told Mary Magdalene, 'touch me not', for something better is to come. But, when the black hour occurs, my fear is that we shall see the devil's greatest trick on the spectrum of believability, and humanity shall be reduced to a trifling."

* * * * * * * *

King and Jix were seated at a table in the lobby of a theater, where they just attended a lecture given by an environmental microbiologist on the process of post-mortem decomposition.

"It's a little early for Halloween," King said while sprinkling his Southwest seasoning into a container of popcorn, "but the lady taphonomist was entertaining."

"That's when I plan to air the podcast," Jix said after taking a sip of chardonnay. "I'm still sussing it out, but it's never too early to do research."

"Pretty macabre stuff for your crowd, isn't it?"

"I'll be coming at it from a different angle, slanting the necrobiome of alien cadavers that weren't recovered and pickled in formaldehyde or stored in cryogenic tanks. Infectious alien pathogens that might still be in the environment of certain locations and could be transmitted by airborne means. Truly exotic diseases spread by little hitchhikers without thumbs. My favorite part of her presentation was how the Toxoplasma gondii parasite alters its host's behavior, getting it to do things they normally wouldn't. Taking chances with risky activity that benefits the microbe in the end. She said the parasite makes rats less afraid of cats, becoming easy targets to be pounced on and eaten. And it can also infect humans. Do you have a cat?"

"Last time I checked – no, thank goodness."

"It's interesting to speculate on any possible effect these alien pathogens might have on humans. What it might cause a person to do for the microorganism's own benefit, but I know that you wanted to talk about something else."

"That's right, I do," King said. "Speaking of spooky behavioral changes, I find myself growing tired of the cloak and dagger aspect of my job. I'm guessing you have in your possession an original copy of *Coronet* magazine, but also purchased several dummy copies to hide in frozen pizza boxes and behind wall sockets for others to find."

"Maybe in the soil of a potted rubber plant," Jix said with a knowing look. "How do you turn off home security cameras?"

"Trade secret."

"Okay."

"Wherever it's stashed, I no longer have the time nor energy to look for it, so if you'd care to answer a question, I'll call off the dogs and keep them from getting dirt on your clean floor. The thing about the magazine is, soon it won't matter, as the article will be irrelevant. Aerospace companies and defense contractors are desperately trying to rid themselves of otherworld material they obtained as part of these legacy programs. The stuff is becoming too hot to handle with all the enquiries from Congress. I'm sure you've seen the grainy videos of metallic apparitions gliding through the air. Some of these bizarre objects floating across the landscape aren't thermal ghosts or sensor artifacts. They're called witches, rubber ducks, jellyfish and stubby cigars. Humanoid aeronaut is the word I hear most, because of the appendage-like arms and dangling protrusions that resemble legs."

"It just looks like a plastic garbage bag to me."

"One of the more famous ones is actually a discarded space-suit – a living exosuit to be more accurate, as the parallel folk it belonged to don't do much traveling in space as we think of it. The damn thing got tangled with a toy balloon, snagged by a mesquite tree and maybe took out an eagle's nest at some point, which is why it's mottled and looks like some tattered monstrosity. Some of the sightings involve other off-world gadgetry that have been dumped in various locations."

"What's your question?"

"Towards the end of the article, a Catholic priest that was once a member of the Knights of Malta alludes to a glimpse of heaven as seen through a secret keyhole. What are your thoughts as to why this was included?"

"In doing research – mostly from tourist brochures – the keyhole is on the property of the religious order. It's on an ordinary-looking doorway that is part of the entrance screen or portal facade to their Villa Magistral. Peeping through the keyhole gives the best view of the dome of St. Peter's basilica, a view that is otherwise not visible. The telescopic view is somewhat illusory as the cupola seems impossibly close."

"Looking though the Aventine keyhole," King added, "one is also able to see three countries in a single glance. This might be important, as a clue, but keeping in mind that St. Peter is the gatekeeper of heaven, was the priest attempting to draw the reader's attention that the occupants of the object recovered near Magenta in 1933 were also looking for a connection between heaven and earth?"

"You're starting to sound like one of my subscribers."

"We both care about Dal – "

"He's okay. His father told me that he's safe. We exchange email when he bribes a guard."

"He is safe for the time being, but I'm formulating a plan to get him out of this program that I was partly responsible for getting him into. Once this happens, I propose that, together – on our own – the three of us take a crack at looking for something lost that would be of great interest to your viewers. Big picture stuff."

"Let's get Dal home first, and see what he says. Are you sure that you don't have a cat?"

* * * * * * *

"That's some wild shit," Dane said while kicking back in the grimy recliner chair in his backyard. In the gathering dusk he was having a beer with Dal, who was sitting at the picnic table, finishing a hunk of peach cobbler. "Usually, slots absorb more than they give."

"True," Dal said.

"And I've seen those toy security vehicles. Was it the High-Trail Crawler with a F-150 Ranger body?"

"I'm not sure. It was hard to see."

"They've got biomimetic shit near the access points, too. Micro-drones hovering like dragonflies along with the big boys."

"But no reptoids with push brooms."

"That guard was just joshing you. Taxonomy is above his pay grade. How'd you like the back strap?"

"It was good. My first time eating Big Horn sheep."

"The tarragon takes it to a new level. I usually pair it with a Bordeaux."

"The peach cobbler is good, too. The crust. You made this?"

"No."

"Who did? Bill?"

"One of your mom's friends named Derethia. I saw her the other day and she gave it to me before leaving to pursue a singing career."

"What the hell are you talking about? You were back in Jaywick, Dad?"

"No, she left Jaywick and came out west. I was surprised when I found out that she knew Corina. A girl that worked for Vennie did. Vennie's the madam of the local brothel called Venus in Bloom. You can get there by taking the same maglev train we rode in Subtropolis. Rumor has it that it was Howard Hughes that made it accessible by an elevator concealed in the barbershop. It takes you right into Vennie's closet."

"No way."

"I've been there enough times not to be Bambi-eyed by the line-up. I'm too old for those girls, but Vennie and I hit it off. Plus there's a store on the property that sells wild boar jerky."

"No, I mean no way that Derethia works there."

"They're regulated, certified and licensed. I think Derethia mostly did the girlfriend experience, and didn't provide sex services or maybe just some vanilla stuff to make enough money to try and become a singer in Vegas."

"I just thought she was still into the church."

"A lot of bawdy house girls go to church. Hell, Vennie has a PhD in Economics. But, I think the church is what caused Derethia to leave Jaywick. She told me that the pastor had all these old dolls from the 1970s. The battery-powered ones that were practically baptized back then. Baby Alive they were called. They had mechanical mouths that little girls put bottles into and spoon-fed from packets of mock baby food. They peed and pooped this goo so that they had to change the diapers. The sicko pastor put long wigs of hair on them that he scissor-cut from women in his congregation that he accused of misbehaving. But, he also fed, or somehow filled these dolls with actual human shit – talking fecal matter – that he collected in Baggies. He was trying to attract demons with the stink so he could practice casting them out. At least that's what he told Derethia."

"I knew Hoburt was fucked up, but didn't think he was that fucked up."

"We've got to get your mother out of that church. When you talk to her, tell her about this. Maybe, when you go back for a visit. I'm working with your friend to make this happen."

"With King?"

"Jix Black. Heard of her?"

"Jix? You've talked to Jix?"

"Yeah, I'm one of her anonymous sources – been passing info to her for the show."

"For how long?"

"Don't fret. I was just joshing about asking if you knew her. After you two met. Hard as it is to believe, but she really likes you. Isn't just using you for info for her show. She's something very special, so don't blow it, sport. As for the lieutenant colonel, I'm still gathering intel, though I think he's also got your back."

As the yard furniture shook from vibrations caused by the underground rail system, Dane got up to grab his binoculars from the picnic table. The sharp turns of bats feeding on insects were harder to see now that the twilight had faded into a blanket of darkness onto which the first stars began to appear.

"There she goes. Your way out of here," he said while grabbing a bottle of beer from the wheelbarrow used as an ice chest.
After taking a gulp, he trained the high-powered optics on a
particular spot in the stretch of desert against the craggy ridges
behind the house.

"What are you looking for?"

"For the last couple of nights that pulsating shuttlecock-orb
of mine has been circling an area in the arroyo – combing a
specific grid – by a mesquite tree out there."

"I don't see anything."

"It's not there now, but I wonder what it was so curious
about?"

When Dal returned to his house and walked into the kitchen,
he was surprised to see Ferrata sitting at the table, eating a slice
of pizza from a carry out box.

"Buonasera, Dal," he said with a cheery smile. "Have some
of Grandmother's pizza if you'd like. I found the place while
doing some sightseeing of the historic mining towns that were
prosperous in their heyday. Goldfield, Tybo and Belmont."

"I'm not hungry, especially for some sketchy pizza."

"You're probably surprised to see me here, but with all the
cavorting that goes on, I thought that some of the residents might
feel obligated to attend Mass on Sundays, once I find a dusty
hovel that will make a suitable makeshift church. Because most
of those at the turkey farm are scientists, I have my doubts many
will require my services, but should anyone, I'll be here on the
weekends."

"I already told you guys about the symbol and that's all I've
got to say."

As soon as Dal entered his bedroom, he locked the door and
went to see if the drawing that Gadzooks had made for his fa-

ther's birthday was still in the drawer. The watercolor was right where he had left it and glancing about at his few possessions nothing seemed to have been disturbed, until he noticed a small crucifix that looked to be made of painted resin hanging above his bed.

* * * * * * *

"I don't have a good feeling about this," Dane told Dal as their shoes crunched some dried woody shrubs. In the early morning before the heat made things unbearable, the two had hiked out to the dry trough, where Dane had seen the orb hanging out. On a nearby rise against further serrated ridges in the distance, they could see a camo dune buggy with two guards keeping a close eye on them as they continued along a rutted trail.

"I don't either," Dal said.

"He shouldn't be here. I'm going to try and push up the time line for the extraction. When we get back, I want you to put some essentials in your backpack and come stay with me. Now, let's fan out a bit and try to find what piqued the interest of that orb. I'll check over there," he said while pointing to a flat stretch dotted with white bursage, "while you look around near the mesquite tree."

After separating, neither seemed to be having much luck.

"Find anything?" Dane shouted.

"No," Dal replied.

"Nothing?" Dane said with a trace of puzzlement in his voice.

"There's an old wooden leg on the ground, but that's all."

"What?"

When he walked over to join Dal, he saw the dusty thing lying on the earth-cracked desert floor. The hardwood prosthetic looked to be old, with its leather straps and rope-work tendons being brittle and having a green patina on the copper strips.

"This must be it," Dane said.

"Aren't we looking for something more high-tech?"

"This was pretty high-tech in its day. Must be over a hundred years old. Let's have a look."

When Dane picked it up, it rattled.

"You know what – it's hollowed out."

After removing a leather covering and holding it upside down, a zinc-capped jar fell out. Inside were silver coins – at least a hundred. Shaking the leg, a couple of leather sacks also fell out. Inside these were twenty or more $20 Liberty gold coins.

"Eureka!" Dane uttered as he examined one of them. "Eureka!"

"They're Double Eagles from 1890... and in near pristine condition. Great find. And the silver ones are Morgans from the same year. I've heard the tales about a mineworker here that got injured and had to have a leg amputated. He must have hollowed out the prosthetic at some point and hid these babies inside. It was probably buried until uncovered by the shifting sands. This will sure help you on the other side."

"You're saying I can have part of this?"

"It's all yours, sport. What do they say – finders keepers. And you'll need it."

"Okay," Dal said with a confused look.

Early that evening the two were at Dane's place. As he sewed some of the Double Eagles into the fabric of Dal's backpack, the black security guard barged into the room.

"Hey, Flash, there's a special delivery I left on the porch," he said while slapping his neck as if an insect was crawling on it. "And if I were you I'd leave it there. I guess you heard about the mackerel snapper that came in last night."

"Yeah," Dane said. "Hey, what kind of security patrols the land around Venus in Bloom?"

"The cathouse. That's near the outermost perimeter of the range, so just a few Wackenhut pussies. Why, you planning on visiting for a little jerky?"

When the guard left, Dane went to the porch and picked up a paper bag. Bringing it into the house, he placed it on the table. Inside was a square clear deli container that was filled with chunks of pink fudge. With hundreds of ants crawling over the sweets, he didn't open its hinged lid.

"That's the signal for ready condition," he said to Dal. "It's a go tonight."

* * * * * * *

Having taken the passenger shuttle to the same stop as before in the subterranean complex, Dane and Dal entered the brightly lit empty barbershop. Walking across the linoleum floor past several old-style chairs in front of mirrors, with its tortoise shell-handled razors, wall decals and stacks of *Field & Stream* magazines, the place still smelled like tonic, aftershave and talc. When they reached the back of the shop with its coke machine, Dane opened a shoebox. Inside was one of the Indentimat biometric scanning devices. Placing his hand in the finger grooves, after a light flashed green, the hinged wall covered with haircut posters swung open to reveal an elevator door.

"Okay, sport, I'll see you soon enough," Dane said as he adjusted Dal's backpack. "We'll have a cold one and some Grippa's chips. Vennie is expecting you. Follow her instructions. Any questions?"

"When did you find the money?" Dal asked while looking his father directly in the eye. "How long have you had it?"

"I guess I can't fool you. A couple of years. It was hidden inside the hollow leg buried nearby."

"Were you worried that the guards would see you leaving it there for me to find? It's a lot of money."

"They respect me. Both the patriot that gave up everything for his country and the next whistleblower to do the right thing. Take care, son."

When Dal stepped out of the elevator into the perfumed closet of the brothel's madam, he found himself staring face to face with an attractive middle-aged woman wearing a black Armani blazer and matching slacks.

"You're Dane's son, I take it."

"Yeah."

"Hello, I'm Vennie. The courtesans are show-ready in the parlor. Go select one that's to your liking."

"What?"

"The girls are lined up in the foyer waiting for you to make a choice."

Rocco chandeliers with sparkling iridescent facets hung above the Victorian furniture. Velvet throws of reds and purples were draped on chairs and crystal decanters gleamed on polished counters with crochet lace doilies. Along with all the antique motifs were two very modern ATMs.

Posing and smiling on an area rug with gold damask patterns were ten girls. Most wore lingerie, though a few were casually dressed.

He was surprised to recognize one of them. It was Jix, wearing distressed denim shorts and a yellow lace tank top.

"How about you?" Dal asked with a sly grin.

"Sure, I'm game," Jix replied. "Follow me to my bungalow and we can negotiate, but, I should tell you right off that I don't have a cheerleader costume."

"Oh, big fucking surprise," one of the girls quipped. "He'd have picked her even if her mattress was on fire."

While heading towards the softly glowing bungalows that were part of the brothel, Dal followed Jix onto a dusty parking lot, where a mid-tier motorhome was idling under the stars. Gray in color with decorative turquoise stripes, the windows were darkly tinted.

As she was about to open the side door, the sound of quickly moving footsteps could be heard on the gravelly surface.

"Hold up there," a man's voice rang out.

Out of the shadows emerged two security guards, whose desert camo uniforms were bulging with field gear. One was a lanky, lantern-jawed redhead with a crew cut, with the other being a stocky Hispanic guy.

"Are you new?" the ginger asked Jix. "I know all of the girls here and haven't seen you before."

"It's my second day," Jix replied, "so I'm like new."

"Still got that new car smell, huh."

As he asked questions, the Hispanic guy was scrolling through a series of head and profile shots of the current residents of the turkey farm on a digital platform.

"Do you have an online profile?" the ginger asked. "Most of the other girls do."

"Not yet," Jix said, "but I'm game for just about anything. If someone wants to pretend they're a plumper that just wants to fix the toilet – as long as they've got the cash – I'll take them as a client."

"Dude, you're on my dime," Dal said while opening the side door.

"Okay, new girl, I'll bring my snake."

Inside the dimly lit motorhome, King glanced back from the comfy captain's chair.

"There he is – none the worse for wear. I was enjoying Jix's cathouse banter."

"I was waiting for you to come out and flash a badge," she said. "I was told that Dal's photo was deleted from the system for a piece of a green cracker."

"For all I know," King said, "my mug's on their list."

"Are we going back to Vegas?" Dal asked.

"We're going through Vegas on the way to our destination."

"Which is?" Dal asked.

"Magdalena, New Mexico. My major concern is a tracking implant that's of my own doing, though only myself and my partner can monitor it."

"Who got chipped?" Dal asked.

Jix and King looked at each other, both trying equally hard to repress a smile.

"Who's ready to go adventuring?" Jix asked excitedly.

* * * * * * * *

CHAPTER X

When Dal opened his eyes, he saw that Jix was gazing down at him while seated on the edge of the double bed in the rear of the motorhome.

"Your eyes twitch a lot while you're sleeping," she said with a bright smile.

"They do? Where are we?" he asked while raising his head from the pillow and glancing about the narrow confines.

"Willow Beach, Arizona. Parked on a campground on the Colorado River instead of boondocking. Just about fifty miles outside of Vegas. It's a little after midnight and gorgeous outside. We saw some bighorn sheep and I made blackberry dumplings. We can have them at the empty fire pit seeing it's still pretty toasty at over a hundred degrees."

While seated in lawn chairs around the fire pit, King was filling in Dal and Jix about some sensitive comms he just received over his encrypted handheld Motorola.

"Word has it that Archbishop Falconieri will be celebrating the feast day of St. Persingula on August 2nd. He's supposed to give a Mass at the Catholic Church in the pueblo and then after the festivities for the patron saint of the pueblo attend a secret tribal ritual. I doubt he's going to this corn dance, but it's his cover for the real reason for him being in New Mexico on that date. That's just a few days away –"

While speaking he had noticed something suspicious at the nearby camping spot. This was a faint red glow coming from near the old pickup with a camper shell parked there. Pointing his IR-sensitive smartphone in the direction of the reflection, he indeed detected the subtle glowing spot of an active IR illuminator, making it likely to his trained eye that someone was observing the three through night vision goggles.

"Excuse me for a minute," he said while getting up and walking behind the motorhome. After stealthily making his way to the other side of the neighboring site, he crept up on the back of the figure, whose focused gaze remained on the fire pit where Dal and Jix were seated.

"What's so interesting?" King asked while grabbing the man's shoulder.

"Shit, you scared me," the guy uttered with a startled look. "That's Jix Black over there. I can't believe it. She's looking for UAPs, isn't she? For her next show. I'm pretty sure I saw a Tetra Class I over the water a while ago."

"And I saw a glowing red blob – emitted by your unit. She's on leave. Please respect her privacy. And what you saw was most likely an owl or a coot."

"Tumbling on its axis?" the guy said as King walked away.

When he returned to the fire pit, King looked at Jix with a troublesome grin.

"I keep forgetting there's a celebrity amongst us. Okay, this interesting date is only a few days away."

* * * * * * * *

"Here it comes," Dal said while seated in the passenger seat with Jix on his lap. "Devil Dog Road. I wonder if Madam Eve is still selling red ice cider? Spell it backwards."

"Okay, yeah, I get it," Jix said. "They're all palindromes. Ha-ha," she giggled.

"What is this nonsense?" King asked with his hands gripping the steering wheel.

"Just word games," Jix said with a yawn.

"Speaking of which, will you two let me concentrate. I'm getting a new message."

While driving the motorhome along the I-40, he kept glancing down at the flexible screen he was wearing like a wristwatch. As a black dot rotated clockwise around the circumference of a larger white circle on the display, he kept track of its position when it came to a stop at a particular radius on the sphere, memorizing a series of 'invisible letters' indicated by the line segment, a procedure made all the more difficult when the grayscale colors reversed, thus changing the encryption parameters.

When the message was complete, he glanced at the device with a confused look.

"RACECAR."

"What does that mean?" Jix asked.

Before he could reply, a black Escalade sped past them on the left. As it did so, the person in the passenger seat, whose features King couldn't make out, waved in a friendly gesture.

"How weird," Jix said as the sign for Devil Dog Rd. appeared in the exterior mirror. "That's a palindrome. Racecar."

* * * * * * * *

A light rain was falling at the Circle K market in Flagstaff, where they had stopped to fill up the tank and grab some snacks.

"I've got some more info from your dad," King said to the others while sitting in the dinette. "Spiller Andrews and Monsignor Ferrata are also heading to the Land of Enchantment. So, now we've got a gaggle on the move. Now, I'm even more convinced they've cracked the code in that secret calendar of theirs. They might have a date – August 2nd – but whether or not they've got precise coordinates of the target is another story. They were last tracked to Verde Valley – which isn't far from here – having emerged from an access point of the DUMB near the cement plant in Clarkdale, I'm told."

"Wow, that's a shocker," Jix uttered. "Lots of my subscribers claim that Clarkdale is a hot spot connected with the Bradshaw Ranch in Sedona. Here, I thought this was just kooky conspiracy stuff."

"All of this is kooky conspiracy stuff," King said. "It's actually a brilliant disguise with all the haulage tunnels moving clinker."

"Sometimes I think half of the stuff you tell us isn't true," Jix said. "It's the spook in you holding onto secrets that you replace with falsehoods. I'm not sure if this is to mislead us or protect us."

"What do you think, Dal?" King asked.

"My dad trusts you."

"Okay then, if something goes south with my boss, Jix, I want you to voluntarily hand over the magazine – the original copy – to protect what I've brought along. It might be a way to unfuck things, if the situation arises. You wanted an adventure. Well, you just might get one."

"What about Dal's drawing from that Gadzooks thing – if it's real – that he hasn't shown me because he doesn't like the way he looks?"

"Let's not worry about that. Now that he's got his Red Bulls and sufficient pogey bait squared away, he can take over with the driving. Wake me up around lunch time."

* * * * * * *

Wafts of Ponderosa pines mingled with the smell of fresh hand-made tortillas as the three walked towards a local Mexican restaurant whose murals on the facade were emphasized with a liberal use of colors. The woody aroma was more pronounced in the afternoon heat, as was the distinct blend of spices that stood out in the small town of Heber, Arizona, a popular getaway destination within the Apache-Sitgreaves National Forest.

As they approached the entrance, the phone was ringing at an old-fashioned booth that had a wooden sculpture of a green-painted alien with bulging black eyes placed next to it. For whatever reason, Dal picked up the receiver and said, "Hello." When he put the phone up to his ear, a man's voice said: "From all evil, deliver us, O Lord."

"It was Ferrata," Dal said after quickly hanging up. "With some bible thing."

"C'mon, how's that possible," King said while glancing about. "Quit dicking around."

"I'm not. I swear it was him."

"We might have to skip lunch," King told Jix, "authentic as it might be –"

The phone started ringing again. Before King could pick it up, an employee of the restaurant grabbed the receiver. "Klaatu barada nikto!" the guy said before hanging up.

"He calls a dozen times every day. Usually, a visitor taking photos answers it. This is a tourist attraction – because of that logger. I guess the caller is afraid of the aliens."

"Ferrata's gotten to you," King said to Dal. "Messing with your head. There's no room for him there."

"The cactus expert got back to me," Jix said while looking at her phone. "He's willing to meet with us."

* * * * * * *

253

"Some of the locals here look like they still eat beans with a prairie knife," King joked as he joined Dal and Jix at a booth in Smoky Jack's. He'd been checking out the old photographs of atomic scientists and rugged miners that plastered the wood-paneled walls beneath blinking chili-pepper string lights.

"Just the drinks for now," Jix told the server. "We're meeting someone. Do you know Walt Wills?"

"The cactus doc," the server said. "Yeah. Hey, be sure to ask him about the time he told us to the call the bomb squad when our potted saguaro started throbbing. I'll be right back with the beers and some water."

As she headed back to the bar, a bespectacled fellow with a heavily tanned face walked in and glanced about. With a roll of Gorilla tape attached to the belt of his khaki desert garb and pair of tweezers in his top pocket, King figured he was their specialist.

"Walt, I'm King," he shouted over the sound of people at the bar and a country tune playing on the jukebox. "What are you drinking?" he asked as the guy sat down.

"Just some water."

"Thanks for meeting with us. I heard that you're the man to talk to when it comes to local cacti."

"What happened to the cactus after you called the bomb squad?" Dal asked as the beers and water arrived. After setting them down, the waitress scampered away with a smile that went along with her playful energy. Judging by his annoyed expression, this clearly bothered the fellow.

"First thing, don't insult my intelligence with urban legends about exploding cacti with thousands of baby tarantulas inside," he said as he removed his glasses and rubbed his eyes. "I value my time and would rather be out in the field, aching back and all, looking for unique species and protecting them from poachers, but I am here to answer any serious questions if you have any?"

"Sorry, doc," King said, "don't mind the boy. I've something I'd like to show you."

From a folder he pulled out a photo that showed a close-up of the illustration of the unique cactus contained in the variant of the 15th-century Book of Hours. The painting was not only enlarged, but also cropped in such a manner that only the cactus, itself, was visible. When he placed this in front of Walt, he was clearly surprised by the image, and even a bit shaken.

"Where did you get this?" he asked.

"My sister Gretta found the painting at a flea market in Gallup, I believe it was, or maybe in one of the trading posts off Route 66. Like you, she loves cacti and has a nice collection. The thing is, nobody's been able to identify it, and, so, we're wondering if it's a real species or just a flight of fancy by the artist? Looks kind of old doesn't it?"

"Saguaro and other natives can live for 175 years," he said. "But, you won't find them here."

"So, if it's real, it's got to be rare," Jix said. "Maybe even a solitary specimen. What do you call it – a monotype? Sorry, I'm not the family cactophile. Could it be a graft hybrid or chimera?"

"Gretta is always looking for new friends," King said. "So, if you know where we could obtain one like it – legally, of course – we'd be happy to donate to your society. Do you know anything about it?"

"It's a columnar cactus. Banded. Not your ordinary trailside cristate, if there's such a thing, especially in the Chihuahuan, where the climate and elevation isn't conducive to saguaros. It's zygomorphic – the bilateral symmetry of the unusual crest, or fan-shaped pattern on the growing tip – even though polyhedral – almost like botanical filigree. I can't determine if it's pubescent, as the illustration doesn't show any fine hairs. I'm afraid your sister will have to make do with her painting."

"Are you saying it's based on a real species?" Jix asked.

"There is one example," he said with hesitation reflected in his gaze, "that hasn't yet been plucked from its habitat. It doesn't have the striking dark pink florets on the crest like in this painting, but perhaps I've yet to see it during anthesis. And that's all I have to say on the matter."

"Would you be kind enough to reveal the location so we can take a photo for Gretta?" Dal asked.

"Too many poachers in these parts. I don't think I can take the chance."

Without saying another word, he stared at the photo, still visibly unnerved by it. Standing up, he nodded to King and walked away.

"I'm glad I didn't wear my What The Fucculant tee," Jix said.

* * * * * * * *

King stopped the motorhome in front of a sign that read:

RESPECT PRIVATE LANDS
OBTAIN PERMISSION FROM LAND OWNERS

"No word back from Walt," Jix said while checking her smartphone. "And nothing from the pictograph guy, Chayton, so it looks like we're on our own."

"Just us and a bunch of dead miners and pot rustlers," King said while glancing about the ghost town landscape of foundation ruins, cattle corrals, old mining equipment and a dusty forlorn cemetery. "From here we have to go on foot."

At the entrance to the mine with the cave murals, another sign was posted:

STAY OUT AND STAY ALIVE

"Who's ready to smell rat piss," Jix said while wrinkling her nose. She once again was wearing her "cavenaut" outfit, complete with the lariat-brown wide brim fedora.

Having made it into the secret chamber with the ancient rock art, all three were illuminating the enigmatic pictographs with their flashlights.

King steadied his beam on the ovoid-shaped feature with the metallic white finish that, oddly, didn't reflect the light.

"What you called super paint is the outer surface of an off-world craft. It's a piece of living skin that was attached here by some means."

"Hey, that's where I saw them," Dal said excitedly. "Those blue markings. They're the same as those on my drawing. Check it out."

"The ones that look like unicode math symbols?" Jix asked while pointing her video camera, documenting the trip.

From his backpack, Dal pulled out the watercolor portrait of him and his dad that the toy oddity called Gadzooks had made. The blue smudges on the paper caused by a leaky ballpoint pen that stained the various geometric shapes of the tiny suction cups on its fingertips matched perfectly with the puzzling graphic devices rendered from vibrant blue mineral pigments on the buff-colored surface.

"The splotches were made by Gadzooks after an old ballpoint pen burst."

"I'll be damned," King said. "I think you're right. I'll bet Gadzooks was here with the little being and made them for nothing more than to say 'I was here'... like those handprints made by the indigenous people after dipping their mitts into ochers and pressing them against the rock. It's just graffiti from a non-earthbound teddy bear."

"I knew they weren't territorial markings," Jix said. "They seemed too out of place."

"I thought the machine-cut cavity must have an analog with its twin ovoid feature due to its being the exact same size and shape, but instead of two pieces of exotic material, suppose it was removed because it contained pictographs of something witnessed by the Ancestral Puebloans. An event having far-reaching significance that the parallel folk became aware of, that some – mostly children - felt compelled to investigate. That's why your Shysie took it after leaving her calling card. She was using it as a map. Due to unforeseen circumstances – military action or exposure to the elements – she left it on the desert floor, sending a message to others of its whereabouts. It could even be that the little beings at the Socorro landing site were looking for it before being startled by the police officer."

"But, why not just copy the map?" Jix said. "They must have camera-like devices. Even Gadzooks could have drawn it. I think it's more likely that someone didn't want anyone to see it or find whatever it leads to. They wanted to put an end to the whole thing, so they removed a section of the panel with the revealing pictographs. Peeled the damn thing right off the wall and disposed of it."

"That's why there's a plan B," King said.

Before leaving, Dal peered into the ovoid piece of metallic skin. In doing so, the red glyph appeared on its surface, looking sharper than it did when viewed in the video footage. When he turned to the others to let them know what he was seeing, Jix's eyes widened as she recoiled in horror.

"What happened to your eyes?" she uttered with both hands covering her mouth. "They're black, Dal. Totally black!"

"It's okay, Jix," King said calmly.

"What are you talking about?" Dal asked with a puzzled look.

"Take a look. Can you see?" Jix asked while digging through her purse. She pulled out her compact and handed it to him without looking directly at his face.

In seeing his reflection with the thin layer of glossy black tissue covering both eyes, his expression was one of complete shock.

"What did it do to me, King?"

After blinking a few times, his eyes returned to normal.

"You see, it's okay," King said. "Both of you calm down."

* * * * * * *

Back inside the motorhome the mood was somber as the three were seated in the dinette.

"Our understanding is that the implants are hyper-spectral lenses that were inserted during your encounter in Jaywick," King explained. "It's a bio-synthetic film that is usually self-activated when your eyes are focused on something designed by the same off-world intelligence, like the composite material in the cave. It's a hard conversation to have, but you're somebody's eyes."

"You knew about this all along," Dal said. "I don't have a gift… any natural abilities like those Inuit native kids. My profile you talked about – what I see – it's all because of the implants. I'll bet my dad knew about this –"

"Knew about part of it," Jix said while gently grasping his hand. "Knew you were an experiencer."

"So how do I get rid of it?"

"The bionics?" King asked.

"Surgery," Jix said.

"Our best people have trouble taking a child's toys apart. I don't know if I'd want a doctor messing with this extra sclera casing that's fused to your eyes. You didn't even notice it until today, and that's only because Jix wigged out. Let's do what we came here for. See what we can find, and deal with that after. Is the black conjunctiva problematic to you?" he asked Jix.

"No, like you said – it's sporadic. Only triggered by certain objects, and how often do you even see such things?"

"Okay – okay, okay," Dal said while tapping his hand nervously on the table. He was ready to move on from the awkward conversation involving the unsightly eye membrane. "I might know a good place to start looking for this piece missing from the cave."

* * * * * * * *

"What you're looking for, it's here," the owner of the Native American trading post said as King opened the tattered screen door and entered the cluttered interior followed by Jix and Dal.

With a forced smile on his pudgy brown face, Bert ran his ringed fingers through his Elvis-style black pompadour as he emerged from a shadowy aisle. Having recently been smudging, the acrid smell of burning sage and pinion permeated the place, with bluish drifts like ghostly fingers brushing the texture of mildewed blankets, rugs and basketry.

"I understand that you occasionally sell museum pieces," King said. "What we're looking for are authentic pre-contact pictographs. Figures composed from mineral pigments."

"What else – Glidden? Let me go get the new catalog," he deadpanned. "Stickmen dancing to plasma discharges?"

260

"Whatever you've got."

"And I'm looking for heads of saints cut from Byzantine frescoes. Seriously, I've got some exquisite newer items with stunning colors and patterns that would be perfect for your den."

"Nothing? Not even from private lands?"

"Nothing that offensive, not to mention sacrilegious. How about some calibrated trends from Bisbee?"

While looking for the source of the pungent haze, Jix saw the smoking smudge stick. She also noticed that it was placed on a tan plate that was ovoid shaped and the same size as the depression in the cave. Then she saw the faint outline and sections of the unique cactus. Except for parts of the cactus on the missing piece of the cave wall, the other markings were faded and discolored, with most of the pictographs entirely obscured by decades of smoke residue deposited on the surface that interacted with the pigments.

"King, come here," she said. "I found it... but I don't think it will help."

"That's an obvious fake," Bert said as he walked over and removed the burning herbs. "Look at the base. It's perfect and the images might as well have been spray-painted. From what I remember, they looked like they were made using magic markers and correction fluid."

"Do you remember what the pictographs depicted?" Jix asked while turning on her video camera.

"A phony map to some make-believe cactus."

When Dal looked at the slice, he was amazed to see a faint image superimposed over the entire smoke-darkened surface. It was the visage of the strangely beautiful doll-like entity with yellowish skin and delicate features. As with the previous times he'd seen visions of the otherworldly being called Shysie, the most unsettling aspect of her pear-shaped face were slanted golden-hazel eyes that sang with a melody of syllables.

As he stood wonderstruck, Jix lifted her gaze to his face before wrapping her arms tightly around his waist. Though she was more curious than concerned, she couldn't see his eyes through the pair of sunglasses he was wearing that still had the price tag dangling from the frame.

"How much for the shades?"

"I thought you said you didn't have a girlfriend," Bert said. "Forty dollars and they come with three ice cold Nehi grape drinks."

"How about fifty, and you throw in the sucker's map? It will look good on my shelf."

"You have a shelf now, too?"

* * * * * * * *

Having agreed to a second meeting, the cactus expert, Walt, along with King, Dal and Jix were seated at a table in Smoky Jacks.

"So, you don't have a sister named Gretta," Walt said. "And you're not cactus lovers. And you've got a show about unsolved mysteries and strange happenings," he added while looking at Jix.

"We're making a doco about the cactus, and here's why."

From his folder King produced a full page from the copy of the 15th-century Black Hours that featured a detailed, colorful miniature of the unique cactus.

"This hand-drawn manuscript is well over 500 years old," he said while pointing out the visually stunning color scheme, "and contains a detailed illustration of the monotype, which it says can be found in Nuevo Mexico."

"Before the Spanish were supposed to be here?" Walt asked. "Before Coronado's expedition in 1540?"

"Apparently so. And we have this," he continued as Dal placed the soot-covered ovoid-shaped slice on the table, "which was found nearby. It's hard to see, but it shows the same crested cactus. We've reason to believe it's a map. Using special scanning techniques we can restore the details. But that takes time. The mystery of the imposter – as it is called in the variant of the prayer book - is beyond the plant's age. Have you heard of a European fellow named Lucketti?"

"He's cactus crook," Walt said. "One of the biggest."

"As we speak, he and others are hot on the trail of the specimen. All we want to do is take video of it. Close shots showing details. We don't plan to reveal its precise location. But, once we announce our discovery, and that we scooped it up for scientific examination, that should put a stop to Mister Lucketti."

"Why couldn't it have been a Spanish galleon?" Walt sighed before talking a gulp of water. "It's a mystery and a very strange one. The taxonomy, it's beyond classification."

After a long pause, he continued with a pained expression on his tanned face.

"Doctors talk about miners with Haunted People Syndrome. Hallucinations caused by manganese toxicity, but I haven't been overexposed. So, what caused the madness? Was it my touching one of the copious hairs the cactus is fringed with – minute ones not shown in your illustration? Or some exotic nutrients in the loam I breathed in? I haven't gone back to that place since the dreams. And you can take that as a warning."

He pulled out a note pad and began to write the directions.

"It's called Dreamy Dust Gulch. It sticks out like a sore thumb, the saguaro does. It's quite conspicuous. I'm not worried about you digging it up and carting it away," he said while tearing out the sheet of paper and handing it to King. "I doubt that it even can be moved… because it *is* an imposter. It might look like a cactus, but that's not what it is. At least, it's not a cactus from this world. What it really is, I haven't a ghost of a notion."

* * * * * * * *

The Ford Grey Eagle was parked on a sandy track near the gulch, which, because of the steep sides, was as close as the motorhome could get to the lone saguaro cactus. The three were excited by the find, which looked, felt (though, they were careful not to touch the fine hairs on the stem) and smelled organic despite the expert's adamant claims that it was a phantasm that haunted this part of the Chihuahuan. There were no florets on the cristate growth, which was the strangest feature, in that each pleat was exactly the same to the minutest detail. Because of this and other factors, such as the awareness that nothing stirred within a considerable radius of the solitary specimen, King also thought it was a 3-D projection or technical apparition. Wearing his Ray-Ban shades, Dal nodded in agreement. As filtered through his hyper-spectral implants, both the bristled trunk and tessellated crest appeared to be comprised of something *similar* to myriad pixels.

When Jix finished videotaping every aspect of it, with nothing else out of the ordinary detected in the area, the scorching temperature caused them to return to the RV and wait for something to happen.

In the fading light, Dal was lying in bed, watching a black and white sitcom from the 1960s on the small flat screen. In a scene where several characters were relaxing on a porch on a summer's evening, one of them was strumming his guitar and singing a bluegrass ditty. As the others sipped cups of coffee while listening to the song, a vivid golden-amber sphere suddenly burst through *the screen door of the house in the comedy*, causing Dal to bolt upright. With his gaze fixed on the glowing orb, it floated about the porch, displaying curiosity at some potted plants there. As he was about to shout to Jix, the energetic ball turned a radiant blue color before making the transition from the screen into the interior of the motorhome. After pausing for a second in front of Dal, it darted away in a pulsating cobalt blaze, gliding silently past Jix as she walked out of the small bathroom combing her dripping wet hair. Instantly, the long blond strands were dried as the plasmoid continued down the narrow hallway, popping a bag of microwave popcorn on a counter in the galley kitchen before shooting up through a skylight beneath which King had dozed off on the jackknife sofa.

What happened sometime later was both confusing and troubling, when all three awoke lying side by side in the double bed at the first light of dawn.

With a metallic taste in her mouth, Jix was disoriented and agitated as she climbed out bed, though Dal and King didn't seem to be fazed by the lingering tang.

"What happened, King?"

"My guess is an incapacitating agent – a vapor with a quick onset time. I detected something sweet and thought you were baking with the stone."

"I smelled it, too," Dal said.

"I wasn't baking muffins!" Jix's voice crackled as she hurried to the kitchen faucet, growing increasingly distressed by the thought of being knocked out by some anesthetic gas. "Or scones or anything. Don't you remember that streak of light?"

"Dal's hitchhiker didn't tuck us in," King said. "Someone breached the Jayco. Maybe security personnel from Spiller's team that didn't want anyone having bleacher seats when things started happening. Hold on – listen." He pointed to the roof as the high-pitched whine of a drone could be heard passing overhead. "Do you hear that?"

When he pushed back the curtain to take a peek outside, he saw a figure in the distance moving along the edge of the steep-sided gulch.

"There are others here. Stay put while I go check to see if it's Spiller's boys."

When he reached a good viewpoint, King saw a flurry of activity within a cordoned off area on the broad arroyo. Several six-wheel off-road expedition vehicles were parked on the dry watercourse fifty yards from the cactus. All had mounted searchlights pointed towards the improbable specimen. Cameras on tripods had also been set up on its periphery and a surveillance drone buzzed while circling at a low altitude. Along with a few large military-style tents were modules that comprised a portable weather station.

While some of the figures were stationed at data processing equipment and others moved about with handheld meters and devices, he recognized the woman who was standing over one of several chalk outlines like you might see to mark the location of a dead body at a crime scene. It was the taphonomist that gave a presentation on the organic remains of cadavers. She, too, was carrying a handheld object – one that was a cause for concern. It was a small fuchsia-colored box identical to the one he had smuggled from the Toy Box and hid inside the motorhome.

Seeing only a few security personnel, King headed towards the zone of operations to confront Spiller. When he reached the cordon, a man in civilian clothes approached him. He had a shaved head and was wearing thick-rimmed acetate glasses that were similar to the pair he had on when King first saw him at the Pit Stop sports bar in Indiana.

"I apologize about last night," the man said, "but we didn't want our racket to keep you up all night."

"That was considerate of you," King said. "What type of field vapor was it? Halothane?"

"Something like that – with a cherry on top."

"You rattled the lady, that's all."

"Yes, the one with a magazine rolled up inside a designer thermos. We found an interesting drawing, too, and maybe some day you'll tell me where you stashed a little box that went missing. We didn't take these items, nor, of course, anything else. My name is Neil A. Shockley. I'm in charge here."

"I always wondered if we might be the child to a parent uSAP. The last time I saw you I was having a pretty good draft pilsner."

"I've wondered the same thing, but when it comes to trying to ascertain what those kids were so attracted to – that they risked their lives – I guess we're in the top slot. Speaking of interrupting your conversation in that bar, you neglected to enter the pit stop – "

"Yes, to which you waved, not thinking we'd beat you here... or did you need us to find the place?"

"I've admired your work. How you find your way through shadowy mazes to piece things together."

"Is Spiller Andrews here? I heard that he was on his way."

"Well, he was supposed to be, but I've been informed that he and Monsignor Ferrata were in a bad car accident in Arizona. Both are in the hospital in serious condition. Ferrata said that he swerved to avoid hitting a walrus – of all things – that was crossing the interstate. Truth be known, both were on my short shit list for letting personal beliefs affect their judgment and being the cause of a schism amongst the team. I can't even rule out sabotage. At any rate, should we need spiritual guidance, the archbishop is here."

"What's the current situation – it doesn't appear that anything's changed."

"Not being a true cactophile, you didn't notice that our radically-symmetrical friend is now crowned with a lovely flowerhead. It's anyone's guess as to what might have caused this nighttime inflorescence, but the timing fits."

"What I did notice was the lady of all things morbid holding that piece of non-human hardware."

"She's combing through the loam inside our bubble and marking off a few possibilities for an alien necrobiome. Those that perished – three, we believe. Unless it was joking – as its been known to do lately – Gadzooks finally confirmed the purpose of the thing. They weren't flight articles, but were to be used by the parallel folk to collect specific, still active microorganisms associated with the decomposition process. The pursuit of this parasite might be a non-earth bound kid's thrill, after absorbing it to induce dreams that lead and guide them into another realm of possibility. To them its not considered a dangerous pathogen, but, rather, a wondrous passport. Our expert has even speculated that a certain microbe that colonizes this alien death community might be designed to facilitate this course of events as part of some rejuvenating process for the otherworldly dead. It's crazy shit, but might be the final piece in this crazy puzzle."

"Similar to the Toxoplasma gondii scheme."

* * * * * * * *

Dal was getting restless inside the motorhome.

"On this date in history we've got the Black Sox baseball scandal," Jix said while reading her notes. "The Declaration of Independence was formally signed into effect – "

"Screw this waiting."

As soon as they stepped outside the RV, they heard King's amplified voice.

"Jix and Dal... Come on down!"

When they reached the edge of the gulch, they found themselves gazing at a hemispherical shell the size of a medium size planetarium dome that was suspended less than a foot above the desert floor. In the wavy heat haze, the color of the dully-lucent surface was hard to describe – a unique interfusion from an enigmatic silver palette. Within the outer shell, Dal could see a strange three-dimensional shape that curled at a point like a twisted prism. It was similar to what a biophysicist would call a scutoid.

Several minutes later they joined King, who was standing next to Neil in the shade under an awning that had been erected a short distance from the mysterious object. As cameras rolled from every angle, the eerie absence of wilderness sounds was more pronounced from where they stood while watching the other team members going about various tasks.

"Meteorological status from all sensors show normal readings across the board," Neil said after getting reports on his handheld Motorola. "It appears there's some kind of optimal climate control for the time and place that is programed for whoever happens to be in the thing – meaning the air conditioning is currently on inside. According to multiple data banks, the thing is behaving as if it's currently habituated."

"Impressive," King said.

"What do you suppose it is?" Jix asked. "An alien space vehicle?"

"We assumed it would be some exotic landing module," Neil replied, "that was cloaked for long stretches of time or invisible while in a higher dimensional phase. Either way, a mathematical disguise enabled it to be rarely distinguished in our perceptible environment. But, I like Gadzooks' take. Instead of arriving in a spacecraft, the object is a piece of the actual world that the visitors came from. Imagine traveling... or manifesting elsewhere in your own house with your own back yard and own weather on that day. All self-sustaining while on other worlds, or having dimensional stability. When all the data collected is analyzed, what might it tell us about degrees of sentience?"

"That it's not a not a binary property," King chuckled.

"Can I touch it?" Dal asked.

"Why all of a sudden are you so gung ho to touch things?" King asked. "Do you plan on bringing a housewarming gift?"

"No magic lozenges lured to the area yet," Neil said. "Are you surprised?"

"Not really," King replied. "Someone's keeping a low profile. That's why they turned Dal here into a walking, talking multispectral camera. Explains why he's so keyed up."

"Warning displays are dark, and other signal indicators look good," Neil said. "If he feels compelled to do so, I say go ahead. He signed enough papers."

After both Dal and Jix touched the bio-fluorescent surface that was constantly fluctuating on the large sphere, Dal pressed his hand more firmly against the softening exterior. The shimmery veneer seemed to have an ephemeral quality about it as he began to peel away layers of what seemed like frozen smoke. Within seconds he was able to step inside the opening he had created, followed by Jix. 'Detaching' further overlays of this silvery glaze, the two moved forward for a few steps, until, inexplicably, after peeling back another layer, they found themselves stepping back outside onto the exact spot where they had entered the curiously shedding facade.

Though the process defied understanding, it was easy enough to repeat a couple of times. Each time they met with the same results, until on their last attempt, Dal detected a blur of color through the mercurial sheet. When he pulled back the thin covering like turning the page in a glossy magazine, a lanky android wearing a motley costume was standing outside waiting for him.

"Zibbles and Zubbles," a voice was heard saying, though the circular yellow lips on Gadzooks' globe-like head didn't move. "Someone called about termites."

Shortly later, when Jix and Dal moved to the area in the lustrous sphere's energetic solder that Gadzooks determined to be an entrance point, the scene was chaotic. As the electric winch of a camo Humvee adjusted the tension of the harness attached to Shysie's exosuit, its arms and legs flailed wildly, kicking up puffs of dust. While a few specialists scrambled about, trying to gain control of the meta-material fabric of the unit, unable to see through its dark, opaque tear-shaped visor, Jix grabbed King by his shoulder.

"If the poor little person doesn't want to go inside," she uttered, "shouldn't you put a stop to it? Call it off, King!" she shouted as the skin-suit continued to resist being pulled.

"You don't understand," he said, "it's already been inside longer than we wanted. It's putting up a fight because it didn't want to come out."

When things settled down with the exosuit, it was time for the person selected by the team to enter the object. With a placid expression, Archbishop Falconieri slowly approached the sphere. Wearing the ceremonial robe and insignia of the Grand Master of the Knights of Malta, he, too, was tethered to the winch by a special harness as he stepped into the unknown.

* * * * * * * *

No communications were received from Xavier while he remained inside the sphere, but, strangely enough, some kind of tinny-voiced radio drama and reports from a local farm show could be heard. It was determined by a member of the team that both were early 1920 broadcasts from the New Mexico College of Agriculture and Mechanic Arts.

While straining to make out these distant voices on his portable Motorola, disturbing thoughts flooded King's mind. When he had first been read into certain aspects of the program, he'd heard the story about a M I hot shot who was the first person to venture into the downed object at a C/R site in the 1940s. Supposedly, when he quickly re-emerged from the gap in the metallic hull, he was heard to mumble that he would rather take a rocket straight to hell than return to the craft's interior. Although the story was most likely untrue, and fabricated to serve as a warning to the overly curious, he couldn't help but wonder how someone like the archbishop would be able to handle standing inside a slice from an alien world, which is what the object was believed to contain.

* * * * * * * *

Night seemed to fall quickly. When Falconieri didn't return at the appointed time, the winch was activated. What it pulled out was an empty harness. The archbishop's fate wouldn't be known until the next morning due to camera interference. When the sphere suddenly became invisible, he was found kneeling by the cactus, whose dark pink florets had also vanished.

"What was the total duration of the entire event?" he asked with bleary eyes.

"Nearly twenty four hours. Shy by only twenty minutes," Neil replied.

"Like Joshua's black hours," Falconieri's quivering lips mumbled.

"What happened to the harness?" King asked.

"If need be, I would have chewed off the cable to escape the grotta."

"What did you experience, Xavier?" Neil asked. "It's hard to make sense of the images."

"Being outside the grotto," he replied. "The distortion of the heavens beyond is caused by our highly-selective perceptual apparatus," he said, somehow able to maintain his normal serene demeanor. "The anticipated technological spectacle – all you'll see are caricatures at best until our faculties develop. To your scientists, our brain's lack of sensory capacities is a mighty terrible devil, indeed. Exposure to unexpected novelty – the anomalies we're bumping into just outside is inducing curiosity that's not destabilizing. We're protected by cognitive limitations, inescapable illusions and false conclusions."

"There's no relevance because of our framing of the world," Neil said.

"Might explain a techno-signature that pricks," King added.

"Si, Kingston."

With his implanted optics, Dal had been able to perceive what appeared to be obscure patterns morphing behind the silvery skin. The sensory input he experienced was neither shocking, profound or overwhelming, simply because of his brain's unfamiliarity with the constantly shifting shapes and colors, as well as the spatial elements involved. Unable to interpret the staggering complexity of shapes, his eyes were drawn to the only delineation that was slightly recognizable: a corridor, whose multifaceted geometry of entrancing water reflected self-rear-ranging garden-circles. Even this design feature was too puzzling to comprehend.

"It's far too different to think about," Dal said. "There were lots of things in there but nothing that's in any way familiar to our story, which is the whole show, so there's nothing to even try to understand."

"Spoken more eloquently," the archbishop said while nodding at Dal with a warm smile, "as one a step up in the interlocking hierarchy of beings."

As Dal, Jix and King made their way back to the motorhome, Dal's attention was drawn to a figure that approached through a billow of dust kicked up by the wind. It was the slim rancher with the sun-creased face and droopy mustache, who always introduced himself as "Toppy." Wearing the same western getup he had on the first time Dal saw him, he tipped his straw cowboy hat while peering down at his fancy snakeskin boots.

"I wouldn't hornswoggle you, friend."

"She was curious about those that made her curious to us," Dal said. "But, I still don't know who you are?"

"Two half brothers make a brother, just like two half sisters make a sister."

"Are we done here?" Dal asked.

"I remember the old Star-Lite Drive-In movie theater in Socorro. Do you have one back home?"

* * * * * * * *

Instead of returning to Las Vegas with Jix and King in the motorhome, Dal rented a car in Socorro and drove to Jaywick. (He had invited Jix to join him, but she told him that she had things that she needed to do, such as editing her next podcast and interviewing the lady taphonomist). While back home, he visited his mom and shared some of his dad's bonanza with her. With Toppy's words about a drive-in movie constantly running through his mind, for the past couple of nights he had hiked up to the forest clearing on a ridge above Sullivan's Field that was once a popular gathering spot for teenagers to watch for strange things in the sky. Though nothing out of the ordinary had appeared, he was still hopeful that one of those white ellipsoid objects would show up to remove his implants. The invasion of privacy they enabled weighed heavy on him, and he was sick of feeling like a freak of nature.

While taking a slightly different path up to the clearing on the third night, he noticed a flash of light on the deteriorated mortar wall of an old structure that was said to be a cellar used to store perishables in the past. Seeing the reflection of the flashlight glinting on the rough masonry again, he stepped onto the exposed stone foundation, snapping twigs as he moved across the uneven flooring until pausing at a raised plank of wood that served as the hatch to the narrow opening of a storage pit.

"Is that you, Dal?" a familiar voice called out from the shadowy cavity. It was King.

"So you're still tracking me," Dal said as King's head emerged from the pit.

"Come down here and see what I found."

While standing next to the wooden cases containing bottles of beer that were stored in the cellar, King held up one to show Dal the purpled-tinted antique glass.

"I couldn't figure out how the glass got tinted that amethyst color, because Wixley bottles were water-clear and the stockpile here in this cold trap had been kept in the dark, which ruled out solarization, which initiates a chemical reaction of the manganese dioxide, or glassmaker's soap that makes glass clear. So, what caused the color change? Answer: The portal foyer is strange indeed, having a synthetic dimension, for lack of a better word, and must emit something that causes an exchange of electrons like ultraviolet radiation does. Okay, I kept mulling over that old newspaper article where an ancestor of yours named Elbert chanced upon one of the small beings that we now know to be the parallel folk. According to Elbert, the being was carrying a tray of beer."

"Maybe they like a cold beer. So what."

"Maybe they do, but, in this case, the beer was a cover for what the being really wanted. Prior to being startled by Elbert, and frightened enough by his coon-hunting rifle to flee, the little thing planned to smuggle something else back to its home world. Something it collected in New Mexico – an alien microbial species."

King put down the bottle of beer and picked up an empty flask.

"This flask contained what it came here for. Who knows what happened to the little being. Had the news of its find got out, it would have saved a lot of energy. But, I've got a container of my own," he said while picking up a small fuchsia-colored box. "After watching how the lady at the Dreamy Dust Gulch used it, I did the same to vacuum up from the flask what's so damn valuable to them in that dust from Magdalena. Seeing how I've had my share of kicks lately, I'm giving it to you. Think of the box as a beacon."

Knowing that the team led by Shockley hadn't relied solely on the high-res body cameras and other micro-sensors attached to the archbishop's garments to capture the event, King wondered what might be left of the optical marvels that were implanted in Dal's head. Evidently, (despite the faintest telltale marks) his asset was completely oblivious to the invasive procedure that had been recently carried out by a skilled surgeon in hopes of retrieving the imagery perceived (and presumably recorded) within the protective sphere by his hyper-spectral "eyes" that transmitted to one of the parallel folk who called himself "Toppy." Though he wasn't privy to the results, he knew that if the team wasn't able to obtain this precious data by what Spiller referred to as a "bidirectional exchange", they would set a trap to hopefully get it elsewhere.

* * * * * * * *

While seated in one of the lawn chairs that were placed on the ledge that offered an unobstructed view of the sky near the clearing, Dal was drinking one of the chilled bottles of Wixley beer that was given to him along with the box King "appropriated from the general's furniture" when he heard the sound of someone stepping on a dead branch. Putting the beer down, he picked up his flashlight and went to check out what made the crackling noise, hoping it wasn't a member of the purple-garbed gang coming after whoever took some of their prized glass.

Glancing about the conifers, he didn't see anyone. But, then the beam of his flashlight was reflected off the surface of the blackboard that earlier generations signed as a guest register while stargazing. Beneath his name, someone had written something. When he moved closer to read what this was, he saw a name scrawled in blue chalk:

Jix Black

He looked around again, but didn't see anyone. After a while, he returned to the seating area to find Jix reclined in a tattered chair drinking one of the sudsy brews.

"Do you think they'll come tonight?" she asked over the pulse of crickets.

"Anything is possible," Dal said while sitting down with the small fuchsia-colored box at his feet. "Anything can happen."

* * * * * * *

ABOUT THE AUTHOR

Black Hours is the latest novel by Blair MacKenzie Blake. Previous novels include *Grumble's Star* (2022), *The Paragon Junk* (2020) and *The Othering* (2018). Other works include *Ijynx* (a collection of occult prose-poems), *The Wickedest Books In The World – Confessions Of An Aleister Crowley Bibliophile* (issued in three impressions), *The Curious Diary Entries Of Verity Pennington* (a short story), and *Remember The Future* (of which he is the co-author). He has contributed essays to ten volumes of the anthology *Darklore* (Daily Grail Publishing), as well as to numerous esoteric-themed magazines, including *The CoSM Journal, Sub Rosa, Silkmilk* and *Dagobert's Revenge*. For over 25 years BMB has been the writer/content manager for www.toolband.com and www.dannycarey.com. He currently resides in Las Vegas, NV.